W9-BTN-738

Murder
In Greektown

Tony Aued

Copyright © 2014 Author, Tony Aued

Blair Adams Books

This novel is a work of fiction. People, places, events and situations
are a product of the Author's imagination. Any resemblance to actual
persons, living or dead is purely coincidental.

No part of this book can be reproduced without the author's permission.
Cover photograph courtesy of Shawn Walkiewicz
Cover design courtesy of Carl Virgilio

Printed in the United States of America

All rights reserved.

ISBN: 13-978-1499227642
ISBN-13:-10-1499227647

This book is dedicated to my former students.

I'm very proud of all of you.

OTHER NOVELS BY TONY AUED

BLAIR ADAMS, THE PACKAGE

BLAIR ADAMS, ABDUCTION

THE VEGAS CONNECTION

THE BLAME GAME

One

The sky was dark and it looked like more snow was on the way. A few homes had their lights on as Chris Banner pulled into the small teacher's lot. It was six-thirty-five in the morning and he was always one of the first teachers to arrive. Chris was in a car pool with the Physical Education teacher, Brittany, and they liked getting to school early. Everyone hated the dark morning sky, especially during the winter, and today was no different. The Detroit winters were often cold and long, but this year had been an unusually rough one; records had been set for one of the coldest winters and most snow ever. It was late February and both the teachers hoped March would bring some warmer weather and melt the piles of snow in the parking lot.

Chris unlocked the gate and pulled his SUV into the fourth spot on the left side of the aisle. It was kind of an unwritten policy that this was his parking spot. The spot was easy to get out of and due to such heavy snow this winter they needed all the help they could get. It was very cold, just ten degrees, and the harsh wind caused him to shiver as he fumbled with the lock. Chris looked up and saw that Tommy Dansforth's GMC was already parked in his spot.

Mr. Dansforth was always the first one in every morning and would unlock the front doors and turn on all the equipment. Dansforth's car was next to Chris and he was surprised that the GMC was already snow covered and had ice across the windshield.

How long had he been here, he thought. Tommy's GMC was bright white and the chrome grill caused the snow to glisten brightly off of it. It was late when Chris left the school yesterday evening and Dansforth's GMC was still in the lot. *Now he's here so early today. He must have more meetings with some parents.*

The two teachers walked to the front door after parking the car and Chris inserted his key in the lock and turned the door handle. The alarm inside the doorway flashed bright red light telling them that it hadn't been disabled. Chris quickly put his code into the alarm system and turned on the hall lights. He was surprised that the lights were not on in the front hallway that led to the Kindergarten and First grade classrooms. *Dansforth usually turned them all on.* They walked down the hallway toward the teachers' work room and were again surprised that the door was locked.

"I wonder why Dansforth didn't turn off the alarm and unlock the work area?" Chris asked Brittany.

Brittany Jackson was in her second year at the school and loved the staff and students. She graduated from Michigan State like Chris. She was a beautiful young lady. She had dark brown eyes and stood about five foot eight inches tall. Last year when she started at the school many of the male teachers were quite impressed with her looks. Her skin was light olive color and she wore her hair short, kind of like Halle Berry. "I'm not sure, Tommy always unlocks this," she said with a puzzled look on her face. They decided to turn on all the equipment. "I have three new posters for the gym wall that I need to laminate," Brittany said. "I'm going to hang out here and get that done first."

"Okay." Chris' classroom was down the hall and just outside of the gym. "Do you want me to turn on the gym lights for you?"

"That would be great." The two teachers were good friends and often helped each other with projects.

Chris Banner taught the fourth grade and had been at the school for the past four years. He was twenty eight and a big guy, close to six-foot-three inches tall and weighed about two hundred pounds.

He towered over the students. Last year during the Elementary School versus the Middle School teachers' basketball game he actually dunked the ball twice. The students went nuts. One of the parents caught it on video and posted it to YouTube. It went viral and had thousands of hits. Chris was embarrassed at the time but soon learned to live with the instant fame. He appeared on The Today Show and Matt Lauer interviewed him for the show. The school enjoyed the notoriety and he was very gracious during the interview.

This was February and Black History month. The hallways were filled with student projects and posters. Each class picked a famous person from Black History and their class was given an area of the hallway to decorate with information, pictures and articles on that person's life. Chris' class chose Colin Powell. It was a great choice. Powell's many accomplishments included being Chairman of the Joint Chiefs of Staff under President H.W. Bush, and Secretary of State under the second Bush. He was the first African-American in either role. The teachers made sure the students understood the importance of so many great black people from history.

The windows in Chris' fourth grade room opened up to the playground. It was nice to look out at the new swing sets and other things that the students and neighbors enjoyed. The desks in his classroom were arranged in four rows with an aisle down the middle. His part of the fourth grade had thirty students. There were three fourth grade teachers in all. Chris had the upper performing group of students. He was in his fourth year at the Charter school and was always helping the other teachers on his team. Chris Banner had been the Teacher of the Year twice at the school and could easily win the award every year.

All teachers liked the mornings. It was great time to prepare the day's activities and lessons. Chris would put key words for the day on the white board and make sure every desk had a clean sheet of paper and pencil ready for the students to start their morning assignments. Students knew that you came ready to work in Mr. Banner's class.

Classrooms were very quiet when the students weren't in. Chris' room was no different. He was working on the white board when a voice made him jump. "Banner, how about MSU this weekend. We're going to clean your clock, buddy." Because the hallway was empty, Bruce's voice sounded twice as loud as normal. Bruce Stanton was a University of Michigan grad and always gave Michigan State fans a rough time. "How much do you want to put on the game?"

Chris turned around laughing. "We've beaten you in football already and will whip you again in basketball this year too!"

As the two teachers continued talking Brittany came down the hallway. She saw the lights on and heard them so she stopped in. "Everything is on in the work room and the laminator is warmed up so if either of you need it, it's ready."

"Great," Bruce answered. "I've got some pages from the Detroit Free Press on Black History that I want to put up in the hallway." He suddenly looked at Brittany and asked, "Why did you turn the machines on, where was Dansforth? I saw his car in the lot."

"Not sure. We wondered the same thing. Nothing was on, not even the lights." They talked for a few minutes then she turned and headed out of the room and into the gym.

"So, we got a bet this weekend?" Bruce was back on the Michigan versus Michigan State basketball game. It was close to the end of the Big Ten season and both teams were ranked in the top twenty. This game would help decide seating in the Big Ten Tournament and possibly affect the Big Dance in March.

Chris finished writing the students assignments on the board and strolled over to Bruce, "You're on buddy. Let's make it ten bucks." He knew Bruce was more talk than action.

"I'm okay with five bucks." Bruce cleared his throat.

Chris laughed. "Guess you don't have much confidence in your team."

It was now close to seven and other teachers were arriving. Mr. Dansforth's room was on the second floor number 215. Dansforth was a middle school teacher and all those classrooms were on the upper floors. He was hired by the school about the same time Chris was. They went through training together and became good friends even though there was a great age difference.

As Chris and Bruce continued talking, Ms. Baker, the Principal came into Chris' room. "Good morning. Have either of you seen Dansforth?"

"No, when I pulled in his car was in the parking lot," Chris said. "Brittany and I were surprised that all the lights were off in the building and the work room was dark."

Baker said, "There was a message on the school phone system," she told them. "It said that Mr. Dansforth won't be in today. The person didn't give her name or any reason why. When I saw his car, I wondered what was going on. If he wasn't coming in why was his car here?" Both men listened intently.

"She didn't give her name?" Chris asked.

"No, like I said when I saw his car it made me question the message."

None of this made any sense. "What can we do to help?" Bruce wanted to know.

"I already contacted a sub and they will be coming in for his classes. I think we should try to get more details. Maybe I missed something. Chris, you know Tommy pretty good. Will you try to give his house a call?"

"Sure, I'll be happy to." Chris was puzzled and moved to his desk to call Dansforth's home. He dialed Dansforth's cell first. While he dialed, Ms. Baker talked to Bruce.

"The students will be a problem without him here. If the sub needs help I know I can count on both of you."

"Of course," they answered. Chris waited on his cell phone for an answer from Tommy Dansforth's cell. There wasn't an answer so then he called his house, but no one answered there either. He hung up. "I'm going back outside to check his car."

"I'll go with you," Bruce said.

They grabbed their jackets and gloves and headed to the front door. Once they got outside Chris walked across Lenox Avenue toward the parking lot as Bruce followed. There were cars now on both sides of Tommy's GMC as they walked around the vehicle to the driver's side door. Once they were along the side of the car both men stopped in their tracks. "What is that on the bottom of the door?" Chris turned toward Bruce and pointed to the ground and door. He stooped down for a closer look.

"Oh shit, I think this is blood!"

They looked at each other. "Blood! Are you sure?" Bruce was stammering.

"You know my wife, Jenn, is a nurse and showed me how to spot different things. This is definitely blood."

"It can't be blood, can it?"

"It's blood alright. We better call the cops." Chris quickly dialed 911 and started to give the police dispatcher the information. Once they finished they hurried across the street back into the school. Both men went into Ms. Baker's office. Chris pulled her door closed when they entered and she looked up.

"What's wrong?" She asked looking up at them. They had serious looks on their faces and were out of breath.

"Ms. Baker, I dialed the Detroit Police," Chris said, breathing hard. Bruce had his hands on his side with a very worried look.

Ms. Baker got up and moved out from behind her desk, "The police! Why?"

"I'm pretty sure there's blood along the driver's side of Tommy's car. Looks like it happened a while ago because it's partially frozen."

She looked over at Bruce who was now looking a bit pale as he listened to Chris explain what they found.

"Are you sure it's blood?" Ms. Baker had now moved around her desk while shaking her head.

"It's blood all right! There's also some along the side of Tommy's driver's door."

The only thing they could now do was to wait for the police to arrive.

Two

The 911 call came into the Twelfth precinct and the captain dispatched Detective Frederickson to the scene. Don hadn't been involved in a big case in years, and had no reason to believe this was anything more than student mischief. The detective's early career blossomed and he was often recognized for performance above and beyond duty. He was promoted downtown and on the fast track when it all hit the fan, as Fredrickson would tell friends. His career was derailed by an Internal Affairs investigation when a partner was indicted with connections to a drug ring. The partner claimed that Frederickson was also involved. Although he was soon exonerated, he was relegated to the city's worst precinct, an outpost at best. Even in the Twelfth Precinct, he was kept in the background of most cases. Don Frederickson was close to retiring but felt that he was still a young man, and at fifty often wondered what he would do once he left the job. Unlike many other officers in this situation; he didn't turn to the bottle and was proud to say he and his wife had a great relationship. Yes, the detective still had his pride and his moral compass was intact.

The initial call stated that a problem occurred in the parking lot at Kennedy Charter Academy on the Eastside neighborhood. A squad car was dispatched immediately and now on the scene. Detective Frederickson left the precinct and headed toward the school with flashing lights and blaring sirens as he weaved through morning rush hour traffic. When he drove down Lenox he passed neighbors gawking from their front porch. The area had changed quite a bit since he was first assigned to the Twelfth. Frederickson thought about how the school had transformed the Detroit neighborhood. When he arrived at the Twelfth, this was a drug haven where prostitutes frequented the streets at night. Houses were boarded up and it seemed that the police had lost the battle. He was pleased when the new police chief had expanded surveillance with more cops on the street. The detective knew that the old school had been renovated and the chief promised that law enforcement would make the area a high priority. His precinct helped round up the drug dealers; prostitutes were arrested and then things started to turn around.

Pulling up in front of the gated lot he observed a young man and a well dressed woman standing with two officers from his command. They were next to the squad car and it appeared that the officers were taking statements. He was surprised that a person from the forensic team was stringing crime scene tape around a GMC in the parking lot. He observed another tech down on one knee taking samples along the driver's side of that vehicle. Still unaware about new developments in the case, he pulled up along the side entrance of the school.

Frederickson had worked with the officers on the scene and felt they were very competent. The men working in the Twelfth respected the detective. He could be gruff but always got the job done. Things were turning around in the city and the Twelfth was improving too. Frederickson was always helping new officers and guiding them through the initial years on the force. He parked his car along the fenced lot and grabbed the copy of the initial report, making a final review before getting out. He was happy to be the lead detective on this case.

As he took one more look at the report a voice called out; "Good morning, I'm the teacher who called this in." Frederickson was startled because he didn't see the man approaching. The guy was now about five feet away and continued talking, "My name is Chris Banner, and I teach the fourth grade. I called this morning when I found the problem alongside Mr. Dansforth's GMC."

Frederickson turned toward the teacher noting that his copy of the 911 call didn't mention what the problem was. When he exited the car, the woman walked over and also introduced herself, "I'm Ms Baker, the principal here. We have a teacher missing, or at least we think he is. Mr. Banner came out to check his car this morning and thinks there is blood along the driver's side." Chris led the detective across the school parking lot toward the white GMC.

The officers working outside had seen Frederickson and nodded toward the group moving toward their squad car. Frederickson acknowledged them, "Morning guys, what have we got?"

"Possible missing teacher?" the officers said pointing toward the vehicle. The officer looked back down at his notepad, "It belongs to Mr. Dansforth, the reported missing subject or at least hasn't been seen this morning."

Chris interrupted. "He didn't show up for work today. We know that he was here late last night but no one has seen him this morning."

The woman added, "I'm so glad you all got here so quick, we're very worried. We haven't had any problems since the school opened. I told the officers that we had a message from someone stating that Mr. Dansforth wouldn't be in, but because his car is still here it prompted us to question the call."

Frederickson asked, "Did the caller give a name?"

"No, and it didn't sound like Mr. Dansforth's wife. He never misses work." It was obvious that the principal was shook up, although she wore gloves, the detective could see she was gripping her hands together tightly.

He was quick to point out, "We always make any issue at a school top priority." Frederickson moved toward the car and noted the stains along the bottom of the driver's door. The technician from the crime lab pointed to a blood trail that extended about three feet from the vehicle. Ms. Baker and Chris stood silently as the detective bent down and seemed to check the samples of the drops on the pavement. He stood up and turned toward the two of them. "We need to go inside and let our people do their job out here." He knew the forensic team preferred to work without someone hanging over their shoulders. Two men and a woman started to walk toward the area where officers and crime scene people were working; "Do these people belong here?" he asked the principal.

"They're teachers and work here," Ms. Baker answered. "I'll get them moving."

More people pulling in the lot had puzzled looks on their faces and some cars moved slowly, stopping from time to time to watch the action taking place. The officers working the scene motioned toward several cars as they moved slowly across the parking lot dropping students off. "We need to get these people to where they belong," they said to each other.

Ms. Baker stayed back at the lot and told the officers she would get the people into the building. She turned and instructed Chris, "Please stay with the detective."

"What about my students?"

"I'll get someone to take care of your classroom and get the kids started." Ms. Baker was the first principal of the new school. She knew with the renovation of the vacant Catholic school that it would bring changes to the neighborhood. St. Philip Neri had been closed for seven years by the Archdiocese and was the perfect size for the new charter school.

The detective watched Ms. Baker as she got the teachers moving into the building. He asked Chris, "When was the last time anyone saw your missing teacher?"

Chris looked down at a piece of paper that he held in his right hand, "He was here last night. Brittany and I left at six and his car was still in the lot. Ms. Baker said Dansforth had a meeting scheduled with a student's parent. I asked around but no one saw him after six."

"Okay, first, who is this Brittany you mentioned?"

"Oh, sorry, Brittany Johnson, she's the gym teacher. We ride to school together." Chris was getting more nervous as they talked and fidgeted with the note pad he held.

"I'm guessing you've jotted all this down on that paper you're holding?"

"Yes, I wanted to make sure I had everything for you." Chris handed him the top sheet of the note pad. The detective looked it over and jotted notes into his I Pad.

Frederickson nodded and asked, "Okay, what else can you tell me?"

"I tried calling Tommy's house, I mean Mr. Dansforth, and his cell phone this morning," Chris added. "There wasn't any answer."

"I'll need all his personal information, address and all the phone numbers on record."

"Ms. Baker will get you his address and phone numbers," Chris said. He knew she was busy getting teachers into the building and his classroom going. The two of them made it to the side door when Ms. Baker followed them into the building. She was holding a sheet of paper in her right hand.

"I figured that you would need this information, detective." Ms. Baker handed him a copy of Mr. Dansforth's personnel information including address and contact numbers.

As she stood in the doorway she saw more students being dropped off by the front entrance and they started to head across the street toward the action. "I'll be back in a minute," she said. Calling out to the new group, she said, "Come on everyone, let's go inside," Ms. Baker directed the three middle school students along with the other teachers into the building. Chris and the detective watched her for a minute before Frederickson asked to see the missing teacher's classroom.

Ms. Baker had finished rounding up the people who had just

arrived and motioned them to the front door of the school. Two students, LaShanda and Harrison didn't move as soon as Ms. Baker requested. "Why are they around Mr. Dansforth's car?" Ms. Baker repeated that there was an incident in the lot and Mr. Dansforth's car had been damaged. The two students nodded but felt that wasn't the whole story. As they followed her to the doorway, LaShanda again asked, "What kind of incident?"

Ms. Baker didn't plan on giving them any more details than necessary but hoped that they would be satisfied with the story that cars may have been vandalized.

Harrison suggested, "The cops should check that old boarded up house down the street, bad dudes hang out there." Ms. Baker looked back at the two story house knowing that it was once a drug hangout.

"Thanks, I'll make sure they know that. Now let's all get inside." The two students moved into the hallway but felt they weren't being told the whole story. They knew from things on their street that the police didn't spend that much time on cars being damaged. They followed her but wondered why the police started to string crime scene tape around Dansforth's GMC. LaShanda whispered to Harrison, "There's more to this." He agreed.

Some of the classrooms faced the east side of the building and students were gawking out the windows hoping to find out what had happened. Ms. Baker had walked back across the street to the parking lot. The officer pointed to the windows and she turned to see what he meant. She waved motioning the teachers to pull the shade and get to work. She was afraid that she would have to answer a lot of questions.

"Thanks," the officer replied, then he told her, "A call will be made to the Macomb County Sheriff and they'll dispatch a squad car to check out Mr. Dansforth's home address."

Meanwhile Chris and the detective had made their way up the stairway to the second floor and were heading to room 215 when Chris slowed and asked, "Do you want to talk to anyone else?"

The detective nodded as he headed toward the classroom. "I'll want to talk to this gym teacher and anyone else that went near Mr. Dansforth's vehicle."

"Okay, I'll tell Ms. Baker and she can get them for you. Brittany would be in the gym and Bruce Stanton, the other teacher that went out with me to check on Dansforth's car, has his third grade classroom on the first floor." Chris led him into the room. "This is Mr. Dansforth's classroom."

When they walked in, the detective saw a woman who appeared to be searching the top of Mr. Dansforth's desk. She was startled when she saw the two men entering. "Who are you?" Frederickson asked in a deep voice.

"This is our Assistant Principal, Brenda Peterson." Chris said.

Brenda Peterson almost jumped. "I was just going over some of the material for the substitute. Ms. Baker asked me to find Mr. Dansforth's handouts for the eighth grade class. But, I could only find the master sheet for the seventh graders." She was almost stuttering as she looked back at the detective.

"Please step away from the desk. I don't want anyone in this room." Frederickson sternly stated.

"Yes Sir, I understand." Mrs. Peterson held some papers in her hand and was visibly shaking. Once the detective said it was okay, she headed down the hall toward the principal's office.

Ms. Baker was in the main office talking to the secretary when she saw Brenda walking into the room. "What's wrong? Brenda, you're hands are shaking!"

"Can we go in your office," Mrs. Peterson said, almost whispering. Ms. Baker feared, *God, what now.*

"While I was going through Mr. Dansforth's desk," she stopped to take a deep breath, "I found blood." Brenda was nervous and looking at the principal for help.

"Brenda, where was the blood?"

"It was on the corner of Tommy's desk. I found it when I was looking for his substitute plans. It was near the computer keyboard."

"Oh no! I have to tell the detective. He should be with Chris."

"Yes, they're up there now. They had just come into the classroom when I found the blood."

"Did you tell them?"

"No, I thought I better tell you first."

"Okay, was anything else out of place?"

"I'm not sure. I just grabbed the lesson plans and hurried downstairs to find you." Ms. Baker flopped down in her chair. "Should I tell the police officer?" Brenda mumbled. "What should I do?"

The conversation in the main office grew louder when several teachers were signing in.

"What's going on?" One of them asked the office secretary.

"I think someone vandalized some cars in the parking lot. I guess it must have been Chris's car. I saw him out there with an officer when I arrived earlier this morning."

"Brenda sure looks upset at something," another teacher chimed in.

"Maybe it's the Dansforth thing. Brenda said he called in. He never misses a day. You know how hard that eighth grade group can be." They both laughed.

"You're right, Dansforth is best at handling those kids. I bet the sub will have his hands full," they grabbed their mail and headed to their classrooms.

Three

The Detroit Police Department had received a lot of negative press for their slow response to calls for help in many of the neighborhoods. Because this 911 call involved problems at a school, and was in the area that had once been a problem, they wanted to be quick to get officers on the scene. The city continued getting its share of bad news. Public school attendance was at an all time low and city government had been taken over by the Governor's new emergency manager.

Detroit was a city that once boasted a population of over one and a half million people, but now it fell to a mere seven-hundred thousand in the latest polls and blight in the neighborhoods was growing at an alarming rate. There were boarded up homes and scrappers were stripping the city of copper and metal. This was once a city of hard working people with a lot of pride but the hope of recovery was wavering. Detroit was the home of General Motors, Ford and many other great corporations who were at a turning point, could the city survive and rebuild? There was hope and a light at the end of the tunnel; new investors had purchased large tracts of downtown land with grand designs to change the crumbling landscape. Casinos dotted the downtown landscape with MGM, Greektown and Motor City boasting huge hotels, gambling and restaurant venues. Two beautiful professional stadiums brought fans of the Tigers and Lions along with cash to spend at the restaurants and casinos. People hoped things just might be turning around; at least the downtown area was improving.

The Free Press seemed to run a story about a murder almost every day in their headlines. There were constant news bulletins about a child missing or a shooting somewhere in the inner city daily. Now an incident involving a middle school teacher missing would surely go national. The city didn't need any more bad press. It was still trying to recover after the Federal corruption trial of the past Mayor. The City Council was in total disarray and the looming Mayoral election didn't offer any new hope. The Governor placed an emergency manager in charge and many factions were fighting the ruling. It was a contemptuous situation with teacher unions, among others, fighting for changes.

Because of the problems in the public schools, charter schools had grown rapidly. There were several corporations that opened these types of schools and Kennedy Charter belonged to one of them. It was often cited as being outstanding in its student to teacher ratio and student scores. More charter schools continued to be built and the demise of the public sponsored education system continued to crumble. The charter schools showed improving student scores and started to extend into the suburbs. The metro area extended into the counties of Macomb, Oakland along with Livingston. In sharp contrast those areas flourished with new buildings, strong neighborhoods, good schools and lower crime rates. Those factors added to the exodus of citizens from the city.

***

Ms. Baker left her office after she filled Brenda Peterson in on all the details of the morning. She knew that Detective Frederickson had to be advised of the blood found on Dansforth's desk. She didn't know if it had anything to do with Mr. Dansforth missing, but the detective needed to know. Ms. Baker walked into the classroom and saw the detective still with Chris. "Excuse me Detective, our Assistant Principal, Mrs. Peterson advised me that there may be something important on Mr. Dansforth's desk.

"Why didn't she say something when she was up here?" He was upset that Peterson hadn't informed him of her findings.

"I guess she panicked. She said it looked like dried blood on the area near the keyboard on his desk."

Frederickson moved closer to the desk and leaned down to take a closer look. Ms. Baker and Chris watched with anticipation. "I want your assistant back up here now," the detective ordered.

"I'll go get her." The principal headed out of the classroom and back down to her office. By the time she got downstairs she was short of breath. Baker put her hand on the door frame to steady herself.

"Are you okay," the secretary asked moving from her desk to help Ms. Baker.

"Guess I took those stairs too fast. I'll be okay."

The secretary wasn't too sure. "I'll get you a glass of water, come on sit down."

Ms. Baker was flushed and panting. She sat on the chair. "I just need to catch my breath. Where did Mrs. Peterson go?"

The secretary was worried but answered, "She said something about needing something from her car and I think she's outside."

"I need her to come back in." Before Ms. Baker could get up the secretary said, "I'll go get her for you. You just need to relax."

Brenda Peterson was in the parking lot and talking to the officers that had been working the crime scene. The secretary crossed the street and called out. "Brenda, Ms. Baker needs you to come to the office. I think you better come in and see if she's okay."

Brenda looked startled. *Oh no, what now!* She thought. She crossed the street and hurried back in with the secretary who was telling her about Ms. Baker's recent out of breath situation. The two ladies entered the office. Ms. Baker had now moved back to her desk and was on the phone. She waved to Brenda to come into her office.

Baker held the phone off to the side, "Brenda, the detective is in Dansforth's room and wants you to come up there. He wants you to show him what you found."

Brenda stood in the doorway for a minute, "Are you sure that you're okay?"

"Yes why?"

"Jean said you were breathing hard and thought you might faint."

"I just came down the stairs too fast. I'm okay. Just see what he wants. I'm waiting for directions from the superintendent on our next move."

Brenda nodded and stopped at the secretary's desk. "Keep an eye on her. We need to make sure she's okay."

"Brenda, what's going on? This is more than some cars damaged in the lot."

"I not sure yet, but I'll fill you in when I know more." With that she headed back up to room 215.

The detective told Chris that he could go wherever he was needed and that he would wait for Brenda Peterson. Just as Chris was leaving the room he saw Brenda turning the corner. He walked toward her. "That guy isn't saying much. He found a spot of dried blood on the desk and wants us to keep everyone out of the classroom."

"Thanks Chris. I'll get with Ms. Baker and see how she wants to handle it." When Brenda entered the room the detective was kneeling along the left side of the desk and he had a pen knife and little plastic bag in his hands. She moved closer and could see that he was taking samples of the dried blood that she had seen earlier.

Without turning to look at her he said. "Is this what you found when you were rummaging around the desk?"

"I wasn't rummaging around," she said sharply. "I'm responsible for the middle school and had to get lesson plans for the sub. I was just doing my job."

Frederickson turned back and looked at her for what appeared an eternity. "I didn't mean anything by that, I just needed to know if this is what you found."

Brenda moved closer and saw that he was taking samples from the same spots that she had seen. "Yes, at first I just thought it was ink or something like that. When I looked closer I was sure it was blood."

"Yeah, me too," he answered. "I'll get this down to the forensic team. Is there a record on file of Dansforth's blood type?"

"I'm not sure but our main offices would have that information. Do you want me to call and find out?"

"That would be great. In the meantime I plan to have a forensic team up here and check things in here out. The room can't be used for a while. We don't know for sure if this is blood or even if it's Mr. Dansforth's."

***

Students that were scheduled to be in their homeroom had been moved to the computer lab. They were being told that Mr. Dansforth wanted them to work on their Black History Projects. Mrs. Peterson planned to alert the middle school staff that officers were checking out the area inside and not to let students in the hallway for at least the next hour.

The initial inspection of room 215 should be pretty simple. The detective didn't see anything out of order. The desk was neat and all the equipment seemed to be there, nothing missing except for Tommy Dansforth. The forensic team was hoping to pick-up fingerprints that didn't belong to anyone in the school. Frederickson studied the spots on the desk and nodded. It was blood, but who's? With six class periods and an average of thirty students per class there would be a lot of fingerprints on the desk. The suspected blood on the desk would be analyzed. Hopefully they had Dansforth's blood type on record.

It was now close to nine-thirty and Dansforth's Social Studies classes were meeting in the computer lab. The substitute knew handling close to ninety students would be close to impossible. Mrs. Peterson headed back upstairs and planned to move the group into the gym.

She moved to the front of the room and everyone looked up. "Class, Mr. Dansforth wanted to make sure everyone was on track with their projects. We're going to go down to the gym, quietly, and we will check your work out. If you need to print your material, Mrs. Kale will make a list and bring your reports down with her."

Students were mumbling and Mrs. Peterson repeated that they would be going downstairs one more time. Rumors had already started and with middle school aged kids they were like wild fire. Peterson raised her voice. "Either we do this right and quietly or you'll lose points from your projects." Books and papers were gathered and students lined up to go down to the gym. Mrs. Kale, the computer teacher, was making a list from those needing material printed and said she would bring it down to the gym.

"Where's Mr. Dansforth?" a few of the students were asking.

"He had a family situation he had to handle. We will get things together for all of you."

"Why are there police cars outside?" This was not going well. Most of the students had lined up to go downstairs but some of the students continued to ask questions.

Peterson didn't want to handle more questions from the students or give them information that may or may not be true. "Mr. Banner found some damage to some of the cars in the lot and the police needed to check it out." She hoped to get the class moving but Harrison McCutchen asked another question."If Mr. Dansforth isn't coming in, why is his car in the lot?"

That caused a lot more commotion and other students started asking additional questions. "Okay, everyone sit back down." Mrs. Peterson was getting flustered. It was obvious the students weren't going to settle for the answers they were given.

Harrison raised his hand again. "Yes Harrison!" She was not happy but had to make sure she gave the students enough information to get them moving.

Harrison asked, "Mr. Dansforth is always here, if he's not coming in we want to know why his car is in the lot? Is he okay?"

Before she could answer, other students chimed in. "Yeah," LaShanda added. "Did Mrs. Dansforth have to come and get him? He hasn't been feeling well lately."

It was clear that the students knew a lot about Mr. Dansforth and his family. Maybe even more than the staff did. "I didn't talk to him. He just left a message that he wasn't going to be in today."

She hoped that would finally satisfy the students. "Let's all get up and head to the gym, now," Peterson wanted to get the classes back on the move. They stood up and got in line and waited to head down to the gym to work on their projects. As they started down the hallway Harrison fell back and got in line next to LaShanda. "I don't think they're telling us everything."

"I agree. But what can we do?"

"Once we're in the gym we can talk about it, they're not telling us the whole story."

LaShanda liked that idea. Mercedes heard them and said she wanted in. Now all three students were plotting on how to find out more about Mr. Dansforth's absence.

***

Once they were notified of the problem, the Macomb County Sheriff dispatched a squad car to the Dansforth residence. The couple lived in a nice quiet condo community off of Hall Road. Their home was a nice three bedroom unit on the third block of Windermere Estates near the corner of Romeo Plank and Hall

Road. The presence of a police car was unusual in the neighborhood. When they pulled up in front of the unit, the officers noticed that there wasn't a car in the driveway. This could be normal because all the units had an attached garage. One officer went to the front door and rang the front bell. The second officer walked around to the back of the unit. There was no answer at the front door. The officer rang it a second time and waited. A neighbor walking down the street was watching with curiosity.

"Is there something wrong, officers," she asked.

"No, we just needed to ask Mrs. Dansforth something."

"Oh, she hasn't been home all day. She left last night in her car."

The officer crossed the street and walked toward the neighbor. "Thanks, that's a great help. Do you know where she was going?"

"No, she was driving but it wasn't Mr. Dansforth with her. Tommy has grey hair and the guy in the passenger seat had dark hair, a beard and was pretty big. I was walking my dog, Muffin, and waved as she pulled out but guess she didn't see me because she never waved back."

"What time was that?"

"Probably close to nine."

"What kind of car was she driving?"

"It's a dark blue Chevrolet SUV. "

"Are you sure about the time?"

"It was well after dinner, and I take my dog Muffin out every night about the same time. Is she okay?"

"We were just checking on a report and needed to ask her some questions. Thanks for your help."

"No problem."

As he started to walk away he turned back and asked, "Where do you live?"

She pointed across the street, one house to the left of the Dansforth's condo. "My name's Anna, been there ten years."

He again thanked the neighbor and walked around the back of the unit. His partner had been there checking it out. There was a neat patio with table and four chairs along with a swing and two large flower pots. They tried looking into the large glass sliding doors but the drapes were pulled tight. The two windows on each side of the fireplace also had shutters that were closed and offered no view into the unit. They moved back around the front of the home and called their findings in.

Anna kept watching as the officers returned from the backyard. She knew something bad must have happened, but what?

_____Four

Students and teachers were all buzzing with questions. The teachers had seen officers on the second floor and now there were two men moving in and around Mr. Dansforth's classroom. Other students from the middle school classrooms were starting to ask more questions and teachers didn't have any answers. The classrooms that were on the east side of the building could see a team of officers working around the parking lot and there was yellow tape around Mr. Dansforth's car. Ms. Baker knew she would have to inform everyone soon what was happening, but she still wasn't sure herself. She had placed a call to the district superintendent for the Detroit Area Charter School system and hoped he would advise her soon.

It was close to the third period at the school and Chris Banner had his organizational time scheduled. He headed to the office and found Ms. Baker with the detective sitting across from her desk. When she looked up and saw him she motioned for him to come into her office. The detective turned and also waved him to the office. Chris felt a lump in his throat. *Oh God, what did they find?*

As Chris entered the room the detective stood and extended his hand. "I'd like to thank you for your help this morning. We'd like you to go over some of the details again."

Ms. Baker stood and moved from behind her desk, "Do you want me to leave?"

"No, I might have a few more questions for you." Chris was visibly nervous. He was asked to sit down and the detective had a notepad on his lap. Frederickson had been jotting down details from Ms. Baker and now planned to ask Chris some of the same questions. "First, I need your full name and address."

Chris complied with the detective's request and then asked. "Have you found Tommy?"

"No, not yet. We're checking the neighborhood and his residence and will be talking to his wife. We should know something soon."

Chris had seen too many episodes of *Law and Order* to feel that everything was going to be alright. He went over the details from the morning starting when he and Brittany arrived at the school and then when he and another teacher went out and spotted the blood by Tommy Dansforth's car. Chris knew the detective had already noted all of this information including when he escorted the detective up to Dansforth's classroom.

Frederickson asked, "Did you touch anything at the car?"

Chris wondered, *why the detective was asking the same questions again*. He thought about it for a minute. Slowly he answered. "Um, well yes, I think just the door, yes I touched the driver's side door." he wanted to make sure he relayed the exact details, "When Bruce and I saw some fluid near the front door I put my finger in it first thinking that it was oil or transmission fluid."

"What made you think that it was blood?"

"I didn't think it was blood at first. Once I put my finger in it and felt how sticky it was it made me think it could be blood. My wife is an emergency room nurse and she has told me how to spot blood."

"Tell me about the car, what doors did you touch?"

"Just the driver's door when I bent down."

"Are you sure, could you have touched anything else?"

"I don't think so; no I'm sure, just the bottom of the driver's door." Chris was sweating. "Just the driver's door."

"I'm going to ask you for a fingerprint sample so that our forensic team can rule you out when they are taking samples from the scene outside, unless you have something else to tell us."

Chris looked at the detective then Ms. Baker. "What do you mean? Rule me out for what?"

"Were you and Dansforth friends?"

"Yeah, we sometimes rode together and we have gone out to dinner with our wives." Chris stood up. "I don't like your questions. Tommy and I were close."

"Okay, just doing my job," the detective answered. "It seems you were the last one to see his car last night and the first one to find it this morning."

Chris raised his voice an octave. "Everyone will tell you that Tommy Dansforth is a great guy and he and I are friends."

"Okay, I got it, like I said before, just doing my job."

"Can I go now?" Chris stood up and looked at the door.

"Sure, we might want to talk to you more if we have any other questions. Who did you say went out to the car with you when you found the blood?"

Chris looked at Ms. Baker before he answered, "Another one of the teachers, Bruce Stanton."

"Thanks for your help."

Chris left the office and didn't have any other response but gave the detective a weird look when he walked out. Frederickson turned to Ms. Baker. "I'm going to need to question this Stanton fellow." She picked up the phone and dialed his room.

Bruce Stanton was giving his class a pop quiz and stopped to answer the phone call. "Yes, I understand. Can I finish this quiz first?"

Ms. Baker asked the detective if he needed Stanton right away. He said, "How about I catch him during his lunch break. Let me talk to him."

Ms. Baker reluctantly handed him the phone.

"Mr. Stanton," he said, "Handle your class and I'll talk to you during your lunch break. Just come to the office and we can meet with you here."

Bruce Stanton said okay and wondered what new news had

developed. He finished the quiz and when they were being collected he dialed Chris Banner's classroom. "Hey buddy, what's going on?"

"Not too sure, but they asked me a bunch of questions including if Dansforth and I got along okay."

"What!"

"Bruce they are going to want to talk to you."

"Yeah, they called and want me in the office at lunch time. Did they find Tommy?"

"The detective really never answered, he just said they were talking to his wife."

"This isn't good."

The detective reminded Ms. Baker that no one else was to know about the existence of the blood they found in Dansforth's room. "Until we know more, I'm treating this as abduction."

_____Five

The Macomb County Sherriff had to get into the Dansforth residence and needed to confirm that Tommy Dansforth and his wife were not inside. An All Points Bulletin had been issued for Mrs. Dansforth's car. Hopefully the APB would result in finding Mrs. Dansforth and help answer some questions about the case. Her Chevrolet Traverse had a GPS built in and it could be tracked. The Macomb County Sheriff contacted Chevrolet and On Star for assistance.

The forensic team at the school had concluded their investigation and Dansforth's GMC was being towed in to the impound lot where more evidence could be taken. Frederickson was completing his fact finding at the school and would be heading in to headquarters.

The blood that was found in Dansforth's room, along with that at the scene outside, was sent to the crime lab. There were new questions regarding what appeared to be a turned in assignment from a student that also had traces of blood on it. It was being dusted for fingerprints and sent to the crime lab for further analysis. The lab would be using an iodine fuming technique to bring out the prints on paper. Latent fingerprints are often left visible on porous surfaces, such as paper. To develop these prints, investigators can use the chemical ninhydrin, which reacts with the make them highly visible. The fingerprint then turns purple and can be easily seen by the naked eye or a microscope. The Detroit crime lab had been strapped for new equipment but their fingerprinting department was rated as one of the best in the state.

Frederickson hoped that the lab would give him some clues in the case. The neighborhood was being combed for some information or the possibility of a body being found. The team on the scene checked the abandoned houses that sat across the street with no results. If the teacher did struggle with possible kidnappers maybe they dumped him somewhere nearby. The detective advised Ms. Baker that he would call her with any new developments. He knew she had to tell her staff and students something soon, especially before the press got the story. He was concerned because Channel 7 was already on the scene. Neighbors had reported to the station that something bad may have happened at Kennedy Charter School.

With so many school shootings nationwide in recent months, news teams hurried to get on top of any story involving schools and student safety. The lead investigative journalist for the station, Carole Newton, contacted Ms. Baker for comments and hoped to get some details for their viewers. The secretary said that Ms. Baker was out but would return the call. Carole was the number one news person in the metro area and had won awards for her work on the recent mayoral scandal. The details on the text messages that she uncovered in that case were key in the corruption case against the mayor and his girlfriend.

It was now close to noon and Ms. Baker had informed all the teachers that they would be releasing students early and parents were being contacted through the robo-call system to pick up their kids at the main entrance. The school sent a message to all families to come to pick up students at twelve-thirty. If the parents or designated person arrived past one, they would have to come to the lunch room to get their student. There would be a meeting for the staff in the gym at two-thirty and more details would be available then. Baker had asked the staff not to discuss anything with students until more information came in. The District Supervisor had followed up with the decision to close the school the rest of the week. At least with it being Wednesday, it only meant being closed two days. Hopefully the police investigation would have some answers by Monday. The supervisor would send Baker an announcement for the press that she could give to reporters.

It was now two-thirty and all the teachers had gathered in the gym as requested on the first floor. They were asking each other questions and everyone was buzzing with speculation. Stories started to spread that something happened to Mr. Dansforth. Bruce and Chris tried to deflect questions but other teachers knew that they had more details than they were willing to share. Everyone by now had seen his car in the lot and news of crime scene tape being put around it and then towed off only fueled rumors.

Ms. Baker and Mrs. Peterson came into the gym along with a distinguished man in a dark suit. Ms. Baker addressed the group. "Please everyone have a seat on the bleachers and we can begin." People moved about and slowly sat on the bleachers along the west wall. "I'm very sorry for all the confusion today and even more so to report that one of our teachers, Mr. Dansforth, may be missing." People squirmed in their seats knowing that the rumors were true and fearing the worst was still to come. "Mrs. Peterson and I, along with Mr. Banner and Mr. Stanton, have been working with the Detroit Police Department this morning. I want to introduce Detective Frederickson who is heading up the investigation."

Detective Frederickson moved to the center of the gym and surveyed the faces in front of him. He opened up the conversation, "I understand that many of you have questions regarding one of your teachers, Mr. Dansforth who may possibly be missing. We understand he is at the forefront of your thoughts. We appreciate that he is a valued member of your educational team and his possible disappearance and the details surrounding this has caused many of you great concern. I can tell you that our investigative team is checking every lead and detail and will not rest until we solve the problem. At this time we do not have confirmation that anything bad has happened to him. We're still checking to see if he may be at his home."

Those words hopefully brought some relief to the staff. Dansforth might not be missing. The detective had to calm the staff and his initial remarks may have done that. He continued, "We have teams both in Detroit and Macomb County working on this case and our forensic team is making progress as we speak. We need your help in solving this as soon as possible." People squirmed as he continued. "Last night it was reported that Mr. Dansforth may have been the last one to leave the school. I need each of you to think back. When was the last time you saw him and where he was? Did any of you see who he had been meeting with or who may have been in the school after hours? Anything you remember can be critical.

People turned to each other and started to ask questions. The room was buzzing and the detective had to get control of the meeting. "I need quiet so we can find out what you may contribute to the investigation." People turned their attention back to him. "Okay, some of you may know something; it could be important. Please raise your hand if you saw Mr. Dansforth after school and what time you saw him. This way we can create a timeline of events." Chris Banner was the first to raise his hand. "Yes," Frederickson said.

Chris stood, looked around the room and offered, "This morning Brittany and I saw Tommy's GMC in the lot around six-thirty. When we left last night about six o'clock his GMC was still in the lot." He added that it was the last vehicle in the lot. Brittany then stood up and confirmed Chris' story. She added, "We both laughed and said that Tommy would sleep here if he needed to." That remark brought a little laughter to the room and smiles to some of the teachers.

It was evident that Tommy Dansforth was considered a respected teacher. His students loved him and although his methods were old school, the staff respected his approach. Tommy previously had a corporate career and once he retired he decided to go back and get a teaching certificate. He brought many things into the classroom, real world aspects that the students could utilize both now and in high school. He showed them old communication devices, like his old manual typewriter, his first cell phone and his dad's 1912 camera. These were things in a museum, not a classroom, but the students got to actually try them and discussed how technology had changed. When his class went on field trips he would often be surrounded by students asking if he had ever used some of the items they were seeing at either The Henry Ford Museum or at The Holocaust Center. He brought in old newspapers announcing the election of John F. Kennedy and then the later assassination. There were also headlines proclaiming the end of World War II, and Martin Luther King's March on Washington. Yes, Tommy Dansforth was important in the classroom and in the lives of his students. But the detective knew that things weren't always what they appeared to be. He needed details not opinions.

"Did anyone else have something to add?" He waited, hoping something new would be added. Teachers looked around at each other, and then Bruce raised his hand.

"I didn't see Mr. Dansforth last night but also saw his car when I left late. There were just two cars in the lot when I left, Chris' and Mr. Dansforth's."

The detective didn't hear anything new and no one said they saw Dansforth in the school after five-thirty. Frederickson now turned his questions to the events of the morning. "Did anyone here go into Mr. Dansforth's room this morning?"

They waited and Ms. Thomas raised her hand.

"Yes, what is it?"

"Each of us locks our rooms at night, only Ms. Baker and Mrs. Peterson have master keys."

Frederickson turned to Ms. Baker. He asked, "Other than Mrs. Peterson, was anyone else in Dansforth's room?"

She stopped to think for a minute, "Just the janitor. He would have gone in to clean the room."

Frederickson asked, "Is the janitor in here?"

They looked around but he wasn't there. Ms. Baker said she would go get him. While she was out of the room Frederickson asked if anyone could add any other details that might be useful in the investigation. No one spoke until Chris stood back up.

"What do we do from here, detective?"

The detective knew that too many details would leak out, many would be wrong and he hoped the staff didn't know about the blood they found in Dansforth's room. He also knew that people often knew some little detail that might seem insignificant but important later on. He addressed the group again, "I'm going to give you my cell phone number. If you remember anything you think might help please call me. I'm also going to suggest that you resist the urge to talk to the newspapers and television people about the on-going investigation. We hope to catch a break soon and don't want too much information out there. Ms. Baker will give the press the official position of the school and my office will handle the press on our side of the investigation." People nodded understanding the urgency to resolve this. He continued, "I know Mr. and Mrs. Dansforth and their family understand that you are worried about them, so say a prayer or whatever you need to do hoping this all turns out okay." The teachers appeared to be happy with the detective's last statements.

Ms. Baker returned to the gym with the janitor. The detective told her he would like to question him with her and she could let the staff leave. She informed the staff, "I have talked to my supervisor and they will have a security team on premises starting tonight to make sure everyone else is safe. If you have any questions please address them to me, not the press." With that the teachers milled around and slowly made their way out of the gym. Ms. Baker waited with Mr. Craft, the janitor, and they sat down on the bleachers with the detective. Her secretary informed her that a reporter, Carole Newton, from Channel 7 was in her office and wanted to meet with her. Ms. Baker hoped that someone from her main office would soon advise her on how to proceed with the press.

Six

The school janitor, Mr. Craft, had been with the charter school since it opened. He was usually there until nine at night cleaning the rooms and building. His normal schedule started at two in the afternoon as he prepared materials needed for the evening's work. There was one assistant, but Craft said he wasn't in the building yesterday.

Detective Frederickson reviewed his notes with some of the details of the investigation before talking to Craft. He called in and had his team run a background check on Craft. *Never know what you might find.* He planned on leaving out the part about the blood found at Dansforth's car and desk when talking to the janitor. Ms. Baker told the detective that Mr. Craft had been with the school since it opened. The detective thought the janitor appeared to be a little nervous, more than he should have been. Frederickson asked, "Mr. Craft, did you see Mr. Dansforth last night?"

Craft thought for a few minutes. "Yes, he was in his room with one of the parents going over some papers when I passed by. He said he would be running late and that he would empty his basket in the trash bin in the hallway."

"What time was that?"

Craft checked his watch for a second. "Maybe close to six-thirty or seven."

"Can you be a little more specific, it's important?"

"I usually do the elementary rooms downstairs first because they're the dirtiest. I go upstairs after that and saw Dansforth. He usually has parents later than most of the other teachers."

"Can you describe the man he was with last night?"

"Don't have to. It was Mr. Sheppard, he's here a lot."

"Are you sure that's who he was with?"

"Oh yes. Sheppard's kid used to be in trouble all the time but lately I ain't seen Mr. Sheppard here with other teachers 'cept Mr. Dansforth."

The detective hoped that this could be his first lead in the case. "Did you see Mr. Sheppard leave?"

"No Sir."

"How about Mr. Dansforth., did you see him leave?" Again the answer was no.

The detective turned to Ms. Baker. "Guess we can let Mr. Craft get to his job. Can we head back to your office?"

"Sure, but I have one problem. The office called and I have a local reporter from Channel 7 in there."

"Okay, you go deal with her but keep it as simple as possible. My office will give them a statement on Mr. Dansforth once we have a little more information."

She said, "Our district office is sending messages via robo call to all the parents and I have a statement from our district to give the news."

The detective wasn't happy about the press here so soon. "Okay, keep it to the missing teacher but nothing about blood found anywhere. You can tell her we haven't been able to get any details about his location and are concerned because his car was found in the lot."

As they headed down the hallway toward the office Mr. Craft came back around the corner. He was waving to the detective. "Hey, I just remembered that the new sixth grade teacher was here late last night too."

The detective looked back at Ms. Baker and asked, "What new sixth grade teacher?"

Before she could say anything, Mr. Craft answered, "The blonde lady. Ms. Blankenship."

"What time was that?"

"Guess I saw her after seven in the work room."

"Thanks," Frederickson said. As he and Ms. Baker continued walking toward the office he questioned her, "What about this Ms. Blankenship? Why didn't she say she was here late during the meeting in the gym? How long has she been here? I'll need more information on her."

Ms. Baker wasn't sure why Mary Blankenship didn't say that she was at the school late. She was pretty sure that Blankenship was in the meeting. They stopped before reaching the hall near her office. "Detective, Mary joined us last month and because the school year was already started she's been staying late to catch up on planning. She's a sweet young girl, first year out of college. I'm sure she's just nervous like the rest of us."

"That may be so, but if she's still in the building I want to talk to her." She knew he was obviously upset. "I'm going to need Mr. Sheppard's information also."

Ms. Baker told the detective, "I will go upstairs and check to see if Ms. Blankenship is still here. If so, I'll bring her down to my office." She climbed the stairway next to the teachers' work room and headed toward the sixth grade rooms. The middle school hallways were lined with lockers and posters for the upcoming Martin Luther King Holiday. Ms. Blankenship's classroom was just down from Tommy Dansforth's. Her light was still on and there was music coming from the room. When Ms. Baker turned the corner and stepped in, the room was empty. The small CD player on the desk was playing a Beyonce song and there was an open bottle of Diet Coke on the desk. Ms. Baker headed back down the hallway and didn't see any other lights on in the other classrooms. Hopefully Blankenship might be downstairs. She headed back down the stairway and hoped she would find her in the workroom.

Detective Frederickson called in to his office to see if the forensic team had found anything in Dansforth's room to help with the case. The chief now wished he had sent another detective to handle the case that was now growing in importance. Hughes didn't trust Frederickson with something this high of a level; after all he hadn't been involved in anything more than petty crimes in the past few years. "Detective, maybe I need to send a second investigator to help with the case."

Frederickson was pissed. "Captain, I have to interview another teacher, then I'll be heading in after that. This is my case and I plan to handle it."

Captain Hughes was in a tough spot. Take Frederickson off the case and lose the respect of the others in the precinct. Although the detective hadn't been handling key cases he was still a respected member of the team. Maybe he'd let Frederickson continue but oversee some of the aspects to help him. The captain agreed, "Okay, but before you come in you better check all the school personnel out."

"I've got a list from the principal of everyone that works here and will make sure we do a background check on all of them."

"Detective, can you email a copy to me and we'll help you get started."

"I'll do it right away."

"See you when you get back."

Once Frederickson had the personnel list he emailed it from the school office in to his precinct. The captain planned to have another detective run the background checks. He knew that Frederickson was determined to handle the case to a resolution. This might be the Frederickson's "swan song" case, but Hughes would make sure everything was as professional as possible. He felt that the detective had a renewed vigor and was looking at every angle. Once Frederickson had all the details handled, he wanted to run over everything one more time. He was upstairs in Dansforth's classroom when the captain contacted him again.

"Detective, we just started our background check and may have gotten our first break in the case. That janitor, he's got a record."

"A record, what did he do?"

"Felony burglary, ten years ago, did six months in jail."

"How in the hell does a guy with a record get a job working in a school?"

"Not sure, check with the principal. You better talk to him again. You sure you're up to this?" The detective hated being questioned on the case already. *Why me*, he thought. "I got it." He planned on heading back to the principal's office. Before he hung up with the chief, he added, "You need to be aware that Channel 7 News is on the prowl for information. Don't think it's a good idea to tell them much?"

"I understand. I know the reporter is here and in the principal's office. I instructed her to let them know that we have a missing person and just that he is a teacher from the middle school. The principal said that their administration sent an email with information for the press. They also will advise parents what is going on and have cancelled classes tomorrow. Their district will have a private security team on premises starting tonight."

"Okay, I'll handle it from here. If you have any other news let me know."

Frederickson pulled his I Pad out and added notes to his case file. He put the janitor's name down along with Mr. Sheppard and now Ms. Blankenship. He planned on re-visiting with Craft first. *Need to check him out one more time.* The other two would also be persons of interest. He wondered if Dansforth and the new sixth grade teacher had anything in common. What about Dansforth's wife. Why hasn't she been found? Then there's that blood in his room. How about the parent with Mr. Dansforth last night? Could the blood in the room have been planted to throw them off? Everyone spoke highly of Dansforth but no one mentioned his wife. There were too many questions and no answers. He walked down toward the janitor's work area and decided to check the APB results on Mrs. Dansforth.

_____Seven

Kathy and Tommy Dansforth had been married for close to forty years. The neighbors told the Macomb County Sheriff that were on the scene, that they were a nice couple. Two kids, the son lived in Georgia and was an editor with a newspaper. The daughter lived in Southern California and was a realtor. People told them the Dansforth's were always traveling in the summer to visit both their kids. When the neighbors were asked, none had the phone numbers of either of the Dansforth's children.

The detective knew things weren't always what they seemed to be. Do you really know your neighbors? Hell, Frederickson lived in the same place for the last twenty years and couldn't tell you one thing about his next door neighbors. Some detective, his wife would say. The Jones' next door, could be mass murderers and you wouldn't even know.

He thought about the man that was recently captured in Cleveland that had abducted three women and kept them for over ten years in his house. None of the neighbors knew anything was wrong. How could things like that happen? Guess everyone becomes focused on their lives and really doesn't pay attention to things around them.

***

The APB hadn't netted anything on the location of Kathy

Dansforth's car. There was always the possibility that the GPS had been disabled. The Macomb County Sheriffs knew that they needed to gain admittance to the home in Windermere Estates. A squad car was again dispatched with a warrant that had been issued to get into the unit. They planned to search the place. Although one neighbor said Kathy Dansforth was seen leaving late last night, maybe she returned late and the car was in the garage. GPS couldn't locate it if it was inside.

This time the squad car pulled up in the driveway of the condo complex and two officers approached the front door. They knocked and waited a few minutes. When no one answered they rang the doorbell, however to no avail. They would have to find an access into the condo. When the female officer walked back to their squad car, a neighbor approached.

"Is everything okay at the Dansforth's' house?"

"We are trying to locate Mrs. Dansforth but it appears that she may have left. Have you seen her today?"

"No, but I have a key to their place."

The officer motioned to her partner. He came walking up to both of them. "This lady has a key to the Dansforth residence. Miss, what is your name?"

"Jenny. My husband and I live right down the street and sometimes when Kathy and Tommy are out of town I check on their place and water their plants."

"We need to get inside and a key would be very helpful. Can you get the key for us?"

"Sure, I'll just be a minute." Jenny turned and walked toward her house. By now more neighbors were standing on their porch and the two officers called the information into their station while waiting for the key.

Jenny returned and handed the female officer the key and asked, "Can I go in with you?"

"We would rather have you stay out here while we check everything out."

"Guess I understand." Jenny feared the worst. Why else would the cops need to get into the Dansforth's' place?

The two officers soon moved back on the front porch and put the key into the lock. Jenny stood on the sidewalk and waited with her hands clasped in front of her. *Please, please I hope everything is okay*, she said softly to herself as the two officers disappeared into the house.

Jenny felt they were gone for a long time when one of them came back on the porch. He waved for her to come up to the porch. She approached and he asked, "What kind of car does Mrs. Dansforth have?"

"A blue Chevrolet SUV, just like mine. Is she okay?"

"When was the last time you talked to her?"

"Yesterday morning, we went shopping and out to lunch. Please tell me what's going on."

"Right now we are just trying to locate her. What was the exact time yesterday that you saw her?"

Jenny knew there was more to this and worried that something bad had happened, but what? She thought back to make sure she remembered what time she got back from shopping with Kathy Dansforth. "Guess I dropped her off about two, maybe a few minutes after that."

The officers knew from the information that another neighbor, Anna had given them, that Kathy had left around nine later that evening. The officer asked Jenny to come into the house with them. She entered the living room and sat on the small brown chair in the corner as he pulled out a note book. "It appears that Mr. Dansforth didn't report to his job today and his car was found in the lot but he isn't around. We tried to reach his wife but she hasn't answered our calls. Another neighbor said she was seen leaving last night about nine or later. Did you see her go out?"

"No, Tommy never misses being at school. Kathy would have called me if something was wrong. Did you try her cell phone?"

"No, we didn't have that number, just the home phone

number."

Jenny pulled out her phone and started to dial Kathy Dansforth's cell.

The officer told her to stop. "I'd rather make that call." She understood. He dialed and it rang three times then went to voice mail. He hung up and tried again. "Sometimes ladies don't hear their phone especially if it's in her purse." It went to voice mail again. "Mrs. Dansforth, this is Officer Johnson from the Macomb Sheriff's office. We need you to contact us as soon as possible." He repeated his cell number and clicked off.

Jenny looked up at the officer. "What can I do?"

"How about you give us your number and if needed we can contact you for more information." Now that they had Kathy Dansforth's cell number they could run a GPS trace and maybe it will show where she was.

Jenny told the officers, "Her car also has a cell phone number." She gave that number to them. "Please call me as soon as you hear from her."

"I'll be happy to. You'll need to contact us if she calls you." He handed her his card. The other officer had been checking out the backyard and garage. She had walked out the rear sliding door of the home and saw three ladies in the yard watching the events.

One of them asked, "Is everything okay, officer?"

"Yes, normal procedures." They just nodded but knew nothing that was happening was normal.

With both Kathy Dansforth's cell and the phone number of her car, there was a great chance that a GPS trace would turn up her location.

_____Eight

Ms. Baker had searched the teachers' work room then the gym, but didn't find Mary Blankenship anywhere. She returned to her office where the reporter was still waiting for an interview. "Sorry to keep you but we've been busy," Baker said.

"I understand," the reporter reached out and handed the principal her business card. Baker read it, her name, Carole Newton, embossed with the Channel 7 logo across the center. "I've been told that there is a teacher that's missing and blood has been found in the parking lot near his car."

Ms. Baker turned quickly and was stunned that the reporter opened with those details. "I don't know where you got your information but we're still trying to locate our teacher, no one confirmed anything about him missing."

"My sources tell me that you also found blood in the teacher's classroom and our viewers will want to know what the police are doing and if they have any leads."

Ms. Baker was flustered and didn't know what to say. She turned and looked out her window as the blood drained from her face. Ms. Baker turned pale and stared out the window. A large van with Channel 7 tattooed all over the side with a large boom on the roof had just pulled up next to the front entrance. Baker didn't hear what the reporter had just asked.

The reporter again asked Baker about the missing teacher but Baker continued to stare out the office window. "Ms. Baker!" Carole said louder holding a microphone in her right hand and waiting for a response.

The principal turned toward Carole and was obviously shaken. She didn't know what to do. Just then Detective Frederickson walked in.

"So where is our sixth grade teacher?" He asked.

Carole could see Ms. Baker appeared to stagger a bit and moved closer to her. "Maybe you want to sit down." She took Baker's hand and helped her to the chair next to the large desk. The principal was flushed and shaking. Detective Frederickson turned around and went into the hallway hoping to find a water fountain. He saw one next to the sign for the girl's bathroom. There were cups in a dispenser on the wall and he grabbed a cup of water and headed back to the office. He, along with Carole, waited as Baker took a few sips and seemed to settle down.

"I'm so sorry to worry both of you but I forgot to take my medicine and didn't eat all day. Guess my blood sugar is too low." Carole went into her purse and pulled out some lifesaver candies. She opened the roll and gave it to the principal.

Ms. Baker was still pale and obviously shaken. "Are you okay?" Carole asked.

"Yes, thank you."

"You just sit here," Frederickson told her. "Where can I get you something to eat?"

"I have my lunch right here. I just need to have a piece of fruit and I'll be okay."

He turned toward the reporter. "Under the circumstances, I think we need to leave Ms. Baker here to rest."

"I understand but I have a few questions and my news crew has just arrived."

"I'll give you what we know so far but let's do it outside."

"Okay." Carole asked again, "Ms. Baker, are you sure you're okay?" Carole wanted the story but was going to make sure that Ms. Baker was fine.

"I'm better. I'm going to eat a couple of crackers and an apple. I'll be fine."

"I'd still like to talk to you but will be willing to come back in an hour or so."

Ms. Baker nodded. "Oh detective, I checked everywhere for Ms. Blankenship and we may have just missed her. I'll ask Mrs. Peterson to check again."

The detective didn't like it that someone, possible key in this case, also appeared to be missing. "You're sure she was here today?"

Ms. Baker moved to the secretarial desk and checked the sign in sheet. "Yes, she signed in at seven-twenty this morning."

Frederickson shook his head. "This doesn't add up. Something's wrong. I need to talk to you about Mr. Craft."

"What about Mr. Craft?"

At first neither of them noticed Carole still writing things down in her note pad. The detective turned, noticed the reporter and suggested, "Ms. Newton, let's go outside to talk?" He moved her toward the office door. "Ms. Baker, I'll be back in a few minutes," he said.

Carole was moving out of the main office and said, "I'd like to get some shots of the school and if you don't mind. We could do it in front."

He looked back and saw Ms. Baker through the office windows. She was in her office talking on the phone. Carole was now outside and waving to the two men in the news truck and a camera man who came out of the passenger side with a high end portable recording camera. He was a stocky guy, maybe in his early thirties with long dark hair. He crossed the street with the camera on his right shoulder. Frederickson had now made it outside and saw the red light blinking on the camera and knew that he needed to keep it short and sweet.

Carole Newton stood smiling as the camera was filming the front of the school. She was extremely professional and the number one field reporter in the metro area. She was five foot eight and slender with light golden blonde hair. She wore a blue dress that had a square cut neck. Always known as the consummate professional, Carole had been lucky to get many of the key stories on the past mayor's corruption trial. Frederickson hadn't noticed what she was wearing before. Once they got outside and he got a good look at Carole, he smiled. Not bad, he murmured, not bad.

As the cameraman panned down to where Carole and the detective stood she turned and started her interview. "Carole Newton here at Kennedy Charter Academy on Lenox on the east side where a middle school teacher has been reported missing. Captain Frederickson with the Detroit Police Department is the detective in charge of the case. Captain, can you tell our viewers what we know so far?"

"It's just detective."

"Okay, detective, what can you tell us."

"This morning we received a report that there may be a teacher missing from the parking lot here at Kennedy Charter. Our officers were on the scene in minutes and we've searched the neighborhood and sent a team through the area without any results. We're still not sure that he just didn't make it to school this morning. I'm working with the school and Macomb County Sheriff's Department where the teacher lives."

"Detective, what is the missing teacher's name?"

"Dansforth, Tommy Dansforth. If anyone has information that will assist in our investigation we would be happy to hear from you. Call 313- 555-1111 and ask for me or our team that is on this case." With that the detective said thanks and headed back into the school.

Carole had other questions and was left standing in front of the school. She turned back toward the camera and decided to re-cap the information for her viewers.

Ms. Baker was watching the action from her office and was happy that she didn't have to be on camera with the news team. The detective walked back into the main office and the principal came out to meet him. "Our main office has sent memos that we will close the rest of the week. With tomorrow being Thursday it makes a lot of sense. They will send all the parents a message saying we have a teacher that may be injured and missing. Until we have more details there isn't much else to tell them. All the teachers will be instructed to report tomorrow in case you need to talk to them again."

"Good idea," Frederickson said. "Hopefully we will have it solved by then. Did anyone ever find Ms. Blankenship?"

"No, she must have left. Her car isn't here and when Mrs. Peterson went back upstairs her purse was also gone and all the lights were off. Somehow we missed her."

He got up and asked for Ms. Blankenship's home address and phone numbers. "I'll try to get her at home."

Once the detective left Ms. Baker tried to replay the events in her mind. She was surprised when she looked up and saw Chris Banner who came back into the main office and knocked on her door. She waved him in. "I'm surprised you're still here," she said.

"What can I do to help? Tommy is a good friend and we're all concerned."

Baker agreed, "Me too, the detective is working on it and maybe he will have some information for us later tonight or tomorrow."

"I didn't like that he thought one of us may have been involved, Tommy is my friend and I don't know anyone that had a problem with him."

"Guess it is just their way of investigating. Don't take it personally, Chris. They're getting Tommy's wife to help fill in some of the details. Guess she would be able to tell them if he came home last night."

"Yeah, you're right."

"I'll call you at home if I hear anything else."

"Thanks." Chris put his coat on and headed outside. Brittany was sitting in his car and hoped he would have some information for her. When he got in she asked, "Do they know anything else?"

"Nope, guess they're going to see if Tommy's wife can help with the timeline. I wonder if he went home last night. Sure hope he's okay."

"I agree," said Brittany.

As he started to back out of the teachers' lot Chris watched a lady holding a microphone approach' *Oh no, I don't need this,* he thought. He slowed down hoping to drive past her when she moved near the front of his vehicle. Chris looked over at Brittany. "Let's not tell her anything." He stopped and rolled down his driver's side window.

"Thanks for stopping. I'm Carole Newton with Channel 7 News and just have a few questions."

Chris wanted to get straight to the point; "Sure, but we're just two teachers here and anything involving the school has to come from our administration."

"I understand," Carole stated. I just wanted to know how well you knew Tommy Dansforth, the missing teacher."

Both Chris and Brittany were surprised that the reporter knew Tommy's name and some of the details. Had she already talked to Ms. Baker or the police? Chris answered her question, "Mr. Dansforth is a middle school teacher here and a great guy."

"Do you have any reason to think that someone may have wanted to harm Mr. Dansforth?" Carole was fishing for a reaction or hoped that they knew of problems Dansforth had with students or parents.

"Like I said, Tommy is a great guy and a super teacher."

Carole knew this was a statement she heard almost every time someone was missing or worse. No one ever had any enemies until once it all started to come out. It would probably be the same in this case. She slipped her card into Chris' hand and said if he or the other teacher thought of anything please give her a call.

Once they pulled out onto the street, Brittany turned to Chris. "Do you think Tommy's dead?" He just grimaced.

Nine

Tommy Dansforth was breathing hard and rolling side to side. A blindfold covered his eyes and his hands were tied behind his back. His feet were bound together and the rope was connected up to his hands. He was virtually immobile. His head hurt and he thought that it must be bleeding. He tried to remember what happened. He was grabbed from behind, then spun around and caught a short man on the side of his head knocking him to the ground. Tommy was able to push him against the driver's door where he saw blood splatter across the side of the car. It all happened in the dark, when all of a sudden someone struck him from behind. *There must have been two of them.* Who did this and what did they want?

He was lying on his right side and the trunk was small and dark, *must be a compact.* Tommy's legs were bent toward his chest and he had tape across his mouth. The tape was pulling on his cheeks and starting to tear at his skin. Pain shot through his back. He wished he could try to search for an emergency handle to release the truck but unless he could get loose he wasn't able to help himself. There had to be some way to get out. Suddenly for the first time he heard voices from inside the car.

"That old sucker is pretty tough. He got you good." The passenger let out a deep laugh as he watched the driver sneer back at him.

"Yeah, I'll get him back. Once we get him to a safe place I'll make him pay for slamming my head into that car door. I hope you know where the hell we're headed to."

"Got the directions but couldn't find this so called River Road. I'll just keep on heading north. We're getting paid a couple thousand for delivering him, so just cool it until we get there. We're too close to finishing this job."

"Guess you're right, I can't believe he was able to get that swing in and knock me down. I'll be more careful when we get him out of the trunk." The two men continued along their route which now took them off road on a very rough unpaved path. The men stopped talking as the road was getting rougher.

Tommy bounced as the car picked up speed on what must have been a gravel road because he could hear stones hitting the undercarriage. Tommy thought the ride along the bumpy road seemed to go on forever as he was being bounced around in the dark trunk. He hadn't heard the men in a while and closed his eyes then the car came to a sudden stop. There were those same voices. They were now arguing about something. One man was yelling about the amount of money they were supposed to get. "It ain't worth the five grand they promised us. We need to ask for more."

"Not now, it's too late. These guys aren't going to give us more money at this point. We need to deliver him and get the hell out of here."

"I've got this gash on the side of my head and this old guy has been more trouble than we were told he would be." The vehicle suddenly accelerated at a fast rate of speed sending Tommy sliding back and crashing into the rear of the trunk. "This is bullshit! I'll be glad to get rid of both of them."

Tommy gritted his teeth and fought back tears. Who were these guys and why did someone pay them to grab him? What did they mean by both of them? The vehicle bounced along as they continued to pick up speed on the gravel road.

***

Detective Frederickson had three persons of interest. He

needed to find this the new sixth grade teacher, Mary Blankenship and then there's Mr. Sheppard, whose son seemed to always be in trouble at the school. When he questioned Ms. Baker about the janitor, Mr. Craft, she said that she knew about his record. She stated, "Craft was from the neighborhood and had been in trouble as a young man. He had turned his life around and the school thought it was good public relations hiring him. They felt he had paid the price for his mistakes," she said. "After all his crime was a long time ago and he hadn't been in trouble since." He understood and his investigation came up with the same results. Craft made a mistake as a young man and had been clean since then. Ms. Baker had told him that Mr. Craft was recommended by the pastor of the church that was adjacent to the school. "He was their caretaker for the past few years and did a great job."

The detective appreciated that the school wanted to help someone from the neighborhood but still had an officer check further into the man's life. He was now sitting at his desk and dialed Mary Blankenship's home phone number. It rang three times when someone finally picked up.

"Hello, can I help you?"

"This is Detective Frederickson, with the Detroit Police. Is this Mary Blankenship?"

"No, I'm her mother. Has something happened to my daughter?"

The detective could sense the fear in the voice. "No ma'am, I'm calling about an issue at Kennedy Charter Academy and need to ask her a few questions." He wondered why the woman immediately felt something happened to her daughter. *Guess it was the police calling*, he figured.

"I haven't seen her since she left this morning. She has a class after school, its downtown at Wayne State University. She doesn't get home until after nine. She always calls me if something is wrong."

"Thank you. Can you please give her my number and let her

know I need to talk to her as soon as possible."

"Sure." She wrote down the number that he had given her and asked again, "Are you sure she's okay?"

"Yes, I'm sorry to have bothered you but I need to ask her about another teacher at the school."

With that Mrs. Blankenship seemed relieved and thanked him. Frederickson looked at his watch and decided to try to contact Mr. Sheppard next. The number he had was a cell phone so he hoped that he would have better results on this call. A man on the other end answered on the second ring. "Bill Sheppard here, can I help you."

"Hello Mr. Sheppard, I'm Detective Frederickson with the Detroit Police and I need to ask you a couple of questions."

"What's that boy of mine done now?"

"Sir, I'm not calling about your son. We have an issue at his school that I need to ask you about. I'm told you had a meeting last night with Mr. Dansforth."

"Oh Tommy. He's been a great help with my son. I just stopped by to bring him the papers to get Devin into the special after school program he suggested."

"What time did you leave Mr. Dansforth?"

"He waited for me until I got out of work and I must have been there for about ten minutes. I'd say I left his classroom around six or six-thirty."

"Did you see anyone else there with him?"

"No, the school looked pretty empty. I don't think anyone else was around."

"How did Mr. Dansforth seem when you left him?"

"Tommy, he was fine, told me a joke that we both laughed a lot at. We walked down to the side door and he let me out. He watched me go to my car, and then headed back into the school."

"Thanks, Mr. Sheppard. If I have any other questions I'll call you." Once he hung up the detective wanted to check on the progress with the search for the teacher's wife. He hadn't heard anything from the Macomb County Sheriff's office and the search around the school's neighborhood hadn't netted any new information. He knew the forensic team wouldn't have anything on Dansforth's car for a day or two at best. He moved from his desk to the break room to grab a cup of coffee when he saw three other officers watching the television.

The television reporter, Carole Newton, was talking to a small group of students and their parents in front of the school. She was questioning them about Tommy Dansforth and they were all telling her what a great teacher he was. One young girl, had tears in her eyes as Carole stooped down to ask her about Mr. Dansforth. "He would always stay late and let us use his classroom computers to finish our homework. I hope he's okay." With that another student put her arms around the girl and they held onto each other. One of the parents told the reporter that Mr. Dansforth had been a favorite teacher of all the kids.

Frederickson stood there for a minute when his captain came into the break room. "Shit, Don, this school thing has blown up. The mayor just busted my balls about having you handling the case and the police chief is on his way here to see what we're doing. Tell me you have something."

Frederickson was pissed. "What in the hell does the mayor mean, me being on the case?"

"Detective, your past isn't a secret."

That may have been a big mistake Hughes made. No one in the break room saw it coming, certainly not Captain Hughes. It was a quick left hook that caught the captain on the right jaw sending him flying into the cupboards and knocking the coffee pot and Styrofoam cups across the room. Frederickson stood over him fist clenched like a boxer waiting for the ref to count his victim out. Officers ran over to get between Frederickson and the strewn body of their captain. One man grabbed the detective and others tried to pick their boss up. Frederickson pushed back at them yelling at the top of his lungs. "Tell that son-of-a-bitch, I'll be interviewing suspects. If he wants any more where that comes from I'll be waiting." With that the detective turned and stormed out of the precinct. He wasn't sure if he still had a job, but if he did he planned on doing it the best way possible. Frederickson planned on heading to Wayne State to follow up with Mary Blankenship who had classes scheduled that night.

Why did he have to catch this case? Could have sat back and watched his captain and another detective scramble with the mayor and police chief. Bet that asshole doesn't get off the floor for a while. Frederickson climbed into to his car and called Mrs. Blankenship again hoping she knew her daughter's class schedule. He thought, *crap, Wayne State is spread across three miles. Talk about a needle in a haystack.* Mary's mom didn't know what class her daughter had or where it was except that the building was on the Main Campus. When he didn't get additional results from the phone call he planned to stop by the Registration Office and get the class location.

_____Ten

LaShanda Ellis sat in her living room with her best friend Harrison discussing the events of the day. Her parents had a nice home a few blocks from the school and LaShanda's dad had recently completed painting the outside of their house. Many of the homes along Lenox had completed a lot of renovation recently. Since the school opened it seemed that more people had moved in and improved the homes along Lenox Avenue. LaShanda's mother brought them both a coke as the two students discussed their options. Harrison thanked Mrs. Ellis and she smiled back at them. "You both know that the police are doing everything possible to solve this. Mr. Dansforth wouldn't want you doing anything to get in trouble."

"Mom, we can't just sit here and do nothing."

"Okay, but I need to know everything you're both planning and Harrison, your mom doesn't want you leaving here without calling her first."

"Yes, I understand, Mrs. Ellis, we just want to see if we can help."

Mrs. Ellis knew that the students liked their teacher and his disappearance had struck them hard. She went back into the kitchen and saw that there was a news update on the small television on the kitchen counter. "Hey kids, turn on the television, there is a news story about the school and Mr. Dansforth."

LaShanda turned on the television and Mrs. Ellis walked back into the living room. Channel 7 News was running a special report and the reporter, Carole Newton, was standing in front of Kennedy

Charter Academy along with a detective. The interview had taken place earlier during the day and the runner board on the bottom of the screen stated that this was a recap of the day's story and Carolyn Clifford from the Channel 7 News desk giving viewers the details. Carolyn was the station anchor for both the six and eleven pm newscasts. The three stood in LaShanda's living room hoping for something new but there wasn't anything that gave them reason to hope that Mr. Dansforth would soon be found.

***

Detective Frederickson walked out of the Wayne State Registration Office on Woodward Avenue and headed to his car. He hadn't heard anything from the precinct and was surprised that Captain Hughes didn't order his arrest. The registrar gave him Mary's schedule. He checked his cell phone before heading out but he had no calls. Blankenship's class schedule took him across Cass Avenue past the Fountain Court to the Department of Chemistry. The lady in the Registrar's Office said the classroom was on the second floor. Frederickson parked along West Warren Avenue near the Science Hall and walked to the Chemistry building. He wasn't happy that he had to try to find Ms. Blankenship at the University, but he knew she could hold some answers to his case. He headed up the stairway to the Chemistry Lab that Ms. Blankenship was supposed to be in. He could see from the glass window that the lab had close to twenty students with the professor writing an assignment on the front white board. He slowly pulled open the door and stood at the back of the room, hoping that the instructor would acknowledge him.

"Excuse me, are you looking for someone," the professor said turning toward the stranger at the door. Everyone spun around and stopped what they were doing.

Frederickson cleared his throat. "Yes, sorry to interrupt the class. I need to talk to Mary Blankenship for a minute."

"Sorry, but Ms. Blankenship didn't make it to class tonight." The professor watched the man wave thanks and walked back out before he turned back to the white board and continued to jot down instructions.

Frederickson stood outside the classroom in the hallway for a few minutes before turning and leaving. He was mad as hell but now was left with only more questions in this case. Mary Blankenship wasn't in the meeting at the school, now she's not at her evening class. Was she missing too? Why hadn't she come forward at the meeting in the gym?

***

The District Attorney couldn't believe his eyes. He stood in his office with two lead investigators watching the Channel 7 News coverage. "How in the hell did this happen?" He was yelling at both of them. "I told you to keep an eye on him."

The two men just looked back at each other. "Not sure, boss. Are you sure it's the same Dansforth fellow?"

Fox yelled, "How many Tommy Dansforth's do you think there are in this city? You two were supposed to make sure that the guy and his family are safe." The D.A. paged his secretary. "Call the Twelfth Precinct, and ask for the captain." *Of all the precincts why did the Twelfth catch this case?* Jack Fox knew it was a dead end for washed up cops. He paced around the office waiting for his secretary to confirm that she had the captain on the line. His two investigators paced in the office and looked back at each other.

The secretary informed him, "I've got Captain Hughes on line one, Sir."

Fox decided to approach carefully, at least until he had the details he needed. "Captain, Jack Fox here. I need to know what the hell is going on with the Dansforth case."

66

Damn, not only the police chief and interim mayor, but now the DA. The captain knew Fox and his reputation. The guy was a real ball buster. Fox always complained about the way the police handled their investigations. "Yes, Jack, my detective is still working on leads and downtown right now interviewing a person of interest."

"Crap!" Fox was yelling at the top of his lungs. "This guy Dansforth and his wife are my key witnesses in a high profile case. Our case is going to a Grand Jury next week and we need him to get an indictment."

Oddly this information didn't surprise Hughes. Did he know more? Although their investigative time had been spent on possible suspects from the school this was a new wrinkle. Could he know that Dansforth was a witness to a crime? Hughes answered, "Jack we had no idea that Mr. Dansforth was…"

"Of course you didn't, your people are so sloppy that my office didn't want any of you involved. Get that damn detective down to my office now!"

Before the captain could answer, Fox hung up. *How did this happen*, he thought. Captain Hughes had to make a choice, either pull Frederickson off the case, especially after the episode in the break room, or leave him on the case and he'll probably screw it up. *That could be his ass too*, he thought. He needed to get the detective downtown to the DA's office.

Frederickson was driving back to the precinct when his cell phone rang. He looked down and saw it was the captain's number. *Crap, what now*, he thought. He decided not to answer. I could say I was in the University and didn't hear the call because it was so noisy. He turned off of West Warren onto Cass and planned on paying a visit to Mr. Sheppard's home. Maybe he needed to meet Sheppard's kid. He could have had something to do with this if he didn't like Dansforth. After all he had just talked to the man on the phone and maybe there was more to him being with Dansforth that evening. As he headed north on Cass toward I-94 the phone rang again. *Damn! I'm never going to get anything done if I got to answer every call.* Frederickson looked down and hit the answer button on his steering wheel and waited for the captain to talk. He wasn't sure where it was going to head to.

"Why the hell didn't you answer your phone?" Before Frederickson could answer, the captain then barked out. "I need you to head downtown to the DA's office now! Looks like our missing teacher may be a key witness for them."

Frederickson almost slammed on his brakes. *What, now his case involves the DA and he has to listen to Fox blow his horn. This investigation is getting worse with each step?* "What do you want me to do now?" Things couldn't get worse between him and Hughes.

The captain was quiet for a minute, "All I know is Jack Fox threw a major fit when he called. Detective, it will be your ass they use for target practice."

What was it? "You threatening me?"

"Detective I owe you one, and you can be sure that it will get paid especially when you're not expecting it. Now get your ass down to the DA's office."

"I'm not answering to that son of a …"

The captain hung up before the detective could finish his statement. He knew this could become the shit storm of all shit storms.

_____Eleven

Jack Fox was still yelling as the two men hurried out of his office hoping to get out of sight before he went totally ballistic. *Too late,* they thought. They had offered Dansforth protection many times but he refused. After all, no one knew that he was the one to come forward about the crime, except for a few people in the DA's office, and the police officer that reported what Dansforth and his wife had witnessed. The Detroit political landscape had undergone a major upheaval since the recent Federal investigations and criminal prosecutions of the Mayor and two City Council members. The Free Press had run an expose on crime uncovered in city hall and those that were either still under investigation or had been sentenced to prison terms. Fox and his office had stayed above reproach during these investigations but if he lost his key witness who knew who else could fall under the federal microscope.

Detective Frederickson knew Fox and he didn't like him. Earlier in the detective's career, Fox had joined the office of Wayne County Prosecutor and started an investigation into corruption in the police force. The case brought national attention to the entire organization due to the acts of a few. Frederickson himself was questioned many times by Fox and accused of wrong doing, he never forgot it. *Now he was ordered to report to the son of a bitch.* Fox propelled his career after that successful case to the office of Wayne County District Attorney.

The DA's offices were located on West Fort Street, so it didn't take Frederickson very long to get there. Walking up the stairs in the office building he saw the sign announcing, Eastern District of Michigan, District Attorney Jack Fox. He prepared himself for a knock down drag out fight. Fox's office was in Suite 2001. The atrium had a great view of the riverfront and downtown. You could see all the way from the Ambassador Bridge and the Canadian shoreline to Belle Isle. It was an intimidating view and Fox used it to the fullest. Frederickson took one last deep breath before entering. *This could end very badly* and he knew it. After the outburst in the break room with Captain Hughes, Frederickson knew he was like a fire cracker with the fuse about to ignite. He pushed the door open and strolled in with his chest pushed out and a scowl on his face. "I'm here to see Fox," he barked out.

The secretary, a pretty young lady was startled when the door flew open. She jumped in her seat when he again loudly proclaimed, "I'm here to see Fox!"

She looked wide eyed at the man now standing in front of her desk. "Yes sir, do you have an appointment?"

The detective realized that he scared her but had grown very impatient with being told what to do and just about had enough. "Detective Frederickson, Twelfth Precinct, I was ordered to appear here."

The secretary pushed back in her chair, pointing to the right, "He's expecting you." She blurted out and motioned toward the large mahogany door. In large gold letters embossed across the front it stated Jack Fox, District Attorney.

Just as the detective thought, *egotistic son of a bitch. I'll be damned if I'm working his case.* Frederickson wished he was somewhere else right now, anywhere else. Detective Frederickson swung open the heavy door into Jack Fox's office and saw the DA standing next to the large wall of glass looking out over the river below. He expected Fox to start on him right away but Fox kept looking out. "Fox, I understand you wanted me to come here!" He stated loudly.

The District Attorney slowly turned around and just looked at

Frederickson. "I know you," he said. "You're still on the force?"

That was the last straw. "You son of a bitch. Yes, I'm still on the force. I'm the senior detective from the Twelfth Precinct, and handling this case." Frederickson was close to exploding again. He already hated the man and now wanted to push him out of those damned windows.

"Hold on detective! I'm just surprised that I knew who was handling the case. I thought that by now you might have been promoted to a captain or retired. I didn't mean anything else." Fox was speaking very calmly and had both hands raised up in front of him like someone signaling for a time out.

Frederickson didn't know what to make of this. *Was Fox being a smart ass or what?* "I'm in the middle of my case and about to interview a person of interest when my dumb shit captain calls and orders me to drop everything and get over here." The detective was now out of breath and had his right hand clenched. "I need to know what's going on." He yelled.

"Sure detective, Frederickson is it, right, let's calm down." Fox was surprised at the comment about the detective's captain, *Wondered what's going on there?* Fox had to calm the situation down, "Why don't you sit down and I'll fill you in." With that Jack Fox moved to his desk and sat back in the large black leather chair. He motioned to the two seats in front of his desk for the detective to have a seat. "Come on, detective, we have a lot of work to do and it will be best if we do it together. Can we get you a cup of coffee or something else to drink?"

Frederickson stood behind the two chairs and tried to gather his composure. *Could the D.A. actually want to share information? What did he mean by working together?* This certainly wasn't the Jack Fox he remembered. He wasn't going to play second fiddle to the DA's office. "I don't need to sit down. I've got a person of interest that I was trying to find and I need to get my job done." Still standing, he was staring at Fox waiting for an answer.

Jack Fox leaned back in his chair, lit a long cigar, and took a few puffs to get it going. "Hope the smoke doesn't bother you, detective, I know it's a no smoking building but if you won't tell I surely won't." He continued puffing on the stogie and waited for Frederickson to respond.

"What's all this about our missing teacher being an important witness for you?" Frederickson wasn't interested in making small talk.

Fox swung around to the large maple file cabinet behind his desk and searched through a drawer on the right side. He removed a manila folder and opened it on his desk. "Here, I had my secretary make copies for you." Frederickson moved closer to the desk. "Dansforth and his wife were going to appear at a deposition next week regarding a murder they witnessed at Greektown." He slid the folder to the opposite side of the desk.

Frederickson moved to the large leather chair across from Fox's desk and grabbed the file as he plopped down into the seat. While the detective leafed through the papers, the phone in the office rang.

Fox turned and answered the call. "Yeah, he's right here. I'll get him for you. Detective, it's for you."

Frederickson looked at him, with a puzzled frown. "What?"

"The call, it's for you, your captain's on the line."

Jesus Christ, I just talked to him, what can he want now. Guess he'll have the DA put me under suspension while I'm right here. Frederickson jumped up as Fox handed the receiver across to him. Holding the receiver in his right hand and before he could say anything the captain rattled off some orders. Frederickson could hardly answer because Hughes was talking a mile a minute. He barely got out, "Yes, okay yes, we're working on background material right now, okay. Yeah, I got it." The phone went dead, the captain abruptly hung up. Frederickson handed the phone back to Fox with an angry look on his face. "Did you contact the governor's office?"

"Hell no, what would he have to do with this?"

"My captain just got a call from the governor's office wanting an update on our case. They're all over him and want us to hand the case over to another group. He told them we were working together and will have an update soon."

Jack Fox was obviously pissed and stood up walking to the office door. "Sally, call the god damn governor's office, and I won't take any bullshit answer like he's out." He stomped back toward the large desk and sat on the same side next to Frederickson. Fox now pounded on the desk and turned toward the detective, "That stupid shit wants to get re-elected or has some big job in mind. His office is getting involved in every fricken case that we have."

Frederickson was surprised at Fox's response. Sally informed Fox that someone was finally on the line. Fox picked up his phone and waited for the person to speak. After holding for a few minutes someone must have come on the line. The detective listened as Fox cut the person to shreds.

"Listen, I don't give a shit if you or your boss wants to know what's going on. We're in the middle of two important cases and the detective in charge is filling me in right now. No, I'm not in a position to give you an update. I don't care what precinct he's from. How about you let me do my job and when and if we have something, maybe I'll let you know." Fox was holding the receiver away from his ears and Frederickson knew the person on the other end must have hung up.

"Okay, detective, it looks like it's you and me versus the high rollers in Lansing."

"Was that the governor?"

"No, he wouldn't have the balls to take the call himself. He had one of his underlings kicking my ass. Guess my move to the state capitol is out." With that Fox burst out laughing. The detective tried to hold his laughter back but he had to laugh at that too. "Detective, I can't do this without your help, and I'll give you anything you need from my office to support you. I'm not sure what the mayor, governor or any of these politicians are hoping to accomplish but it's our job and we'll handle it how we think."

Frederickson looked Jack Fox straight in the eye. "You know, way back I felt you destroyed my career. Guess you were just following the evidence. My partner was deep into bad shit and I didn't have a clue. I can see how it looked like we must have been in it together."

"I'm really sorry about that, Don. Sometimes I guess we go head first into something without looking at possible repercussions. I wish once you were cleared you got back with me. I could have helped fix everything up for you."

The detective was surprised again at Fox and his statement. "Well I could have done a better job myself instead of holding a hard on for everyone."

"Me too?"

"Especially you." It was silent for a minute then the detective stood up. "Jack, sorry it went that way. I'm partially to blame and could have been more cooperative instead of fighting the investigation."

Fox also stood and extended his right hand. "We're partners now. I promise to share everything I have with you."

"Deal." Both men shook hands and got down to business.

"Detective, the missing teacher is my main witness in a murder that happened a few weeks back. I couldn't tell anyone because I'm sure there's a leak in the police department."

"Where did this murder take place?"

"The Greektown Casino garage. Dansforth and his wife had been eating in Greektown, at the Pegasus and after playing the slots they headed to their car on the sixth floor of the parking garage on Monroe. Dansforth said they were in their car getting ready to pull out when shots were fired in the row across from their car. They both saw the shooter."

"Who was it?"

"That's the thing. They tried looking through mug books for

us but couldn't identify the shooter until last week. He comes into my office holding the Sunday Free Press. I've got the guy he tells me. I look at the newspaper and he's pointing to the lieutenant governor's photo in the Parade section."

"The lieutenant governor is the shooter?"

"No, he was pointing at the lieutenant governor's family photo. He tells me it was the guy's youngest son. I asked, are you positive, he says, that's the guy."

"Holy shit!" Frederickson was stunned.

"My staff has been checking all of this down. We got surveillance from the Casino security team and the kid was there. He was playing poker with a guy that won big, really big. We found out the kid has a gambling problem, a big problem. He followed the guy to the parking garage, we have him on video."

"Then why do you need the teacher?"

"We have photos of the kid going in the garage behind the big winner but the video in the garage isn't clear. I only have the shooter from the back. Dansforth and his wife are our only eye witnesses."

"Is that why the governor's office is involved?"

"Could be, like I said, I think there's a leak in the police department. Someone has tipped them off and the lieutenant governor's kid is in the wind. No idea where he is. Detective, I can't trust anyone, especially cops right now."

"Why are you telling me all of this?"

"Detective, because of our history, I feel that you might be the most trustworthy person in the department. Plus we have a lot in common. Officials in Lansing have me frozen out, and the governor's office is on my ass. We're both fighting something bigger than either of us. You have been frozen out in your precinct too. Detective, I feel I can trust you."

"Jack, I promise everything you told me will be kept safe."

"Thanks, now let's get these guys." The two men huddled in the DA's office planning their strategy.

***

The ride must have been hours long since Tommy was awake and he knew that he could be anywhere by now. He hurt everywhere and was dizzy from rolling around in the trunk. They easily could have driven into Canada or taken him to one of the many small islands off the river. Harsens Island was just about fifty miles north of the city and accessible by ferry boat. There were many desolate spots, especially in the winter. Tommy knew that he had been out cold for a while, but had been awake for at least a couple of hours. He tried unsuccessfully to free his hands or feet many times and now only waited for his captors to take the next step. The car had rocked along and the ride had been a lot smoother since they left what must have been a dirt road. *How he wished he knew what was going on. Why did these men want him?*

The vehicle slowed down as it approached a sharp turn along the road and came to a stop. "Get out and open the gate for me," the driver told his partner. He handed the man a piece of paper with instructions on it. This led to a private stretch that had a gate that required an access code to open. As his partner punched in the numbers, the heavy metal gate slowly squealed as it slid from right to left allowing the car to enter. Once they pulled through the opening, his partner punched in another code and the gate moved back into a locked position.

"Shit, it's cold as hell out there," the man said as he jumped back into the vehicle. "We're finally here so let's get the job done and get the hell out." This would be a good payday for the two of them, even though one man had taken a hard hit from Tommy when they grabbed him in the school parking lot. "I'd still like to get one more lick at that old man before we have to leave him here."

"Yeah, I understand, however, maybe we don't get paid if he's not in good shape."

That conversation made Tommy feel a little better. At least

they weren't sent to kill him, but what was next? He pulled again on the ropes but the binding that held his hands behind his back only seemed to get tighter. The ride now turned very bumpy again and Tommy bounced along as the vehicle accelerated. *How much longer would this be* he thought. A sliver of light had shown through the tiny gap along the edge of the trunk along right quarter panel. Tommy figured that the vehicle must have some damage to that side. It also let a lot of cold air into the trunk and along with the binding the cold air caused Tommy's hands and feet to become numb. Even if he could get loose, he probably couldn't stand up, let alone fight back. He tried to kick at the trunk lid hoping to make enough noise to alert anyone near, but his legs were bound so tight that it was impossible to hit the trunk lid.

The tape across Tommy's face had pulled his skin so tight along his cheeks that he knew that he should stop trying to get it off. Maybe this was close to being over.

Twelve

Frederickson knew he had to drive to his precinct after meeting with the DA. That was something he didn't look forward to. Hughes said he'd get even, but what did he mean by that. He was hoping to get a call from the officers dispatched to the Blankenship address. He had just turned off of the Lodge Freeway when his cell phone rang. "Detective, this is Officer Ryan. We're standing on the porch of the Blankenship residence and no one is here."

"Shit, it's eight o'clock. Where could they be? I talked to her mother a little before six." This wasn't good. After the meeting with Jack Fox, he was sure that Dansforth's disappearance had to be related to the incident at Greektown. He also wondered how the new young teacher and her disappearance now fit into the investigation.

Officer Ryan added, "Don, we've checked next door and they haven't seen Mary or her mother. What would you like us to do?"

"Stay there and keep an eye on the place. Maybe someone will return soon. Check in with me in an hour."

"Got it."

Things really didn't add up. Where was Mary Blankenship? She wasn't at the school's meeting or was she. Not at her evening class and now not at home. And why is her mother gone? Is this girl involved, and if so, how? The detective needed a break in the case. He pulled into the parking lot of the precinct and had an idea. They needed to flush out whoever was involved in this and maybe he could use the press to his advantage. He remembered the reporter, Carole, from the school earlier. Maybe he could use her to his advantage.

Carole Newton had finished reporting for the evening and was about ready to leave the station when she got a call. Grabbing her cell phone she was surprised to see who was calling. "Ms. Newton, this is Detective Frederickson. We talked earlier today at Kennedy Charter Academy."

"Yes, I remember. What can I do for you detective?"

"I need a favor. Can you meet me at our precinct tomorrow around eight?"

"Sure. Can you tell me what this is about?"

"I will tomorrow. See you then." The detective hung up.

When she got off the phone she wondered, *was there a break in the case? What did the detective want from her?* It was Carole's experience that when the police wanted to offer information they always expected something in return. She didn't know what she had to offer but wanted to know what the detective planned on telling her.

Frederickson had a plan but he needed help from the press. The search hadn't netted anything. If this was an abduction, the people who took Dansforth would be seeking a ransom. They would have certainly called with a demand for money by now. He planned to call Jack Fox with his idea. Detective Frederickson walked into the precinct knowing that every eye watched him making his way to the bullpen. Captain Hughes was in his office and looked up as Frederickson sat at his desk. The captain moved out of his office and walked toward the detective's desk. One of the officers saw that this might be the second confrontation of the day and decided to move towards Frederickson's desk. "Hey Don, Heard you were at the D.A.'s office, did he give you more details about the case?"

Frederickson was surprised about the question, especially from this officer. He now saw the captain who was about five feet away. Don realized what the officer was doing, and appreciated it.

"No, he just wanted to make sure that we knew how important the Dansforth case was. Guess the teacher might be involved in something the DA has going on."

The officer nodded, "I have some of the details that we worked on for you at the school, do you want to go over them now?"

"Sure, that would be great, thanks." Frederickson pushed the chair next to his desk and the officer sat down. The two men began discussing the case as Hughes continued to watch them from a few feet away.

The Captain started to move closer and joined the conversation, "Detective, how about if I call the DA and see if I can get more details from him."

"Good luck with that, when I asked him questions about his case he nearly bit my head off." The detective hoped to keep his captain concentrated on their part of the case and not their confrontation from earlier.

"Okay, but if necessary I'm calling downtown to see what they know. Did he offer anything that could help us?"

"Not really, he just wanted to make sure we were following procedure. Doesn't trust our methods, I guess."

"He's not the only one, guess the mayor and governor's office want to take our case over. I got my ass handed to me on a platter because you're involved."

"Guess it didn't help that it's in our precinct either." Frederickson knew that tossing it back at the Twelfth would piss the captain off.

"Well I told them we're on it and making progress, now it's up to you to make it work." Hughes turned back toward his office, looking back at Frederickson and the officer who continued to cover details in the case. Hughes knew everyone in the precinct was watching them. Either he yanked Frederickson into his office or just concentrated on the case at hand. He decided to just go with the case for now.

Once the captain was out of listening distance the officer asked, "You really think the DA is up to something?"

"I think he's just interested in us solving this. If we say he has a person of interest that has been brought in for questioning and the news runs it, who knows." Frederickson knew that he needed to get both the DA and the press in on the story to have any chance of it being believable. "It's been done before. Maybe someone thinks we have a witness or suspect and either comes forward or panics. We need a break, and this is a chance to make it happen."

Captain Hughes was still watching from his office and continued to give Frederickson a cold glare. The detective saw it but ignored the Captain's look of disgust.

***

Carole Newton decided to go back in her office. She wanted to do more background on both Tommy Dansforth and the lead detective. So far her only information was from the people she interviewed. The search for information on the missing teacher, Tommy Dansforth, resulted in four reference sites. The first one covered his corporate career and she pretty much got that from the principal at the school. The others she found were his facebook, and school related post. Nothing showed up that she hadn't already found out at the school. Tommy was well liked and involved with his students, like a lot of teachers, both in school and with extracurricular after school activities. She turned her attention to Detective Frederickson. She found his record on the Detroit Police personnel site. He started as a beat cop on the lower east side of Detroit. The area was much different than it is today. It was a collage of ethnicities. Although it was predominately Italian and Polish, the Irish cop got along very well with everyone. There were many articles regarding an arrest that the detective made that broke open an investigation into police corruption. Carole stopped when she found another one that said Frederickson later became the main suspect in an internal probe. The investigator into the probe was the current District Attorney, Jack Fox. This piqued her interest. As she continued her research, the last article told how Frederickson was exonerated of all charges. There really wasn't any more reference to the investigation. The only outcome she surmised was that Frederickson was sent to the Twelfth Precinct as punishment for whatever his part may have been.

"Carole, I thought you left." She turned to see her station manager standing in the doorway.

"I was on my way out when I got a call from the detective on the teacher's case. He wants to meet at the precinct tomorrow morning."

"Is there a break in the case? Did they find the teacher?"

"I asked but he just said they needed our assistance."

"Watch out for cops bearing gifts."

They both laughed. "I'll call when I find out what they want."

"Sure, you know you're my best reporter, so go with your instinct."

"Thanks, boss."

Carole watched as he turned toward the exit. She appreciated that he trusted her and hoped that there was a break in the case. She was also happy that Frederickson was willing to give her the story.

_____**Thirteen**

The car finally came to a stop. Tommy Dansforth was in pain from rolling side to side in the trunk as the car bounced on the rough road. The voices from inside grew silent and he lay with anticipation of what was next. Is this where it all ends? Who ordered his abduction? His only clue was the upcoming trial he was supposed to be a witness in. Maybe he should have agreed to the offer of protection from the DA. There weren't any sounds from either outside or inside the car. Then he heard doors slamming and voices outside.

"Where in the hell have you two been? You were supposed to be here hours ago." The voice was gravely and deep. Not one Tommy had heard before.

"Problems! The old shit didn't go down very easy. Then we had an issue with the directions. What road is Highway 29? It ain't on the map."

"You dumb shit. River Road is Highway 29. I told you take River Road all the way to the ferry landing."

"You never said River Road."

Tommy knew from the argument outside that he was north of the city, either in Marine City, Algonac or they may have crossed into Canada. There were ferry crossings at both cities. He wondered where exactly they had taken him.

The argument outside had stopped and Tommy heard the car doors slam. It seemed oddly quiet and then the trunk popped open. The light beam aimed directly in his eyes temporarily blinded him.

At least two men were over the top of him pulling him out of the trunk. Tommy's legs were numb. He was tossed onto the ground and pain rose through his limbs as he hit the gravel.

"You just lay there, old man," the order was barked out loudly.

Tommy couldn't move if he wanted to. His legs were stiff after hours of being constricted in the trunk. He was rolled over on his stomach as one of the men straddled him cutting the binding from his legs and feet. Tommy's face was pushed into the gravel as sharp stones cut into his cheeks.

"Don't try anything funny, I've got my gun this time and won't hesitate to use it."

This was one of the voices he had heard arguing in the car. The two men were now grabbing his arms and pulling him up. Tommy tried to stand but it was close to impossible. His legs wobbled and they pinned him up against the back of the vehicle as one man continued to press his body against Tommy's, keeping him up. The tape was ripped from his face and Tommy briefly let out a cry. He wanted to know why he had been grabbed. "What the hell's going on?" Tommy's voice cracked with the first words he had spoken in close to sixteen hours.

"Drag him into the cabin."

"I'll get him."

That voice came from a new person speaking. Tommy hurt everywhere. This person wrapped his arms around Tommy's chest and jerked him off the back of the vehicle and started dragging him. The man must be huge because Tommy's legs were dangling in the air as he was being carried off.

"Stop, stop, I think I can walk!"

The giant man continued carrying him along. His arms were like a vise squeezing Tommy's upper body and causing more pain. Tommy struggled and found enough courage to kick back at his captor. His legs were starting to gain some feeling and he didn't know what was next but he wasn't giving in. He soon realized that his feet were pretty far off the ground and he was being carried. The large arms were wrapped around Tommy's upper body were carrying him like a rag doll. It was hopeless. Tommy had no options other than to see what was next. It was extremely cold outside and the wind rushing across Tommy's face stung his cheeks. The tape that was pulled off his face had torn his skin and the cold multiplied the pain. His arms were tingling and hands were numb. Ropes bound his hands and seemed to be wrapped around his upper body.

In the distance there was a sound of a door opening and more voices came from inside. "Put him over there." The warmth of the room hit him and felt good. After hours in the cold trunk he was happy to be somewhere other than the brutal cold. Tommy was slammed into a wooden chair and his arms were again restrained to the back of the chair. He scanned the small cabin room left to right and once he saw her tied up in a chair he gasped and was horrified. There in the corner was Tommy's wife, bound and gagged to a chair. He screamed out. "Let her go. She hasn't hurt anyone. What in the hell do you want with us?"

His wife shook her head from side to side. She tried to signal to her husband, but the gag was so tight, there wasn't anything she could do.

"I said let her go!" Tommy was still yelling when a man from behind punched him knocking the chair and Tommy over. His head hit the floor and he was on his back with his legs dangling in the air.

"I said shut the hell up, old man! Either you need to stop yelling or I have no problem slitting her throat."

That threat stopped Tommy immediately. He knew these guys were serious. He looked up at the huge man standing over him and spoke again, this time in a more begging tone. "Please don't hurt her. She hasn't done anything to deserve this. I promise to do whatever you want. Just let her go."

"That's better." The man pulled Tommy up and placed the

chair back on the floor. "Sit down!" Tommy nodded and sat back on the chair. "I'll loosen her gag if you shut up." Tommy just shook his head up and down too scared to say anything that would bring more pain to his wife.

For the first time he checked around the cabin and saw that there were two more guys on the other side of the room talking quietly. Maybe they were his captors. The big man was moving toward Tommy's wife and pulled a knife from his pocket. Tommy arched his back hoping the man wasn't going to hurt her. The huge man blocked Tommy's view of his wife. He walked around the back side of his wife and snarled back toward Tommy. "Remember our agreement." Tommy just kept his eye on the giant guy. Then the man put his hands on the back of her head and cut the gag. He then moved around the front of her and leaned down. Pointing his big hand in her face, he said, "I don't want you to say anything. Do you understand?" She nodded. Turning back toward Tommy he said, "I'll remove the rope from her arms but understand I don't have a problem killing either one of you." Cutting the ropes but leaving her hands bound together, the man kept an eye on Tommy. He pointed his knife at Kathy Dansforth's throat. "Remember what I said."

Fourteen

LaShanda was just saying goodbye to Harrison when her cell phone rang. "Hey girl, my mom got a call from the school and they're cancelling classes tomorrow."

She turned to Harrison. "Wait Bernice is calling."

"Sure," he said.

She continued talking to Bernie. "Yeah, we got the same call. Guess until they know what's going on we won't have school."

"They said that Mr. Dansforth is still missing and no one knows where he is."

"This is crazy. He wouldn't just go off like that. Harrison and I think someone isn't telling us the whole story."

"Harrison's at your place?"

"Yeah."

"Sweet."

"No nothing like that. We're just talking about the thing at school."

"Sure, but that boy is hot." With that both girls laughed.

"We're going to head over to school tomorrow and check out the parking lot. Wanna come along?"

"Count me in, I bet we can figure this out. What time?"

Come on over to my house about nine. We'll go from here but don't tell anyone else. Too many people will only cause them to make us leave."

"Okay. See you then."

LaShanda planned on filling Harrison in on the plan. "Maybe we can check around school better than the cops. I know a couple of kids that live on Lenox but don't go to our school. They will be able to give us some dope on the neighborhood."

"Sounds good, I'll see you tomorrow." With that Harrison headed down the street to his house. LaShanda stood at the end of the porch and smiled watching him when her mom came outside.

"I told Harrison's mom that I'd call when he was on his way home." She dialed the number and gave his mom the information. Both women commented about the incident at the school and expressed concern for Mr. Dansforth. They knew he was a positive influence on their students and hoped that everything would turn out okay. In this neighborhood you never knew for sure.

It was light outside the next morning as Harrison strolled down the street to meet LaShanda. Once he was close he could see that she was already outside waiting for him. "Wow, you're out here early."

"Bernie should be here in any second." Harrison knew that Bernice was LaShanda's best friend and it didn't surprise him that she was tagging along. "That's cool." The two of them turned when they heard Bernie call out.

"Hey, I'm not late, am I?"

"No, we were just waiting outside for you." LaShanda smiled as Bernie winked at her. The three started down Drexel Street heading for Lenox. LaShanda told them that she called one of her friends last night and they gave her a few tips on the street that they could check out. "Can't tell my mom about this, but my friend said that the second house on the corner down the street near Kercheval used to be a drug house. It's abandoned now. I think we should check it out."

They all agreed. When the three students turned onto Lenox they were surprised to see Mr. Banner outside in the school parking lot. Harrison waved as they got closer. "What are the three of you doing down here," Banner asked.

They looked back at each other not sure if they should tell him their plan. "Well, we were wondering if there was any news about Mr. Dansforth."

"Sorry to say but the police haven't found anything yet. Everyone is still hoping that it's just a mistake and he's gone somewhere." Banner wasn't sure how much information the kids knew or what he should tell them.

LaShanda nodded but had a puzzled look on her face. "How come you're outside?" She could see that the lot was almost full of other teacher cars and the spot where Mr. Dansforth usually parked was still roped off.

"Ms. Baker wanted something from her car. I told her I'd come out and get it. All the teachers are in today and Ms. Baker bought donuts for the training room. She needed help bringing them in." Banner pointed back to Ms. Baker's car as he walked over to get some boxes from the back seat. The three students offered to help. "Sure," he said as they watched him retrieve three flat large boxes that had Kroger Bakery written along the sides. "You guys shouldn't be out here. How about coming in. Do you want a donut?"

The two girls said thanks but they already ate. "I'll take one," Harrison answered. Banner opened the box and extended it toward the student. Harrison reached into the top box and was happy to find a large bear claw within his grasp. "Thanks." LaShanda told Mr. Banner, "We're just heading down the street, thanks for the offer but we'll be okay."

Banner didn't have the authority to make them come in and told them, "Be careful and stay out of the parking lot. The police have more work to do and don't want anyone near the roped off area." With that Mr. Banner headed back in to the school.

"I think he knows something more but can't tell us," Harrison said. They watched as the front door closed behind Mr. Banner and turned looking at the parking lot and the crime scene tape that surrounded about four parking spots near the entrance. "Let's check it out," Harrison said chomping on his bear claw.

LaShanda thought better of the idea. "Better not, someone is probably watching from Ms. Baker's office and we'll get in trouble. Let's go down to the house I told you both about. Maybe we'll find something down there." It was agreed and the three headed down toward the opposite corner from their school. Lenox was a long narrow street with mostly old two story houses on both sides. The houses were built during the early 1950's and most were two family flats. Although many of them needed outside work, some had been freshly painted and there was only about three or four that had been boarded up. One of those was the house LaShanda's friend had described to her. They stopped in front of the boarded up run down house and looked at each other.

"Not sure we should try to get in that thing." Harrison said.

"Harrison's right. Look at that porch. Those steps are falling in."

"LaShanda, how long did your friend say this been empty?"

"She didn't say, just that before the school moved in it was a crack house."

"I think we'd be better off if the cops checked this out."

Bernie agreed. The three turned back around only to see Mr. Banner heading toward them. He was about two houses away and motioned for them to come with him. "Crap, now what," Harrison said. They walked back to where Banner stood and waited to see what he wanted.

"You three shouldn't be out here, Ms. Baker wants you to come into the school. Why don't you tell me what's going on?"

The three students looked at each other before Harrison answered. "We just wanted to see if we could help with finding out what happened to Mr. Dansforth."

"I know you're worried, we all are. I think it would be best if you all come into the school and we can talk."

The small group headed back up Lenox and entered the side door of the school. Mr. Banner had them follow him into his classroom where Ms. Baker was sitting. "Thank you Mr. Banner, I'll take it from here," she said.. The three students figured they were in real trouble now.

Fifteen

The small cabin was just across the water from Marine City on the Canadian side of Lake St. Clair. The two men who grabbed Dansforth were met at the ferry crossing on the Canadian side once they called to say they were on the ferry. They were all driven to the hideout that was hard to find. Once they delivered Dansforth, they had to wait around for their payout. They were getting restless and just wanted their money and to get back across the Lake. "Hey! What about our money?"

'We'll get it for you but first we have to confirm with the boss that everything's okay."

"Bullshit. We brought you the guy you wanted. We want to get out of this God forsaken place. Whoever heard of Sombra anyhow?"

"You dumb shits need to shut the hell up." With that the man that seemed to be in charge said he was going outside to call the boss.

Dansforth now had the information regarding where they had been taken to. He knew that Sombra is a village located on the St. Clair River, in southwest Ontario, Canada. He had been there and knew it was known for their quaint specialty shops. Dansforth knew that the population was probably only a hundred people and not many people would want to cross the river this time of year. Tommy Dansforth was securely tied to a chair but wanted to help his wife, somehow there had to be a way. He called out, "You need to untie her now!" They just ignored him. He shouted out, this time very agitated. "I said untie her!"

The big man with a thick dark beard turned toward him. "Shut up, old man." He now moved to a few feet in front of Dansforth.

Tommy didn't let up, "You're screwing with the wrong person." With that last statement the men burst into laughter. "Hell, you're the one tied up. What do you think you can do to us?" Dansforth looked over at his wife. She had tears in her eyes. He knew they were right. What could he do? But he wasn't giving up, "At least take the ropes off her legs."

"Say please." The big guy now stood with his hands on his hips with a sinister smile on his face. Tommy looked back at his wife. He felt helpless, "Okay, please take the ropes off her legs."

"That's better." The large man moved over to Tommy's wife and untied the ropes from behind her feet. He moved around in front of her and bent looking into her face just about an inch away. "Lady, I don't want to hear a sound unless I say you can talk. If you do anything funny, I'm going to knock the crap out of your husband."

Kathy Dansforth nodded and dipped her head to the side so that she could make eye contact with Tommy. He tried to garnish a smile back at her letting her know that he was okay.

The big guy turned back to the far side of the cabin where Tommy was strapped in the chair. "Now I'm going to make this clear. Both of you will be my guests for a very long time so any funny stuff and you'll never leave here." He continued to stare at Tommy who was now feeling the glare of his dark brown eyes boring a hole in his face. The men in the cabin had been talking and motioned to the large man. He moved over to where they were standing while still keeping an eye on Dansforth and his wife. The head guy was filling them in, "I got a text from the boss. He said the shit has hit the fan. The television is carrying the story about the two of them missing. The boss had to get his office involved in this."

"What the hell did he expect? Big Sam said, grab them, so we did."

"Yeah, I told you that but we wanted them taken from their home." Big Sam clenched his fist and pounded his fist into his left palm. He was looking at the two men.

"I'm not blaming either of you or the big man" Bud quickly said. "The boss is pissed that you grabbed the guy from the school parking lot. The school thing brought immediate response and more police action than if we took him and his wife from their home in Macomb County. With the call the boss had sent to the school the night before there wouldn't be so much attention."

"That was our plan and we grabbed his wife from the house but the teacher wasn't around. Once we got into the house we had no choice, grabbed the wife and had to head to the school after we delivered her to Big Sam."

"The big guy answered quickly. "Don't blame your shit on me." He again sneered at the two abductors.

"Hey, we did what you told us to. Grab them from home, I don't know why he wasn't there, the wife said he was still at school." It only made sense to us to get him from the school. How about you just give us our money and we'll get out of here."

Tensions between the men was growing. Dansforth could see that they were arguing and hoped it would work in his favor. Maybe if this grew it would give them an opportunity to escape. He kept wiggling his hands that were bound behind the chair. If only he could get loose. He kept an eye on the big man as he continued trying to loosen the ropes.

"Hey, what are you doing?" The man on the other side of the cabin was now looking in Dansforth's' direction.

Tommy stiffened in his chair. He saw the big man approaching but as he got closer Big Sam appeared to be looking past Tommy to the other side of the cabin. Tommy was relieved that they were yelling at one of the two guys that had grabbed him in the school parking lot.

"Put that cell phone down."

"What?"

"I said put the cell phone down, now!"

"I've got to let my people know that I'm going to be awhile."

They were now a few feet apart and both yelling at each other. "You dumb shit. I said put the phone down. You could be traced from anywhere on that thing."

Tensions had been running high as the men were now staring at each other like two heavy weight boxers waiting for someone to ring the bell for round one. Just then the man they called Bud, who seemed to be in charge, came back into the cabin. "What the hell is going on in here?"

"This dumb shit is using his cell phone. I told him to put it down."

"I'm done with him telling me what to do." The small cabin was about to explode with the men in a fist fight.

Bud moved into the center of the room. He held his arms out separating the two men and spoke low but with authority. "I understand that we're all under a lot of tension, however Sam's right, give me the phone. Those things have GPS and can be tracked anywhere around the world. We have to be careful. I'll give it back to you when you leave."

The abductor looked back over at Big Sam who had been yelling at him then over to Bud who calmly asked for the cell phone. "Okay, but if he yells at me one more time it will be his last."

The men continued to stare at each other as the guy extended his hand out with the cell phone. "Thanks, now you need to keep an eye on our two friends and the rest of us will resolve the problem that the boss is calling us about." Bud had to keep control but it was obviously more difficult with the new issue of the police and media coverage at the school. Bud's biggest problem might be controlling the big man who had a vicious temper. "I told all of you, no cell phones."

"But you've been using one." The man said back to Bud, after the argument with Sam.

"I've got a few, all burners, no way to track them. This is my gig, and I said no one is to have a cell phone, understood."

Sam watched this then turned and moved to the other side of the cabin still grumbled. "This ain't gonna be forgotten."

Sixteen

Detective Frederickson knew his captain was looking for some way to get even. He wanted to get out of the office as soon as possible once the meeting with Carole was completed. Jack Fox agreed to his idea to use the press and said he'd go along. The meeting was set and the Channel 7 reporter, Carole Newton, should be arriving at the precinct any minute. When the detective talked to Jack Fox he was surprised that Fox agreed to the plan. If only now he could get Channel 7 to run with it.

The morning traffic was crawling along on Interstate 94 as Carole moved into the right lane to exit the freeway. She had never been to the Twelfth Precinct before but her GPS was guiding her. She was glad that the road was plowed the night before and she didn't have to veer off the highway. Once she exited at Connor Street she turned left toward Jefferson. The precinct was just ahead on the right side near the Jeep Assembly Plant.

Frederickson paced across the room and filled his coffee cup waiting for his guest to arrive. He planned on playing it straight up. Just present the facts, although he made them all up, and hoped the reporter ran with them. Jack Fox gave him some suggestions but said he would let the detective run with his idea.

An officer approached his desk, "Detective, you have a lady at the front door asking for you. Do you want me to bring her in?"

"Yeah, I'd appreciate it if you have her sit at my desk; I have to get something from the back." He wanted to make Carole think he was busy with leads and moved toward the storage room. The detective's desk was piled with folders and a stack of manuals.

Once Carole was sitting at his desk he returned carrying a folder and leafing through it. When he saw Carole who now was sitting across from his desk he smiled, "Glad you could make it." He pulled his chair up next to where she had sat, "Can I get you a coffee?"

"Thanks," she was surprised that he was being so nice because yesterday at the school he didn't even want to talk to her. Carole had been trying to read some of the opened folders on his desk but they were turned to the other side and she would have to lean over to them to read what they said. She stood back up and watched to see where the detective was going for coffee. She could see he was standing with his back toward her across the room at a counter, probably the coffee pot. She took that opportunity to check out the folder on the desk. It was opened to details about Tommy Dansforth and she quickly could tell it was a listing of his address and other personal information. Before she could read more Frederickson returned.

"Something wrong with the chair?"

"No, I had to take my coat off and was just wondering where to put it."

He gave her a funny look. "You can give it to me and I'll hang it up for you."

"Thanks," she took it off and handed it to him. "So detective, why am I here?"

Frederickson knew he had to string together a believable story for her to buy it. "Looks like our missing teacher is even more important than we first thought. I got a call late last night from the DA regarding our case." Carole leaned closer to the detective's desk as he shuffled papers obviously looking for something in particular. "Guess that Dansforth and his wife are key witnesses.

This immediately grabbed her attention. "A witness, I can see how that changes things."

"You know Jack Fox, he's is all up in arms over losing him and he's pulling out all stops to find them."

Carole right away knew the case he was talking about. "Detective, this is big. According to my source the suspect in that murder is connected to someone in a high political office."

"Yeah, we don't get that kind of information down here." Frederickson wanted to find out everything that the reporter knew. Fox was right, the news is out there but how did the reporter know key details?

Carole continued, "It's still only rumors, but according to my source, the main suspect may be connected to someone pretty important in Lansing. The capitol has been abuzz for the past week over this."

Frederickson pretended to be searching through some papers on his desk as Carole continued to spin the story on a possible tie-in to the state capitol and the story that linked it to a Greektown murder. "Wow," he said, "hadn't heard anything about that." *Got to tell Jack when she leaves, he thought.* "Good, here's what I was looking for." With that he withdrew a manila folder from the middle of a stack. "Jack Fox, the DA, met with me earlier and he is enlisting our help. His people are hoping to flush out some information and he feels that if we plant a story in the news it would do the trick."

"What kind of story."

"One that will get back to the guys that took Dansforth. Did I tell you that his wife is missing too?" The detective was playing all his cards to get the reporter to buy into his idea.

Carole didn't have that detail. "No, we were wondering why she hadn't come forward in the investigation. My contact at the Macomb Daily was looking into it for me. So tell me the plan."

Frederickson laid it all out. He told Carole about the father of a problem student that he talked to and then the new sixth grade teacher that didn't show up at her evening class at Wayne State. He said all of them were initial suspects and only the sixth grade teacher remained as questionable. "Do you have an APB out for her?" Carole inquired.

"Yes, but she's off the grid. I have men stationed in front of her home but both she and her mother are now gone. We're not sure what to make of it but she may be involved. She could have been a plant to grab Dansforth. She just joined the school staff."

Carole was surprised that Frederickson was being forthcoming and much of this was new details for her. "What's in it for me if I go along with this?"

"You and your station would be exclusive on everything from our end and with the DA."

Carole nodded and waited for details. Frederickson spun the information just the way he had gone over it with the DA. It included a report that the police had a possible witness from the teacher's abduction and a good description of the men and car used to take Dansforth from the school parking lot. They bounced questions back and forth off each other and finally Carole stated, "Detective, the only way this is going to bring what you want is you'll have to be willing to go on the air with me, telling the public what you have."

He was hoping that he wouldn't have to do that but if she was willing to air the information then maybe it was his only choice. "I'll have to get it cleared with the DA." The detective got up and crossed the room to a small office that was dimly lit in the corner. He was in there making a call for over five minutes and Carole decided to call her manager with an update.

The station manager was pretty excited with the prospect of scooping everyone. "If you could pull it off, get him to do the interview right there now. I'll send a camera team over and we can get it on the end of the morning news."

_____Seventeen

Carole Newton was pleased that the detective agreed to go on camera with the story detailing that they had a witness to the abduction of the teacher from the school parking lot. She knew her camera team would take about thirty minutes to arrive so she prepped the detective on how she would open the story. "This would be carried live," she told him so they had to be prepared.

District Attorney, Jack Fox had been informed what was going to take place by Frederickson. The detective was in his office discussing the plan with Carole. The hope was with the news that would be reported that a witness came forward with new details; that the captors would be spooked and maybe slip up. It was a long shot but it had been close to twenty-four hours since the case was opened and nothing positive had developed. Confirmation from the search in Macomb that Dansforth's wife was also missing had the police going in two directions. The detective had his teams split up tracking both the aspects of Mrs. Dansforth being taken from her home in Macomb County and the door to door canvassing of the east side Detroit neighborhood. The police continued to search the empty lots around the school as well as knocking on doors to see if anyone had actually seen anything yesterday. Frederickson had received a call from Ms. Baker at the school saying some students were out and felt that a possible link could be to a known drug house at the end of the street. The canvass would start there and move up the block.

The news flash came across the bottom of the television screen. _Teacher missing from school parking lot, a break in the_ *case would be detailed soon.* Channel 7 would have the scoop before any other station could get their reporters on the scene. The on-air news person announced that they would be going live to the Twelfth Precinct and their reporter, Carole Newton, was there with the lead detective. The information that Frederickson planted about a witness was big news, and the other stations would be sending their field reporters to the police station hoping to have their own take for the noon audience.

The report caught a lot of people flat footed, including the staff at the school. Ms. Baker had finished a meeting with all the teachers that were there for an in-service day. Before she could get back to her office some of them were telling her that it was announced that there might have been a break in the case. She still had the three students in her office that Mr. Banner had brought in from earlier. She wondered could this nightmare all come to an end soon. Four teachers were now in her office and they turned on the television to Channel 7 to see what the new developments were.

The television anchor was telling viewers that their reporter, Carole Newton, was currently at the Twelfth Precinct and she had an important break in the case of the teacher that may have been abducted from the school parking lot. It was now eight-fifty-five and the local news was about to switch to Good Morning America. This might get national coverage for both Carole and Channel 7. The camera team had set up just outside of the captain's office and Frederickson and Carole had all their details ready. Another camera team had gone to Kennedy Charter and planned to film the parking lot and neighborhood for their viewers. The on-going investigation would get all the coverage that was possible.

Carole opened the segment re-capping the case for viewers with footage from the school parking lot and neighborhood she shot yesterday being shown on the screen. The screen showed Carole turning to introduce the detective from the Twelfth Precinct. Frederickson made sure he didn't give any names but told the audience that his investigation uncovered that neighbors had given officers a solid description of both the car and people probably involved in grabbing the missing teacher. He also said there may be a witness regarding the teacher's wife who was also missing. The District Attorney watched from his office as the newscast continued hoping this latest ploy might bring some positive results. He knew without his only witness there was no hope of a trial. The pending Grand Jury would have to be postponed.

Once the interview was over Frederickson thanked Carole for her help. "I promise you'll get everything I have on the case as soon as I get it." The two shook hands and Carole and her news crew packed up their equipment. The station was already getting requests from the national morning news shows for interviews. Savannah Guthrie from NBC was on the line with the station manager and he was setting up an interview with Carole once she got back from the police station. The station's phone rang off the hook as CNN and Fox News also called for updates and possible interviews from the reporter handling the coverage.

***

In Lansing, the state capitol, another interested viewer watched shaking his head. Outside of his office staffers could hear him yelling. "Son-of-a-bitch!" His chief of staff opened the office door and asked, "Everything okay, Sir?"

"Rich get in here now!" The man was pacing in the corner of his office and everyone outside knew something bad had happened, but what was it?

Back at the cabin things had turned pretty ugly last night after the confrontation over the cell phone. The guy in charge, who they only referred to as Bud, was trying to sort out what his boss had wanted. *Handle all the loose ends he was told. This can't get back to me. The boss was in a panic.* Bud knew what he had to do. He planned on having the young man who looked to be just a teenager into watching Dansforth and his wife. He told the two abductors, the big bearded guy and his partner that he would get their money. When they were counting it out, Big Sam slipped out of the cabin and positioned himself outside near the back of the car that they had transported Dansforth in. Bud told the two abductors, "Okay, all the money is there. You two need to find your way back to the ferry and hide out of sight for at least a week or two." They agreed and the big bearded guy asked for his cell phone. "I turned it off and you need to wait until you've crossed back into Michigan before turning it on." It was agreed and they headed out to their car.

As the two of them made their way out of the cabin the big bearded guy was still pissed. "I wish I could get my hands on that asshole that called me a dumb shit. I'd like to kick his ass." Both of them laughed as they were a few feet from their car when out of the shadows bullets flashed. Both men fell to the ground, blood gushing from their bullet riddled bodies. The gun didn't create any sounds, as big Sam used a silencer and the shots killed the two abductors. Bud wanted to make sure it didn't bring any unwanted attention in case hunters or snowmobilers were around.

Bud appeared from inside the cabin and instructed Big Sam. "Drag the bodies to the back. We'll bury them in the morning."

The big man stood over the body of the bearded guy and smiled. "I knew you were a dumb shit." With that he kicked the bloody body of the bearded guy in the head. "Guess he who laughs last, does laugh best." He had a good chuckle as Bud grabbed the sack with the money. "Why don't we just toss them in the river? They'll freeze over and won't be found until spring. They may go downriver with the ice flows all the way to Cleveland."

Bud said, "I'll need to make a call first, just get them in the back and we'll see what the boss wants us to do."

_____Eighteen

Big Sam and the kid followed their assignment from Bud; they moved the two dead bodies to the back of the unit and waited for further instructions. Tommy Dansforth and his wife had heard the talk about bodies and figured something had happened. Thieves and criminals never trusted anyone, especially each other. Tommy knew that if they were quick to kill the men that took him from the parking lot that he and his wife didn't have much of a prayer. It would only be a matter of time before they would kill them too.

Bud was telling Big Sam and the young guy to put the bodies along the wall near the propane tanks in the back when a phone rang. It was the old fashion wall phone that hung in the kitchen area of the cabin. Bud removed the handle off the cradle and seemed very anxious as the person of the other end of the line gave him some information. "Yes, I understand. I've already taken care of both of them. Yes, we should have found someone more reliable for the job. Yes, I got it." He turned to the big man and motioned him to follow along outside.

Tommy Dansforth hoped to get his wife's attention without alerting the young man in the cabin. He had kept on struggling with the ropes behind the chair. His wife was across from him and she wasn't looking good. Tommy asked, "Hey, could you please get her some water?"

"No can do."

"She's going to pass out. Please, I'm begging you, just a small glass of water."

"Bud said, do nothing unless he approves. He'll be back in a minute."

Because the young man was left in the cabin to watch them, Tommy was hoping he might be able to get free somehow. If he could get the guy to walk in front of the chair he might be able to trip him. He was desperate and figured they were running out of time. "Come on, just a damn glass of water."

"Old man, you're one big pain in the ass." With that the young kid turned toward the cupboards and grabbed a plastic coffee cup from one of the shelves. He filled it with water from a bottle in the fridge and walked toward Kathy Dansforth. He was about three feet from Tommy when the cabin door opened.

"What the hell are you doing?" Bud was standing in the doorway questioning the kid.

He stuttered, "I'm just getting her a cup of water." He was close to where Kathy Dansforth was seated.

"Who told you that it was okay to get her a drink?"

The young man was shaking, "Sorry, uncle."

Bud continued to stare at him. "I'll tell you what's okay. Dump the water."

Tommy thought he needed to do something to maybe get the young guy on his side. He also hoped to use the revelation of the kid being Bud's nephew. "It's not his fault, I asked him to get her a cup of water."

"I don't care what you asked for. It's not his fault; you're becoming a real problem old man. Nothing happens unless I say it, okay."

"You don't have to be an asshole, my wife needs a drink." That was the last thing he should have said. Bud had an angry sneer on his face and quickly moved in front of Dansforth. He clenched his fist and punched Tommy in the face knocking the chair he was attached to over, sending Tommy crashing to the floor.

His wife cried out, "Don't hurt him!"

"Shut up, bitch!" Tommy's nose was bleeding from the punch

and his feet were dangling in the air as he lay on his back, still attached to the chair he was tied to. Bud turned his attention back to Tommy as he was now straddled over the top of the man on the ground. "This is your last warning old man. He pointed his finger in Tommy's face; one more problem and you'll join the other two men in the back." Bud turned to the young man who was still standing in the middle of the room. "Now get him back up." With that Bud went back outside.

As the young guy moved over to prop Tommy back up, Tommy said, "Sorry, I didn't mean to get you in trouble."

He didn't answer at first. Once Tommy was upright, the young man whispered, "Bud has a lot of pressure on him. You better just be quiet."

Tommy nodded and mouthed, "Thanks."

The good news was the fall helped loosen Tommy's hands a little more from the weight of his body sliding off the seat. The bad news was Tommy thought his right hand might have been broken. Pain shot up his wrist and arm and he dropped his head not wanting Kathy to see how much it was hurting.

The cabin door again suddenly swung open with a loud thud as Bud and Sam pushed inside. "Shit, it's colder than hell out there. It's impossible to dig in the frozen ground. We'll figure out what to do with them later."

"We just have to hope that they aren't discovered until spring." Bud was holding his right hand close to his face and studying it.

"Something wrong, Boss?"

"Yeah, I think I broke my finger on that old shit's face." With that he let out an evil laugh that made Kathy Dansforth shudder. Bud turned to the young man who had backed all the way into the kitchen. "Get us a cup of coffee, kid."

"Yes Sir."

Bud waved the burly guy over to the small table. "We'll figure out how to get this done and catch the ferry back across to Marine

City." The sun had started to come up over the horizon and shown through the trees into the front of the cabin.

Tommy didn't like what he was hearing. Were they about to kill both him and Kathy? What did Bud mean, let's get this done? He continued to wiggle his wrist although the pain in his right hand was shooting up his arm. He just couldn't sit there and do nothing. He wasn't sure what he would do even if he got free. There were three of them and they all had weapons. It had been over twenty-four hours since he was abducted from the school parking lot. He hoped by now the authorities had a search party out looking for them.

***

The television in the main office of the school now had a huge crowd of teachers pressed around hoping for some good news. The reporter was familiar to all of them, and Ms. Baker informed them that Carole Newton had been at the school yesterday asking about the events with Mr. Dansforth. The television report so far only re-capped the facts from the previous day and when the lead detective stated that they had creditable witnesses from the neighborhood everyone stood silently. His statement was that they had the description of two people that grabbed Dansforth and a partial license plate. There was a quiet cheer from those gathered. "Maybe now they will catch the guys and Tommy will be safe," was heard from a small group near the back.

Once the news bulletin was completed, Ms. Baker stood and turned the television off. "This may be the break the authorities need. I think we should all think back to the events of yesterday and if anyone remembers anything that may seem important let me know. I'll call whatever you think of to the lead detective if we have any new information." The group of teachers all nodded. "I have one more question. Did anyone see Mary Blankenship in the gym during the meeting yesterday?" It was quiet and people started asking each other as to help remember if she was there.

Mr. Banner asked aloud, "Why, what's important about Mary?"

"We're just concerned because she didn't report this morning and hadn't called in yet?"

That made sense. No one seemed to be sure if Mary was in the gym or not. Once the conversation was over Ms. Baker instructed them to return to their rooms. "We will possibly have classes on Monday so I suggest you plan accordingly. I'll check with our administration and let everyone know what I find out. All parents got the robo calls that told them we have a missing teacher, and now the news is giving them more details. Don't tell parents or students things we don't know for sure. Our administration has a guard hired to watch the lot for your safety 24/7 until this is all figured out." That news helped the mood of everyone. After all could this be something personal or just an isolated incident. Once they all dispersed she remembered about the students that Mr. Banner had brought in from the neighborhood. Baker headed back down to where she had left them and would tell them about the news conference. She couldn't have them searching the neighborhood. Their safety was critical. Hopefully this would all be over soon and Mr. Dansforth would be okay.

_____Nineteen

Detective Frederickson was completing his conversation with Carole Newton as the news crew gathered their equipment. "Detective, you didn't tell us if your team had discovered the owner of the vehicle that you described in the interview."

"We're working on it, Carole. We only have a partial plate number and there are hundreds of vehicles matching the description. My team is working with the DMV trying to narrow down the options."

She wanted to get back to the station but had to make sure she had everything that the detective knew on the case. "You'll call me if something else develops?"

"Of course, that's the deal and you'll do the same, right?" The two had a pact and had to trust each other. Carole thanked Frederickson and grabbed her coat. Two officers watched as she made her way out of the precinct. "I think she bought it," Frederickson said as Captain Hughes approached his desk.

"You know this is all on you, if it doesn't work, you're the one on the line." The captain had the detective right where he wanted him, give him enough rope and maybe he'll hang himself. Both men knew that once you passed the twenty-four hour point, the prospects of finding the abducted person dropped dramatically. With the aspect of Tommy Dansforth being a witness in a murder case, those numbers fell even further. Frederickson wanted to contact Jack Fox and plan their next step which included a re-canvassing of the neighborhood. It's possible that someone actually may have seen the abduction and the news story would bring them forward. The detective contacted the team that was stationed outside of Mary Blankenship's home hoping the teacher or her mother showed up. With her disappearance more questions about her involvement had arose. Could she be involved, and if so, how? If Mary was at the meeting, she never came forward about being there late around the time Dansforth was meeting with parents. She wasn't at her class at Wayne State and now she and her mother haven't been home since the detective called Mary's house. What did she have to do with this, if anything? His call to the team staked out at the Blankenship address didn't bring any new results. He filled them in as he got ready to head back out to Kennedy Charter Academy. Frederickson planned on talking to Ms. Baker about the new sixth grade teacher, Blankenship. He hoped she had shown up at the school but so far it was a dead end. He also needed to let her know that the janitor wasn't involved.

***

The television special that Carole Newton just completed created a buzz across the state, and nowhere bigger than in the state capitol. Calls had gone out from the office of the lieutenant governor. He had been watching the morning news update from Detroit and paced nervously waiting for an important call. His staff originally questioned how they could help; not knowing what exactly had triggered his recent outburst. They were sent off on other tasks as he hoped to be alone waiting for the call. When his cell phone rang he looked at the screen making sure that it was Bud on the line. "What the hell is going on?"

"Everything's okay, Boss. I have everything under control."

"Bullshit! The news is stating that they have identified the people that took Dansforth from the school parking lot."

"Boss, I told you we took care of it. We got rid of those two bumbling idiots."

"That may not be enough. There was a television report stating that they have identified the car and with GPS will soon be able to run a location on it. It's going to lead them right to you."

"Okay, we'll get rid of their vehicle."

"Bud, they can't find it. If they see it's in Canada they will soon be checking video surveillance from every border crossing."

"What else do you want me to do?" Bud was upset with his micromanaging.

"You've got to get the car out of the area as soon as possible."

"I know what to do, and I'll do it right now."

The lieutenant governor clicked the cell off. Buying the burner phones was a great idea. He and Bud both had multiple sets and agreed that they would toss the first set today. They couldn't take any chances. Things had already gone very wrong. The lieutenant governor put in a call to his source in police headquarters. His message was quick to the point, "Get me all the information that this detective at the Twelfth detailed this morning and get it now." Before the man could answer the caller hung up. He figured with a bunch of mismanaged cops at the worst precinct in the force that nothing would come back to them. How did this detective all of a sudden get so resourceful?

***

Bud was pacing outside the cabin. He knew that he had to send someone to dump the car. He couldn't trust that his young nephew would do it right. He planned to send Big Sam to do the job. The big burly man wouldn't be happy handling this task because he liked hurting people not hiding cars. Bud pulled up the hood of his jacket as the cold wind off Lake St. Clair blew through the woods. Although the sun was coming up, the ice on the lake caused temperatures to drop as the winds whisked across the channel. "Let's put the bodies in the trunk of their car. When you dump it in the lake, open the trunk. Tie some weight on them and the bodies will float away separate from the car."

"Okay boss, good idea. But I think we need to have the kid do this."

"Trust me it would be better if we leave him here. They're tied up so it should be pretty easy."

"You never should have brought him into this. The kid is as dumb as a box of rocks."

"I've told you Sam, I'm responsible for him. He can be trusted. You just handle your part of this."

"He ain't getting any of the money for just being a lookout."

"I told you, he will share my part. Don't worry about the kid, he's okay." Sam didn't like the idea or having the kid tagging along. Once they finished their conversation, Bud turned back to the cabin and said, "Hey it's cold as hell out here, let's go inside." They pulled the door open and Tommy turned to see Bud with the big man following behind. They were still talking very low, "Here's how I want you to get rid of the evidence. Travel toward Sarnia, you can maybe dump the car into the channel past the Blue Water Bridge. You know, the marina next to the casino. The current in the channel there will take it deep down into Lake Huron." The big man shrugged, as Bud continued. Tommy was sure this was the end. They would dump him and Kathy into the water and they'll never be found. When Bud handed the big man a set of keys and reiterated the orders, Tommy looked over at his wife. Was this going to be their final fate?

The young man standing over near the cupboards in the cabin asked, "Uncle, what do you want me to do?"

"You stay here while we go outside and get everything out of that car. Watch these two." With that, the men turned and headed back outside. Before walking out, Bud motioned his nephew to come close to the door. He whispered something into the young man's ear and walked out.

Tommy needed to do something now or there wasn't hope for him and Kathy. "Hey kid, what's going on?"

The young man waited until the door shut and Bud was out of the cabin. "Guess we need to dump the car those two used that took you from the parking lot. I need you to just be quiet so I don't get into any more trouble."

"No problem. Do you know what else they're planning?"

"Just that they want me to stay here watching you. Now please be quiet."

"Sure kid, thanks." With that, Tommy breathed a sigh of relief.

_____Twenty

Frederickson parked in front of Kennedy Charter and placed one more call to the team watching Mary Blankenship's place. "Might as well forget the stake out," he told them. "I'm waiting on some detailed history on Blankenship from the principal here and we'll need to run a background check on her." He clicked off and grabbed his folder from the front seat.

Ms. Baker knew that she had to make sure the students that Mr. Banner found walking in the neighborhood understood that it wasn't safe for them to try to carry out their own investigation. She went over the television report with them and that she told the investigator their idea about the crack house. "If you think you have any more ideas or information that would help the police we'll report it to them for you. Mr. Dansforth would be pleased that you all care but he wouldn't want any of you to be in danger."

Harrison nodded and turned to LaShanda. He said, "Thanks for telling the cops about the house we think might be involved."

LaShanda told Ms. Baker that some of her friends that went to Cody High School said that the house on the corner of Lenox was known by the kids as a drug house and that the guys that lived there were involved in a lot of bad things. Ms. Baker said, "I've written all the information down. I have a meeting with the lead detective in a little while. I'm sure if this helps in the current investigation, or not they will use this information and close that place down." The students were happy that they had helped. She called Mr. Banner to walk the kids along with Bruce, and the gym teacher to their houses. She wanted to make sure they all headed home and were safe. She also placed a call to each of their homes advising the parents what she had done, hoping that they would help keep them at home. Ms. Baker wrote the information down for Detective Frederickson, along with the files she had on her new sixth grade teacher, Mary Blankenship, and waited for the detective. She wondered why the new teacher hadn't shown up today and what might she have to do with the disappearance of Tommy Dansforth.

Detective Frederickson was hoping the news story they ran this morning would bring some worthwhile leads. The team of officers canvassing the neighborhood this morning were supposed to report to him if they had any new details. When he entered the school he was directed right to Ms. Baker's office. "Good morning, detective." Frederickson wasn't known for his social skills but he acknowledged her and smiled. She told him, "I have some interesting information for you." That perked him up, maybe a real break in the case.

He set a folder down that he brought on the chair across from her desk as she handed him two different packets. He leafed through the first one as Ms. Baker explained. "Some of our students wanted the police to know about a home they told me about, near the corner off Lenox and Vernor. They said it's known to many of the students as a drug haven and that the residents may also be involved in other crimes. I put the address and location in the packet."

As he reviewed the information he said, "This is very helpful. I have a team of officers outside canvassing the neighborhood and I'll get this to them right away. Don't want them walking into a problem." He took his cell phone out and called the information in to the lead officer.

Before he looked at the other information she had, she asked, "We all saw the television report this morning, are there any new details that you can tell me about?"

Frederickson didn't want to address the news conference or give her false reports. He looked at Ms. Baker and thought about telling her why they reported that they had a real lead in the case. "Ms. Baker, there a lot of things happening and because of the sensitive nature of the investigation it would be better if I didn't say too much."

She pressed her lips tightly and nodded. "Guess you can't tell me more. Hope you can understand that all of our students and staff care a lot about Mr. Dansforth and are praying for his safe return."

"I understand. The only thing I can tell you is Mr. Dansforth and his wife were witnesses to a crime a few weeks ago and we are trying to see if that has anything to do with his being abducted." After he said that, he wished he hadn't. "That information isn't known to many people, so please, I must beg you not to tell anyone what I just told you."

"Sure, I appreciate you telling me. That's surprising; he never said anything about that here."

"We're not sure what, if anything, that may have to do with this but we are looking into everything." Once that was said he opened the second packet she had for him. It contained everything the school had on Mary Blankenship. Nothing immediately jumped out. She grew up in the area and attended Wayne State University, with a degree in Secondary Education. She's the only child of a single mother. The address that they had on file was the same one she had grown up at and the one they had staked out the previous night. None of this made any sense. Why had she disappeared? Frederickson thought this was another dead end. He flipped through the papers and on the third page he saw that Mary was divorced from a man that she now had a standing personal protection order from. He continued reading. Mary's ex recently became violent and followed her after their separation. He served six months in the city lock-up after hitting a court officer at the divorce hearing when he reached out trying to grab Mary. He swore that he would get her. Frederickson turned to Ms. Baker. "What do you know about Blankenship's ex-husband?"

"I didn't realize that she was ever married." Ms. Baker was surprised to get this news.

"It says here in your file that she had to get a restraining order after her divorce became final. It appears that he is a violent man."

"We never talked about her personal life, other than she said that she lived with her mother. Detective, she's only been with us a couple of weeks. I'll ask a couple of the other sixth grade teachers to see if they are aware of anything else."

"Could you ask them to come down to your office?"

"Sure." Baker turned and picked up her phone. The detective listened as she talked to the two other sixth grade teachers. "They will both be down here in a minute," she relayed to him. "Maybe they can shed some light on Blankenship's marriage and problems with her ex."

The detective again leafed through the packet that Ms. Baker had prepared for him. As he turned the last page again revealing the bad marriage issue one of the sixth grade teachers came into the office. Frederickson looked up and saw that she was young, maybe just out of college, but looked more like a teenager. She wore jeans and a Central Michigan University sweatshirt.

Ms. Baker introduced her. "Detective, this is Ms. Styles; she's our English and Social Studies teacher for the sixth grade."

Ms. Styles reached out and said, "Call me Beverly," please.

He smiled. "Sorry to take you away from your classroom. I have a couple of questions but these are all very confidential."

"I understand. I don't know what else I can add for you, but I hope you can tell us more about the news story from this morning."

"Sorry, I don't have much to add just that we are conducting another neighborhood canvass." Just about then the second sixth grade teacher arrived. Ms. Baker waved her into the office. The two teachers looked at each other and Beverly raised her eyebrows.

The second teacher was also very young looking, dressed in jeans and wearing a Detroit Mercy sweatshirt. Ms. Baker noticed that the detective seemed to stare oddly at the two teachers.

"Detective, because we don't have any students I told the teachers to dress casually."

"Sorry, that's not why I'm staring. Guess I'm getting old because both of you look like you could be students, not the teacher."

Beverly started to laugh. "Last year one of my sixth graders asked how old I was. When I asked why he wanted to know, he said maybe I could date his older brother." That brought laughter from everyone in the room. May have been the first time any of them had laughed since Mr. Dansforth was reported as missing. The detective apologized about the remark on their ages. "No apology needed. We're glad to have someone say we look so young."

He began his story again, "I started telling Ms. Styles that the questions we are about to ask each of you are confidential and must not be retold to anyone especially the other staff members."

The teachers looked back at each other knowing that this was about to get really serious. *What could they know?* They nodded and Ms. Baker reminded them about school policy. Frederickson suggested that they have a seat as he got up and moved over to the office door. When he pulled it closed, the room was filled with silent anticipation.

_____Twenty-One

Bud stood outside of the cabin watching the car pulling out of the wooded lot. He had to call back to Lansing letting the Lieutenant Governor know that everything had been handled. Bud needed to figure out what his boss wanted them to do next. With the news that was just released they might have to move the couple to another location or do away with them too. The little cabin seemed to be perfect. The ownership belonged to a multi-national corporation headquartered out of Toronto with offices across Europe. It would be almost impossible to trace the ownership down. The lieutenant governor had handpicked the hiding place. Bud decided to check on his nephew before making the next call.

The cabin was hidden deep in the woods from all the roads that surrounded it. The gravel drive was cut into the lot from the dirt road that ran off a secondary road that was primarily used by local hunters and snowmobilers. Although the snow was deep, Bud made sure there was a good path for them to enter and leave without getting stuck. Now he feared that moving the couple would bring unwanted attention; especially since the press released pictures of Dansforth and his wife.

Tommy Dansforth continued trying to make inroads with the young man assigned to watch them. While Bud and the big man were outside, he tried by asking him some personal questions. Kathy recognized what he was doing. "Guess your uncle is pretty important to you?" The young man didn't answer but moved to the front of the cabin and looked out of the small window. "I've been teaching for a while and many of my students are in a similar situation you're in."

The young man quickly turned, "You don't know anything about me." He sneered at Dansforth.

Just then Kathy spoke up. "He didn't mean anything bad. It's just that we both are concerned that whatever happens, you don't end up in prison."

"I'm not going to prison. My uncle will take good care of me."

"I'm sure that was the plan," Dansforth said. "The problem is, his plans seem to have gone wrong." The young man was quiet and looked back at Dansforth. Tommy continued, "Last year I had a great student who was kind of forced into helping his dad who robbed a party store."

Now the young man's face relaxed and he listened to what Tommy was telling him. "How could you help him? You're just a teacher."

"That's right, but my student was troubled and one afternoon after classes he stayed back and wanted to talk. At first he asked about his grades, but I knew there was something else troubling him."

"You mean he told you straight up about the robbery?"

Dansforth felt he was getting through to the kid. "No, not at first. He told me that his mom and dad had separated and that he would stay with his dad every other weekend. His dad didn't have much and one night his dad drove up to a store and told him to get behind the wheel. At first he didn't know what was happening, but when his dad told him, as soon as I come out and get in the car you need to take off, the kid knew what was going to take place."

"Guess the kid didn't have a choice." The young man was now engaged and that's what Dansforth had hoped for.

"You're right. He didn't. But he was a great kid and it bothered him so much that he wanted to make it right. I'm sure he struggled with ratting out his dad, but he couldn't live with knowing what had happened."

"Did the dad just rob the place or more?"

"No, he shot the clerk. The next day the kid saw the news story showing that the store was robbed and that a single mom was shot and in serious condition."

The young man was caught up in the story that Dansforth told him. He continued to ask questions and then he told Tommy about his relationship with his uncle. "My uncle is really an okay guy. When my dad died, my mother struggled to pay the bills. Then she hooked up with this guy. The new boyfriend treated me like shit. They got married and had a kid of their own. It really got bad after that and he finally kicked me out and my mom didn't do anything to stop him. I was only thirteen. That's when my uncle took me in. He's been great to me. This is the first time he's wanted me to help with something like this."

"I'm sure he means well, but now that everything is going south. You really seem like a nice young man and I'd hate to see you waste your life and end up in prison." Just then the door to the cabin flew open. "Crap, that snow is blowing so hard that I can hardly see the clump of trees out front." Bud was holding a box filled with various items taken from the car. The young man spun around hoping that his uncle didn't realize that he had been talking to Dansforth. "Do you need me to help with the stuff from the car?"

"No, I'm going to have to figure out what to do with these things, everything okay in here?"

"Yeah, sure, no problem, uncle." The kid looked over at Dansforth and was glad the teacher just hung his head without any expression. "These two have been quiet the whole time."

"Good. I need to make a call and when big Sam finds a place to dump the car I'll have to pick him up. You sure you're okay here?"

"Absolutely."

"Glad, keep your eye on them. You better toss another log on the fire. It's cold in here." With that Bud moved to the back of the cabin while the young man did as instructed. Bud dialed someone on his cell and waited for an answer.

Tommy wished he could hear the conversation. The wind was howling through the cracks in the cabin's front door and it sounded like a train going by. The weather outside must be getting worse. The small window in the front of the cabin rattled and the young man finished stoking the fire. Bud moved closer to the front window and looked outside. He wondered, *How long before Big Sam gets back?* Bud waited on the phone for an answer.

With this new information that Dansforth overheard and with Bud leaving his nephew at the cabin to watch them, it could be just what they needed. He hoped that his earlier conversation with the young man made an impact.

_____Twenty-Two

The meeting back at the principal's office began to shed light on Mary Blankenship's rocky marriage. The other sixth grade teachers told the detective that Mary had confided to them that her ex-husband had recently been stalking her, both in the school parking lot and at her home. She and her mother reported it to the local police but they had never been able to catch him in the act. The key thing they revealed was that many times she and her mother stayed at an auntie's house. It was Mary's mother's younger sister and they said they felt safe there. Although the teachers didn't know the address, they knew she lived in Indian Village and they had a first name for the aunt to give to the detective. After the meeting he sent the information back to the Twelfth Precinct team. Hopefully they will be able to track down the aunt's address and find Mary there. His team also tried tracking down the ex-husband to make sure he hadn't been involved in Mary's disappearance. Once the teachers returned to their classrooms, Frederickson and Ms. Baker reviewed the files she had for him one more time.

Although he couldn't give Ms. Baker too many details, he did share some of the investigation facts, but said nothing about what event Dansforth may have seen or why he was a key witness. Once they finished their conversation Frederickson wanted to talk to the two teachers again that found the blood on the side of Dansforth's car. Ms. Baker offered to call them but Frederickson said he'd rather meet them in their classroom. She walked him down the hallway toward Mr. Banner's room and left him there. The detective wanted to make sure that with a night of rest, Mr. Banner or Bruce may have remembered something else that they may have seen. Chris Banner had more questions than answers for Detective Frederickson. Unfortunately nothing new was added to the investigation. It was the same story with Bruce.

As he walked back down the hallway, Frederickson's cell phone rang. He stopped in the hall while Captain Hughes informed him that they had some new details on Blankenship. He learned that they located Mary's aunt; she lived on Iroquois Street in Indian Village, just as the other teachers had told him. The captain had sent two sets of officers to check things out. When they approached the home on the lower east side of the city something seemed out of order. The house, a well kept two story brick home seemed empty, however there were two cars in the side drive. The officers had circled around the place checking the yard when they were sure they saw a figure watching from an upstairs window. "Detective, you and I need to discuss this morning's incident privately, however with these events, it is better to put it off until we've solved this case. Rest assured it will not be forgotten." Once Hughes finished talking, Frederickson remained quiet on the line.

Frederickson knew he had to address the situation but was determined not to apologize. "Captain, our team has always been looked down upon by everyone, and when we start accusing each other of being poor performers, it only makes the team weaker. I'll do everything in my power to make sure this case receives the best detective work possible."

Hughes knew he wasn't going to get an apology with that statement, but maybe didn't deserve one. "Agreed, but the chain of command stays in place and when I need you to follow an order, you'll do just that."

"No problem."

"Regarding the events here in Indian Village, I wanted you to know what we've found and give you a heads up on our plan of attack."

"Sounds like a good plan, Sir. I'll head that way as soon as possible to assist in any way you need."

"Good." The two men hung up and Hughes turned to the men on the scene and gave them his orders, "Pull back and move your squad car down the street where we can still watch the house."

Frederickson headed back into the principal's office and informed Ms. Baker, "I have to handle something else. I'll be back a little later."

The captain wondered why he hadn't seen this type of solid investigative work from his detective since he had been in the Twelfth. He heard nothing but negatives about Frederickson, maybe he judged him wrong. When the captain was transferred in a few years ago he was told that Frederickson was a bad apple. Keep an eye on him and don't let him get involved in anything big. Frederickson didn't seem to be a bad apple now; although he wasn't going to forget that incident in the break room, in fact Frederickson appeared to be the best investigator the Twelfth had.

Baker watched out her window and saw the detective jogging toward his car. *Oh no, this wasn't good*, she thought. Baker feared what had happened now. The events of the past few days were taking its toll on the school's principal. She had one teacher abducted from the school parking lot and now another teacher missing, perhaps due to a domestic situation. She didn't know how much more she could take.

The detective jumped into his car and headed down Jefferson Avenue toward the recently built complex of new homes along the Detroit River across from Indian Village. The officers convened at the corner of Iroquois Street near the parking lot of the Indian Village Marketplace, a new grocery store that served the neighborhood. Along with the team of officers that had positioned themselves while watching the aunt's home, and the captain they went over the situation. Hughes said, "Okay, go over what you saw again." The captain and detective listened to the report that the two officers gave them. "Detective did you find out anything new from the teachers at the school about Blankenship?"

Frederickson updated the group, "It appears that Blankenship's ex-husband has been stalking her both at home and in the school parking lot. I did check and there's multiple reports filed by Mary reporting sighting her husband both at school and home."

The captain instructed his team, "We know her ex has a record and has been jailed over abuse charges. We don't know for sure if he's in there or if he's armed. We need to approach carefully." They planned their moves while a call had gone out for a second team of officers to the scene.

Frederickson and his captain walked up the street together but neither said anything to each other. The second team of officers from the Twelfth Precinct would be on the scene in a few minutes. The detective finally said, "We need to ascertain the situation without a possibility of expanding the problem."

"Agreed, I think we should make a canvass of the neighborhood down at this end of the block and see if anyone may have information for us." The two agreed and once the second team was in place they would start the process. Iroquois Street was one of three streets that comprised the area known as Indian Village. The Village was over one-hundred years old and included more than three-hundred-fifty beautiful large homes. It was located from Jefferson Avenue north to Mack Avenue. The officers knew that many of the residents were affluent and would be more than willing to assist with their investigation. All the men were in place and the captain dispatched his two teams along the street to see if anyone could shed some light on what they may have seen or if they knew Blankenship's aunt. "We need to be careful," he told them. "I don't want to create panic just that we are looking for someone that may have been seen in the area."

The police would only question those homes that were far enough from the aunt's house so that if someone was holding Mary or her family they wouldn't see what was taking place. The first few houses did not have any residents home. This wasn't unusual with many of the people being professionals and probably at work. They approached the fourth house from the corner and before getting to the top of the porch a lady opened the front door.

"Is there a problem, officers?"

"Good morning. We are checking with residents regarding a possible missing person. Have you seen this lady or her daughter here recently." He showed her a photo's of Mary and her ex.

She moved to the porch while leaving the front door slightly opened. A little girl peeked out from the archway as she started looking at the photo the officer had. "Mama, Billy is throwing cereal at me again."

"One minute officer, would you both mind coming inside, it's a little cold out here." They all moved into the front hallway as she called out, "Billy, come here now!" She stood there for a minute when a young boy, maybe seven or eight crept toward the hall.

"What mom?"

"You need to come over here." As he moved closer he saw the two officers with his mom and sister. Panic filled the young boy's face. "You called the cops. I didn't mean anything. Why did you call the cops?" The two officers smiled and jumped into the fray. The mother was quickly amused. The first officer motioned the boy to come closer. He knelt down and said, "We got a report that you have been mean to your sister."

"I'm sorry, why did you call the cops?" Before anyone could answer the officer added.

"We need you start behaving and be nicer to your sister or we'll be back." The little girl stood closely behind her mom and had a huge smile on her face. The mother added, "Billy, I've told you unless you behave you'll get in trouble."

"Sorry mom, honest I didn't mean anything bad."

The officer, still knelling, looked directly into the young boy's face. "It's important that you are nice to your sister and you should be protecting her, not hurting her." The boy nodded a yes as the officer reached out to shake the his hand. "Let's shake on this."

The boy shook the officers hand and turned toward his sister. "I'm sorry." His mom leaned out and hugged him. "I've told you the same things, Billy. Now both of you go back and eat your breakfast while I talk to the officers."

The two young children scampered away and the lady turned to the officer that had knelt down and gave her son the warning. "Thank you so much. You have a great way with kids."

"I have three little ones of my own so I know how tough it can be."

"Now, how can I help you?"

They again handed her the photo of Mary Blankenship that they got from the school and another of her ex husband. She studied the photos for a minute. "I've never seen this man, handing the photo of the ex husband back to the officer, but I know this person, it's Louise's niece, Mary."

This was a big break. "Are you friends with Louise and her niece, Mary?"

"Oh yes, Mary has baby sat for me for a long time."

The first officer quickly sent his partner back to find the captain. This could be the opportunity they needed to get into the home. "I've sent my partner back to my captain. Do you mind if we ask you a few more questions?'

"No, I'll be willing to do anything to help. Mary is a sweet person and my kids just love her. I hope she's not in any trouble."

Just then there was a knock on the front door. She opened the door and the captain introduced himself, "I'm Captain Hughes from the Twelfth Precinct. We might have a situation down the street and are trying to take every precaution possible." The lady listened with anticipation. "I hear you know both Mary Blankenship and her aunt."

"Yes, I told your officers that Mary has baby sat for me for a few years while she was attending classes at Wayne State."

"We are concerned because Mary didn't show up for her

classes last night at Wayne State and she didn't report to her school this morning. We're told that she has made previous complaints about her ex husband recently. Do you know anything about that situation?"

"Not much more than that really, just that the marriage had been bad for a while. I do know that Mary and her mom stay with her Aunt, Louise at times."

"Neither she or her mom are home, we thought she might be at her aunt's home."

"What do you want me to do?"

"Do you have the phone number for her aunt?"

"Yes. I'll go get it for you."

While she moved from the hallway, the first officer contacted Frederickson. "Detective, we might have a break. The lady at the house here knows both Mary Blankenship and her aunt. She's getting the phone number for us."

Frederickson hoped this was the break they needed. "I'm on my way."

_____Twenty-Three

The area around Indian Village was quickly teaming with police action on the corner of Jefferson and Iroquois Streets. Roadblocks were set up just past the Village Marketplace on the corner of Jefferson and at both ends of the street as a precaution and officers were stationed along the area. Detective Frederickson had arrived and along with Captain Hughes were both at the neighbor's home and happy that she was able to give them the phone number of Blankenship's aunt. The plan was set. The neighbor would call the aunt under the guise of asking if Louise could get in touch with Mary for a weekend babysitting assignment. Captain Hughes gave the final instructions to the woman. "It's important not to alert her on what we think might be happening. We will be listening in on the other line. Just see if anyone answers and if it's your neighbor, ask if you can get Mary's phone number."

While this was going on in the living room, an officer sat at the kitchen table making sure the two children were quiet. Although she was very nervous, the neighbor was happy that she could help. She lifted the receiver as Captain Hughes picked up the second line. He pointed to her as she dialed the phone number. How lucky, the captain thought, that the neighbor still had a land line phone. If she only had cell service this would have taken much more technology.

She signaled to the captain that the phone was ringing. "Hi Louise, its Julie. I haven't seen you in a while, hope you're doing okay." The answer was short. Julie knew that this was unusual for

Louise who liked to talk. "I was hoping that you could help me get in touch with Mary." Louise didn't respond. "Louise, is everything okay?"

Julie could hear what sounded like a deep voice in the background. Then came an answer, "Yes, Julie, I was just getting something off the stove."

The captain whispered to Julie. "Try to get her to talk to you. Maybe she'll give you some sort of signal."

"Louise, you know how much we have wanted to get out of town and Tom has a meeting in your favorite city, Chicago. Hopefully Mary could watch the kids for us."

The answer again was short and methodical. "Yeah, Chicago. Sure wish I was there now." It was quiet for what seemed an eternity.

"Louise, can I get Mary's new phone number from you?" Julie was doing great and Captain Hughes was pleased with her performance.

Louise answered, "I don't know her new cell phone number. Do you want the number to their house?"

"I think I have that one, but you better give it to me anyway." While she waited Captain Hughes instructed her to ask a few questions about Mary's new job. "Hey Louise, how's Mary's teaching job going?"

This answer was also quick and short. "Their number is 313-888-1212. I haven't seen Mary in weeks. Sorry, Julie I have something on the stove." With that she hung up.

Julie turned to the captain. "Something is really wrong. Louise is very close to Mary and her mom. They almost see each other daily and I know that she would know how the new job was going. She always tells me what's going on when we talk."

This was the confirmation that something was wrong at Louise's home and the officers needed to take the next step. Captain Hughes had to make sure that the neighbors along the street were clear of any action that might take place. Louise's home was a two story brick dwelling with a large wraparound porch and circular driveway. It sat close to fifty-feet off the street and would be easy to isolate it from the homes along both sides. Captain Hughes now had a second volatile situation. He turned to Frederickson, "We haven't any real leads in the abduction of Tommy Dansforth and now I have a possible domestic dispute that may have multiple hostages."

Frederickson turned to Hughes, "How about if I continue on our abduction case while you and the rest of the team handles this issue."

"Sure, we've got this one."

The detective moved back down the street toward his car, turning back once to answer a question from the team on the corner of Jefferson. Once he updated them, he got in his car and checked his cell phone for any missed calls. Nothing, he shook his head. His case was going cold and he needed to check in with Jack Fox in the DA's office.

***

At the cabin Bud was huddled in the corner giving his nephew instructions. "Listen kid, these people need to be kept here safe and sound without any problems. I need to head up St. Clair Highway to Sarnia and pick Sam up. He's dumping the car in the lake just past the casino there. The current hopefully will take it deep into Lake Huron. It won't be found for a long time. Everything will be okay; I promise that I'll get you out of here as soon as Sam gets back." The young man listened as Bud continued. "I shouldn't be very long, you going to be okay kid?"

"Sure, no problem, uncle. I'm worried about the big guy, he don't like me."

"Listen I'm in charge, it will be fine."

The young man was conflicted. He didn't know that this would result in two people murdered and now whoever his uncle reported to was changing the plans. His loyalty to his uncle was strong, but he wasn't sure how to handle the things that the teacher said to him. He wondered, *how could he get both his uncle and himself out of this mess?* Maybe Dansforth had made an impact on the young man.

Bud asked the kid one more time, "Sure you're okay. I'm going to take the car; do you need anything out of it?"

"No, I've got everything I need. I'll be okay." The young man looked over at Dansforth's wife. "Is it okay if I give the lady a glass of water?"

"Yeah, but you can't untie her hands. Just tip the cup so she can sip the water from it. Be careful, we're almost done here." Bud didn't have a choice; he had to leave his nephew at the cabin. What could happen, his two captives were tied up and as long as the kid just left them that way everything would be okay. The trip to Sarnia to get the big man would take over an hour. Bud turned toward Dansforth. "If you want your wife to be okay you'll just stay still. I promise you'll be sorry if you try anything." Bud nodded toward his nephew as he walked out. "I'll be back soon."

The young man moved toward the front of the cabin and watched out the small window as Bud pulled out of the wooded lot. He reached into his pocket and looked at what appeared to be something small he held in his hand. Bud had said no cell phones, so he couldn't tell anyone that he had one, but this was different. He held it close to himself and appeared to be pulling it apart. Shaking his head he stuffed it back into his pocket. His hands shook and he turned to look back out of the window. A noise came from outside and the kid looked out only to see the sun glistening off the bright white snow. It was almost blinding as the glare reflected off the glass. He continued starring out and Dansforth looked over to his wife. He tried to make head motions to give her a signal that they needed to do something and do it soon. After what was close to five minutes, the young man turned toward the couple who were separated by about fifteen feet. "I'm going to say this just once. My uncle isn't going to hurt either of you, he promised me that. But if you try anything, all bets are off."

Tommy knew that had to say something. "I appreciate you telling us that. I also wanted to thank you for getting your uncle to agree to give my wife a drink." Dansforth didn't want to move too fast, but wanted to re-open dialogue with the young man. The young man looked at Dansforth then back over at his wife. "I know that my uncle seems like a bad guy to you but he's just following orders. None of this is his idea. He would never hurt anyone and promised me that you both would be free soon."

Dansforth nodded then again thanked the young man. "Maybe so, but that big guy with him shouldn't be trusted."

"Big Sam will follow orders from Bud, I know that."

"Hope you're right kid, I sure hope you're right." Dansforth knew that the kid was struggling with loyalty to his uncle and understood the problems with the big guy. Sam had already complained about Bud bringing his nephew and now with problems cropping up who knows what he would do. "Hey kid, she could really use that water now." The kid turned toward the small kitchen area. The cup that he had gotten earlier sat on the counter when he planned on giving Kathy Dansforth water before. He dumped the contents and filled it from a bottle in the fridge. Turning he looked at Dansforth who had been continuing to struggle with the binding behind his back. Dansforth leaned back in the chair. "Sure getting pretty stiff. I could use a chance to stretch my legs."

"Sorry teach, ain't gonna happen." He walked across the room and looked down at Dansforth's wife. "I thought a cup would be easier to drink from."

"Thanks, you're a kind young man," she said and leaned forward as he tipped the cup toward her. Kathy's lips were chapped and the water both refreshed and hurt at the same time. "Thanks, I needed that."

He watched her drink and could see that her lips looked like they were bleeding. "Wow, your lips look bad. How about if I see if we have anything to put on them."

"That would be great."

"Do you want another sip of water?"

"No, but anything like Chap Stick or Vaseline would be helpful."

"Not sure what I can find but I'll check it out." Turning back toward the kitchen he checked Dansforth one more time. Pointing at him he said, "Please don't try anything."

"I won't, just want to thank you for helping my wife." Dansforth watched the young man head back to the kitchen. Once he was sure that the kid had turned away, he again fidgeted with the binding. Eureka, it was loose and he thought that he was close to getting one hand free. If he could just distract the young man, maybe, just maybe he could get them out of this mess.

_____Twenty-Four

The lieutenant governor's staff knew that after the outburst the other day that there must be something very wrong but he hadn't confided in anyone. The past few hours he remained holed up in his office and when one of the girls asked if they could order some lunch for him, he about bit her head off. "What the hell could be going on," the pretty young blond receptionist asked Rich, his Chief of Staff.

"No idea, but knowing him, we're better if we just leave him alone. If he needs something he'll let us know. I've got to attend a meeting. I'll be back in an hour."

They were holding all incoming calls and cancelled the afternoon appointments. There was always something happening in Lansing and everyone was surprised that they hadn't heard any rumors or scuttlebutt that would tell them why the lieutenant governor was on edge. Every once in a while they could hear the lieutenant governor speaking loudly on the phone. The receptionist said to another of the ladies in the office, "He must be on a cell phone, none of the lights on the office phones are lit up."

"I heard that he has several cell phones. Probably a personal one, I try not to get too involved, it always bites you in the ass when you do."

"Guess that stands to reason. Jobs like this are hard to come by. I know political figures have to be careful using cell phones."

Just then the office door swung open and the lieutenant governor stood in the doorway. He was an imposing figure, close to six-foot-five and a thick head of hair. "I'm not going to need you all to be here the rest of the day. Take the day off and I'll see you tomorrow morning." With that he turned and shut the door.

"Wow that's different. I've never had that happen, at least not in an election year," one of the women said. "I've worked in the capitol for close to twenty years and seven for him. He's never done anything like that before."

"Hey, I'm not going to complain. There are alot of things I can do at home," another woman said. They all started picking up when the young receptionist asked, "Who will answer the phone?"

"I'll put it on message for you. Guess you're new and that you're not used to this. It happens usually on an election night when returns are coming in or when a journalist is trying to get a scoop. No one wants to be in their office when results are coming in or have to listen to reporters with their questions."

The office started to clear out in less than twenty minutes when Rich, the Chief of Staff came back in. He wondered why everyone was starting to walk out. "Where's everyone going?"

"He told us to take the afternoon off."

"What! There's no reason for that. Let me check with him before you all go." He knocked on the office door but there wasn't an answer. He tried the door knob but it was locked. "Sean, its Rich, can I come in?" Still no answer. He called out a second time. "Sean, I need to come in and talk to you."

The answer finally came back, "Rich, I'm on an important call."

"Sir, are you sure you want to send everyone home?"

The lieutenant governor now yelled out, "Rich, I want you to leave too. Get the hell out of here." Rich turned red faced and didn't want the ladies to see how embarrassed he was. "Sorry, guess we all should leave. He'll be okay. Tomorrow's another day." With that everyone walked out and Rich locked the exterior door to the main hallway. As he walked down the hallway of the Capitol he wondered what was going on. Rich didn't plan on leaving but instead headed across to the Senate Building where his best friend worked for the senate whip. Rich knew there was something really wrong but what could it be.

***

Detective Frederickson waited on the line for the DA, Jack Fox, to answer his phone. He wished that the news report he planted on Channel 7 earlier would have flushed someone out but so far nothing had developed. He also wanted to inform Fox that the other teacher that hadn't reported to school was probably involved in a domestic dispute. That eliminated all the suspects and only left the Greektown murder events for the reason for the abduction of Dansforth and presumably his wife.

When Fox came on the line he was talking at a very fast pace. "Sorry to keep you waiting detective. We've got a new development. I contacted the Border Patrol last night to keep an eye out for anything suspicious that could be related to our case. I just got a call from the Michigan Border Patrol chief that they have something along Lake St. Clair for us. Late yesterday an old four door Chevrolet crossed by ferry from Marine City into Canada. The two guys in the car seemed squirrely but nothing else seemed out of order. Detective, the description matches the one we used for the news report."

"Hell Jack, we made all that up."

"Yes, I know but I've asked for a copy of the video of the incident just in case. If the abductors took Dansforth to Canada it might be their smartest move." This made sense.

"Can I head over to watch the video with you?"

"Absolutely, come on over."

The detective heading downtown. He thought about how his relationship with the DA had come full circle. When the case started he wanted to toss the guy out of the office window. Their past history was bad. Now they were partners sharing information. *Guess you can teach an old dog new tricks*, he thought.

***

Tommy Dansforth kept working to get his hands free from the binding that held them together behind the chair. When he was knocked over earlier and the chair crashed to the floor it helped get the ropes loose around his waist and he was able to wiggle in the chair. He feared that even once he was loose that his legs had gone numb and it would be hard to even stand up, let alone overtake the young man that was watching over them. The young man called out to Kathy Dansforth. "I found a can of Crisco, it seems slippery, would that help?"

Kathy looked back at Tommy before answering. Once he nodded she said, "Sure, anything will be a plus. I really appreciate this." Dansforth turned back toward the kitchen and saw that the young man was holding a small blue tub of Crisco in his hands. The kid was making his way toward where the two were still strapped to the chairs. "I could also use some of that for my lips if possible." Tommy said.

"Let me take care of your wife first and see if that helps." He was about two feet from Kathy and had a paper towel in his right hand. "I'll spread some of this on the towel and then put it on your lips."

"Okay, just please do it softly. They are so sore and I'm afraid they will bleed even more." Kathy said. The young man was happy that he could help. He thought back about growing up. He was very close with his mom and they shared so much together. When his dad died, and she took in a boyfriend, things started to fall apart for him. It went real bad once she re-married and became pregnant. The guy became mean but never where the kid's mom saw what was happening. When the young man finally told his mother, she didn't believe him. Things digressed to a point where the new husband often hit him and the mom never stepped in. He was just thirteen and they kicked him out. His father's brother, Bud, quickly took him in. He owed Bud a lot and would do anything to help him. He moved in front of Dansforth's wife and handed Kathy the paper towel with the Crisco dabbed on the corner.

Once Kathy had applied the Crisco to her lips she ran her tongue across them to help spread it. The greasy substance designed for cooking seemed to help.

"Maybe let's apply it one more time. It seems to really help. Thanks so very much. You're a nice kid." Kathy was taking up the conversation where Tommy had started earlier.

"I'm not a kid. I turned eighteen last month and don't want to be called kid."

"Sorry, you're right. Guess because we're older you just seem so much younger. Enjoy your youth. What's your name?"

That took him by surprise. He figured they knew his name. *Bud surely had called him by his name, hadn't he?* "Andrew."

"That's a nice name. Do you prefer Andrew or Andy?"

"Guess everyone calls me Andy, but my mom always used to call me Andrew. I was named after my dad."

I understand, "My name is really Mary but my middle name is Kathleen and everyone calls me Kathy."

"Why's that?"

"My grandmother is a Mary, my aunt is a Mary, so using my middle name became a lot easier. It caused a lot less confusion especially when we were all together."

Andy laughed. "That's kind of funny. Wonder why they named you Mary."

Kathy was pleased that she was able to make a connection with the young man and kept watching Tommy who continued trying to free his hands. While this conversation was going on; Tommy kept working hard on the binding holding his hands together. The knots in the ropes were loose from when he was knocked off the chair. Although terribly hurt, and regardless of the pain he twisted and tugged at the binding. Finally, his right hand was now loose. He couldn't believe it. He was finally loose. Now what would he do?

Twenty-Five

Detective Frederickson sat with the District Attorney watching the surveillance video that the Border Patrol had sent over. They saw what the Border Patrol Chief had described as two squirrely guys in an older four door dark Chevrolet. They watched as the two men, the driver with a dark beard and his partner were questioned by the border guard. Although it was night and the video was grainy, they had a pretty clear view of the driver.

Fox was surprised, "Hey, they never checked the trunk." Frederickson agreed. "Did you ask their captain why?"

"No, I need to find that out. I've also asked the crime lab to run a facial recognition on the driver. He appears pretty clear at one point. So far nothing has come to light but I'm confident that we'll get results soon."

"Great plan. I didn't see the Border Patrol check the interior or trunk?" Frederickson pointed this out again.

"Neither did I. I know their chief won't be pleased either. He's meeting with the two border agents at the station as we speak. I've contacted the Marine City Police with this information and also contacted the Royal Canadian Mounted Police through the FBI office to get them involved in the search."

"I'm not real familiar with that area. What's across the lake in Canada from Marine City?"

"There's a ferry crossing that's pretty busy during the warm months but very few people cross there during the winter. A quaint little town, Sombra, is on the other side. It's mainly a summer resort community with a very small population in the hundreds."

"That should make it an easy area to search."

"Yeah, you would think so, however we've got to get a buy in from the RCMP and the FBI. Plus it's a highly wooded area and used mostly by snowmobilers and hunters this time of year."

"Why did you get the FBI involved?"

"Anytime we have an issue that extends into another country they have to be involved. I've talked to the local Bureau Chief, Brian Sikorski. He's sending a request to Ottawa for assistance and authority to make a combined search of the area. It will have to be a multinational investigation. The Canadian authorities may need more details and could consider it a U.S. Border Patrol issue."

"Shit, this could take forever and we don't have that kind of time."

"My other concern, detective, is I really don't want to get too many people involved with the Greektown issue. I'm not too sure who I can trust at this point. I'll just leave it that we may have a U.S. citizen and his wife abducted and taken into Canada."

Frederickson looked over at Fox, "I appreciate being brought into the loop on this. Glad you feel I can be trusted?"

"Right now you are the only person outside of this office that I'll share details about the case with."

"Thanks, Jack. Never did I think it would become an International incident."

"Detective, this is still your case, I'm glad you're willing to share it with me. Guess our two cases intersected which is a good thing." The two men continued talking about the two cases and details on the Greektown murder. Fox went over the details again with the detective making sure he hadn't left anything important out. "Like I told you yesterday, about two weeks ago a young man was shot in the Greektown parking deck off of Monroe Street. They have cameras that cover the deck however the shooter had his back to the camera and there was only a view of him from the back. It was a few minutes after the shooting that a 911 call came in giving the details and location of the incident. The caller identified himself as Tommy Dansforth and said he'd wait for officers to arrive. He was told to stay in place and not put himself in danger."

"Where was Dansforth when this took place?"

"He and his wife had just got into their car. It was parked on the same floor of the deck. They had a clear view because they were parked across the aisle just three vehicles away from the action."

"Were they able to identify the shooter?"

"Originally, Dansforth and his wife, were only able to give the officers a good description of the suspect. Of course they drew a composite and we checked for the usual suspects, but nothing jumped out. Like I was telling you before, it was days later when Dansforth came downtown with an article from the Free Press. He said that he was reading the lifestyle section when he saw a photo of the Lieutenant Governor, Sean Johnson, and his family being featured in a story. Dansforth was certain that Johnson's younger son was the shooter. He was positive. We've been running a background check of his whereabouts on the night in question. The kid has an extensive gambling problem and is a frequent patron of both Greektown and MGM casinos."

"And you could confirm that he was there that night?"

"Yes, we've reviewed the video and have confirmation from Greektown Casino security showing him entering the casino on Monroe Street an hour before the shooting. There's a video of him leaving the casino from the overpass walkway on St. Antoine toward the parking deck elevators just a few minutes before the incident and another of him exiting the elevator on the same floor as where the shots happened. He appears to have been following the guy that was shot. I've put a pretty good case together but the identification by Dansforth and his wife are critical to win the case. Everything else could be argued as circumstantial."

"What was his motive?"

"The guy that he shot had a big night at the poker tables and the security video shows the kid was playing in the same game. The guy won thousands."

"Does the lieutenant governor know anything about this?"

"Unfortunately, I think someone from the downtown precinct had to get the information to his office. That's why I've been keeping everything close to the vest. I can't trust anyone outside my office on this case."

"Although robbery looks like the motive that could be pretty weak with all the money the family has. Can you make it stick without Dansforth?"

"That's the main problem. It appears that the lieutenant governor has been taking measures to cover any reference to money problems. The kid's bank account is now flush with cash and he hasn't been seen in over a week. He may even be out of the country. I can't force the issue with the Grand Jury indictment so that's at a standstill now."

"We'll find your witnesses, Jack."

Fox appreciated the detective's positive attitude. "No one outside of my office knows the details I've told you. I know I can trust you."

The two men stood and shook hands. "You know I'll never tell anyone what you just told me."

Fox shook his head, "I know."

Frederickson headed back to his car and planned on checking on the progress on the standoff on Iroquois Street and the search for Mary Blankenship. The officers at the scene relayed to him that the negotiator had everyone in place, and would to try to make contact again with Mary's aunt or whoever was holding the ladies. The detective wanted to do something to help, however until Fox called back with more information, and he knew more about the search across from Marine City, his best bet was to go back to the action in Indian Village. He debated about calling Carole Newton from Channel 7. Maybe he could give her the details taking place on Iroquois. This would keep her on his side and concentrate the reporter on handling the coverage of the hostage situation that was going to get the news team's attention anyway.

_____Twenty-Six

The standoff on Iroquois was coming to a dangerous point. Captain Hughes had men stationed both in front and back of the home and they were able to get a sniper positioned across the street with the permission of a homeowner. They had evacuated the area and were ready to make their next move. The captain planned on making a second call to Blankenship's aunt. This time he would get right to the point. The man holding the family had to know the odds he faced. Give up now or face grave consequences. The phone hook-up was completed. Hughes was stationed across the street with three of his men and a second captain from the Tenth Precinct. The phone rang several times before it was finally answered. "Hello Louise, this is Captain Hughes from the Twelfth Police Precinct. I need to talk to the man that's holding all of you."

"No one else is in here." Hughes knew that Louise was being prompted into that answer and that she was alone. "I wish that was true but if no one else is there you need to open the front door and come on out."

There wasn't another answer for a few minutes when a man's voice came on the phone. "You all need to leave us alone now."

"We just want to talk. How about you letting me in and we can discuss what you want."

"I want to be left alone with my wife."

His admission that Mary was inside now confirmed what was strongly suspected. "What's your name?"

"My name's not important. I just want you to leave me alone

with my wife. Leave us alone, now!" The next sound was the receiver being slammed down.

Captain Hughes had dealt with this type of situation before but reported it downtown and knew a hostage negotiator would soon arrive. He had the family history details with everything the negotiator would need. Hughes just hoped he might be able to defuse the situation himself. Knowing that the ex husband had recently been released from the city jail regarding violating the protection order Mary had against him, made this possibly more dangerous. The man could be unstable. Hughes moved back to his post across the street confirming with the men stationed around the home. He also wanted to see if the sniper had a view of anyone inside.

"Captain, I've been able to get a clear view into the front room of the home. It looks directly into the large dining room but no further. There is what appears to be an older woman sitting in the front room with a younger woman next to her. Neither of them has moved and may be tied up."

Armed with those details Captain Hughes was happy that they had a clear view into the place. Hopefully they wouldn't lose it. He could see one of his men walking toward him escorting another officer. *Must be the negotiator*, Hughes walked toward the men who approached the area. He introduced himself, "I'm Captain Hughes, I appreciate you helping us here." He filled the negotiator in on the hostage situation and that they had a man stationed across the street with a clear view into the home.

"Do you have a line of communication opened?"

"We have talked to both the lady that lives there, Louise, and then on a second call finally were able to talk to the ex husband that is holding the three women, his ex wife, her mother and aunt. After trying to open a dialogue he hung up."

"Where are all your men stationed?"

"I have men at both the back and front porch of the house, plus, the man I told you about across the street on the roof of the home over there," the captain pointed out the location of the home where the man was positioned on the roof.

"First I'd like to try to re-open the negotiations."

Captain Hughes handed the negotiator the phone number and hook up. "Hope he answers."

"Don't worry captain; I've done this many times." With that the man looked over a list of the people that were probably being held in the home. "Captain, did he request anything before hanging up on you?"

"Just wanted us to leave him alone with his ex wife." The man turned and dialed the home and waited for someone to answer. One, two, three, four rings without an answer. "He's not going to answer that thing." The negotiator kept waiting and let the phone continue to ring.

Finally someone picked up, "Why are you still out there, I told you I want to be left alone with my wife."

"Sorry about that James, but we've never talked before."

"How do you know my name?"

"Simple, you told the police captain that Mary was your wife and our records show that she was married to a James Walls. Our records also show that you are now divorced."

"Yes but we're trying to work things out, and I can't do that if you and the police continue to interfere."

"James, my name is King, and I'd love nothing better than to help you both work it out. How about you both come on out here and let's see how we can help."

The man was taken aback by this approach. "We're doing okay up here. You all just need to leave."

"James, I'd love nothing better but, you see this police captain called my boss and got me all the way down here; either I come up with a solution or it's my ass. Can you help me out here, James."

"What the hell do you mean? I don't need you here. Just tell your boss it was all a mistake."

King already had James engaged in a conversation and getting him to talk was the first rule all negotiators followed. "James, I'd love nothing more. But you know the type, I sent you down there and you better come back with a resolution. I gotta do something. How about you or Mary come out and talk to me so I can send all these other cops home."

"Ain't gonna happen, King."

"You've got to give me something, James. How about the other women in there? Why don't you send them out? It will show the captain that you're a good guy and not looking for trouble."

"If I send them out, will you leave?"

"James, I'd like nothing more than that. At least it will help me convince this police captain that we can send some of these cops out of here. After all, you're not a bad guy, are you James?"

"No, I'm not a bad guy. I love my wife and really don't need the two old ladies. I'm sending them out. I expect to see the police pulling out, King."

"We've got our first deal there, James. I'm unarmed and going to cross the street. I just want to help the two ladies to a car so we can get them out of here. That okay with you, James?"

"No funny stuff, King, or they won't make it across the street."

With that King confirmed that James had a weapon. "Take it easy there, James, look out the front window; I've got my hands up and I'm walking alone." King looked up and could see a figure from a small side window, then the front door opened a few inches. One lady walked out of the home and down the stairs. She crossed to where King stood and he put his arm around her. She was crying.

"He said unless he sees some cops leaving he won't let my sister leave."

"Don't worry, we plan to follow our agreement. Let me get you across to the men stationed there."

As they walked across the street she turned and looked back at the home. "My sister, Mary's mother, isn't well. She has a bad heart and needs her medicine."

"I'll take care of it. Everyone will come out of this okay." King handed her to Captain Hughes. "You need to pull some of your men out and he has to be able to see what we're doing."

"I'm not doing that!"

"I made an agreement and it's the only way he'll let Mary's mother out."

The captain didn't like this. He wanted to be in charge and now the negotiator was removing men from the scene. He turned to an officer. "Tell the guys hiding at the back and front of the home to pull back and move out here where they can be seen."

"Are you sure, sir?"

"Shit, just do what I said."

"Captain, keep one man at the rear of the home, please," King told him.

Three officers came out of the front and back of the home and another from down the street. Hughes told them to pull back to the corners at the roadblocks."

King called back to the home. "James, thanks for holding up your first part and I've held up my part. Now send Mary's mom out. She needs her heart medicine and we surely don't want anything bad to happen, do we?"

"Once she comes out, King, I expect the rest of those cops to leave us."

"I can't promise that James. What I can promise is I'll get everyone else out of here but, you, me and the captain. How's that buddy?"

James told him, "I need to think about that."

"Well, James, we followed our agreement and now it's your turn. Don't put me in a bad way with the captain and my boss."

"Give me a few minutes." With that James hung up.

Minutes later the front door again opened and an elderly woman moving slowly walked out the front door. King hurried back across the street and helped her down the last few steps.

"Mrs. Blankenship, I'm Captain King, is your daughter okay?"

"James has a gun. He says unless she takes him back, he's going to kill her. Please help my daughter." With that she broke down in tears.

King got her over to where her sister and the captain were standing. They had men take both women over to Julie's house where they had dispatched an EMS team waiting to help. "Okay Captain, we've got a fifty percent success here but now it becomes harder. Mary's mother told me James has a gun. He's also saying either he and Mary get back together or he's going to kill her."

Hughes asked, "Okay, what's our next move?"

_____Twenty-Seven

Tommy Dansforth knew this might be their last chance to escape. They had to try something before Bud and the big man returned. His wife was occupying the young man while he finally got his right hand loose from the ropes that bound him to the chair. Andrew was standing with his back to Dansforth and Kathy had asked him for one more application of the Crisco that she was using on her lips. Tommy kept watching him as he used his free hand to get the ropes loose from his feet. Once he accomplished that he gripped the arm of the chair and swung it with his free hand as hard as possible hitting Andrew across the back of his head sending the young man sprawling to the floor. Tommy's legs were so weak that he too fell to the floor next to the young man. Kathy screamed. "Honey, are you okay?"

"Did I get him?"

"He's down and out."

"Then I'm great. See it pays to watch those old cowboy movies." He slowly crawled to his knees and over the top of the young man lying about two feet to the side of Tommy's wife. Tommy pulled the ropes loose that had bound his legs to the chair and wrapped them around the right hand of the young guy first and pulled the left arm back so he could tie the kid's wrists together. "I don't want to hurt him any more than I have to but I have to make sure he's immobile."

"Can you drag him to that radiator near the window? You can tie him to that."

"Good idea." Tommy's left arm was still tied to the piece of the broken arm of the chair that he used to clobber Andrew with. He pulled those ropes off it and used them to bind Andrew to the radiator that was on the side of the main room. Once he accomplished that he moved over to help free Kathy. It took a little longer than he hoped and his right arm was killing him. "Kathy, I'm sure that it's broken."

"When I'm free I will check it out. Maybe we can find something to wrap around it."

Tommy got her free and held Kathy in his arms as the two hugged. "I don't know how much time we have but we have to get moving as quick as possible. I saw a couple hunting jackets and hats on the rack over by the rear door. I hope they left a car here with the kid. I think I saw him looking at something earlier, maybe he has a cell phone." Tommy searched the kid's pockets and found a cell phone tucked in a small jean pocket. "I got his cell phone."

"We can call for help."

Tommy flipped it opened but the screen was blank. He tried turning it on but nothing happened. "Kathy, I need two hands here." She moved over to him and took the phone, her hands trembled but she followed his directions.

"Open the cover on the back." He watched her pry it open and she turned toward him.

"There isn't a battery in it, no battery, why?"

"Maybe Bud or the big guy found it. Put it back in his pocket, not going to do us any good." He grimaced in pain.

"Let me look at your arm." She knew it was bad, but didn't know if it was broken. "I'll tie it in a sling for you." She ripped part of her sleeve from her sweatshirt and manufactured a makeshift sling. Once she had done that Kathy moved over to Andrew and checked the back of his head. "Tommy, it's bleeding badly," she moved over to the sink and got a wet rag.

"What are you doing?"

"Tommy, he's bleeding. I can't leave him like this."

"His uncle is probably going to kill him. It will only look

worse if he sees that we took care of him. Leave him alone. The blood and cuts might save him. Maybe they will accept that we overpowered him. Honey, it's really best for him."

Kathy knew he was probably right. "But he's just a kid."

"I know. They're all kids when they get started."

Kathy left the wet rag on the sink and grabbed the jacket and hat that Tommy handed her. "Glad they left our shoes on. It would be impossible to leave without footwear." They continued looking for keys or any transportation but nothing was available. "We got to get out of here." Tommy looked out the small window and saw that the front of the cabin was pretty well hidden by a group of pine trees from the road. "At least the sun is out." He turned to help Kathy bundle up. "Put this scarf around your face. Let's see if there's any food we can grab. Don't know how far we're from anything. I'm pretty sure we're in Canada, maybe in a small village, or hunting area."

"Why do you say that?"

"The big guy said that they would head up to Sarnia."

"That's going to make it tougher for us."

"Now that we're free, we may have the upper hand. We just have to get some help. Let's see if we can find some food."

Kathy opened a few cupboards and found part of a loaf of bread and small jar of peanut butter. She also grabbed a packet of cheese crackers and stuffed it in her pocket. "I got some stuff."

Tommy saw that there were a few bottles of water in the fridge. "I'll grab these too." It was hard stuffing things in his pockets with one arm in a sling but the arm felt better immobilized. They filled their pockets with as much as they could.

Suddenly from the front of the room a voice called out, "Help, you can't leave me here like this." Andrew was coming to and crying.

"You have to be quiet. I'm not going to hurt you but we're getting the hell out of here."

"Bud's going to have a fit when he gets back and Big Sam will kill me. There's something I gotta tell you!" The kid had tears streaming down his face and sobbing.

"Tommy, he's right," Kathy said.

"Yeah, well he should have thought about it before helping his uncle abduct you from our house. He's not innocent, just in the wrong place." Tommy looked down at Andrew. "Sorry kid, I'd like to help you and promise when we reach the authorities I'll let them know you were forced into this." Tommy stuffed a rag into Andrew's mouth and tied a gag around his head.

Andrew turned his head back and forth, trying to talk but the gag stopped any chance of that. Kathy looked down at him, "It would be better if you stop trying to fight it. I'll make the police will know you tried to help us but couldn't." She stood back up and headed toward Tommy who was gathering food. They grabbed the sack with the water and food and took off out the front of the cabin.

Once they were outside Tommy said, "We're going to leave tracks in the snow, I'll double back in a few spots to try to confuse them."

"Maybe you can break a branch off one of the pine trees and brush off some of the tracks."

"Great idea."

The road was over two-hundred feet from the front of the cabin and the gravel along with the fact that the two captives had been bound and seated for close to twenty-four hours didn't make it any easier. They held each other's hands and once they were in the clearing Kathy started to cry. "What's wrong honey?"

She was softly sobbing, "I just knew they were going to kill us."

Tommy Dansforth knew his wife was strong, when she broke down he felt almost helpless. He held Kathy tightly with his one arm for a few minutes. "Honey, we're out and we'll be okay." They hugged and he lifted her chin with his hand and kissed her softly. Looking into her eyes he promised that they'll make it. "We really need to get out of here honey."

"You're right." They headed down the road sticking close to the tree line. They zigzagged through the wooded area hoping not to leave a clear path of the direction they headed. Tommy knew that at any moment they might need to duck back into the woods. They couldn't flag any vehicle down; it could be Bud and the big guy coming back. They had been out of the cabin for about fifteen minutes and really didn't know where they were headed to. "I wish I had an idea which direction the lake was? If we could get to the lake I'm sure there might be a cabin with someone or a boat we can use to get across."

"Tommy, the lake is frozen. It's cold as heck out here. I read in the paper last week that the ferry had to have the Coast Guard ice breaker to free a crossing for them. We should try to find a town or something while it's still light outside. Do you have any idea what time it is."

"No, let me think for a minute. The sun came up about two hours ago. It usually comes up around seven thirty this time of year. It must be after eleven because it was at least an hour after Sam had left when Bud went to get him."

"How about you keep brushing away our tracks and I'll lead us out of here."

"Okay, you lead and I'm ready to follow." For the first time in two days the two laughed. "Come on boss, which way?" he asked.

"Just stick close to me," that brought out a few more chuckles from the couple.

_____Twenty-Eight

Frederickson put a call to his captain. "I just left Jack Fox and he filled me in on his part of the case."

Hughes was upset, "What do you mean his part of the case?"

Frederickson remembered what Fox had said. _The lieutenant governor has people and friends everywhere._ "You know, the story we put together for the news today."

"Yeah, guess it's better to keep him on our side. We're working here with this negotiator from downtown, a guy named King, have you ever worked with him?"

"Sure, they call him Sky King. He seems to take everything he touches right to the top of the news. A few years back there was a hostage situation on Warren Avenue that started as a drug bust, King was the negotiator once the thing got out of control and the men were holding a woman and young child in the home. I heard he's pretty cool and got everyone out safe and sound. He's been in on a lot of big hostage things since and is very solid. Good guy to have on the team."

"That's good to know. Wonder why I hadn't heard of him before."

"You were in the Sixth Precinct and on the west side, they probably used another guy. I plan to call Carole Newton, the television reporter, and get her in on the deal here on Iroquois."

"Sure, guess we owe her and never know when that will come in handy in the future. King has cleared out some of my men as a token so that Mary's ex would release the hostages."

"How'd that go?"

"He got the guy to let her mom and aunt out of the house; just working on getting Mary out now."

"I'm on my way back." Frederickson planned on calling Carole at Channel 7 while he headed to the events taking place on Iroquois. He knew that if he kept her in the loop with the on-going events that would be covered by pretty much all the news channels, she'd continue to let him know things she had found out. *Maybe she'll be the first reporter on the scene. He would make sure she had full access to everything.*

Carole Newton was surprised to hear from the detective. She informed him, "Our traffic chopper reported action taking place along Jefferson and we didn't know exactly what was going on. Thanks for the heads up, detective. I'm going to head over there with a camera team. Where should I meet you?"

"I'll tell the officers stationed on Jefferson and Iroquois that you're cleared from me. I'll give them the approval to let you up to the command area. I wanted to make sure that I gave you whatever we could."

Carole Newton, and the Channel 7 News team headed down Jefferson, speeding toward the action taking place in Indian Village. Her cameraman made sure the station was putting together an intro into the action by pulling video from old files of an aerial view of the Village. Most Detroiters were familiar with the historic area; however many in the suburbs may not know it very well. Always good to give the viewers the best details as possible and Carole was an expert at that. She knew that the other local stations would be on the scene but with help from the detective she may have the real scoop. Carole thought, *this has been a good news week for me.*

King knew that getting Mary Blankenship out wouldn't be as easy as it was with her mom and aunt. Her ex was determined that he was going to get back together with his wife and King had to make him think that could happen. He and the captain made a obvious show of moving the police that were leaving past the front of the home, so that the man holding his hostage would see that they were keeping their part of the bargain. King needed to get the man back on the phone. James gave him what could have been an ultimatum; get back with his wife or else. The only way a hostage negotiator could succeed is by keeping the subject talking. King placed another call into the home hoping this time James would pick up. This was the third time King dialed the number so far without results.

Suddenly he had someone on the line. "You need to stop calling me!" the man yelled.

"James, hang on there. You're doing great and I might have a way for you to get everything you want and not face any charges." King could hear breathing on the other end of the line but James didn't answer his last statement. *Maybe he's thinking about what I said.* "James, my boss down here is pleased that you let Mary's family go. He's willing to work with you and Mary to make sure we can clear the way for you to get back together."

"How the hell can you do that?"

"Mary's mom told me that if you both sat down and talked to a marriage counselor there was hope that you can reconcile the marriage."

"I thought the old lady hated me?"

"No James, she just wants what's best for her daughter. She knows Mary still has feelings for you." How King wished he could talk to Mary and give her some directions to help in the negotiations. King needed to talk to her mom one more time. He turned toward Hughes who stood a few feet away, "Captain, could you see if Mary's mom is okay enough to come and talk to me."

Captain Hughes headed back over to Julie's house. He didn't know why King wanted Mary's mom back at the scene but King was in charge. Once Hughes was in the home he saw that the women were still with the medical personnel. "Mrs. Blankenship, how are you feeling?"

"How's my daughter, is she okay?"

"Everything is going good. We've been talking to her ex husband and things are progressing well. Mr. King wanted to know if you would be willing to come back out there and help him."

She jumped up off the couch and said, "Let's go!" She hurried to the door and left Hughes trailing. The captain and Mary's mom headed back to where King had set up his command post. As they made their way to the area, Carole Newton and her camera team had arrived. Mrs. Blankenship addressed the negotiator, "Mr. King how can I help you?"

King was happy that the lady appeared okay after the ordeal that she went through and hoped that she could shed some light on her daughter's state of mind. King covered the phone receiver as he addressed the lady, "Mrs. Blankenship, if you could help me it would be greatly appreciated." King held his index finger up as James asked him a question.

James asked, "You need to tell me exactly how this thing can work out for me and Mary?"

"James, her mom is standing here with me right now and wants to thank you for letting her and her sister get some help from our medical team. Would you be willing to talk to her for a second?"

"I'm not sure."

"How about letting her at least talk to Mary for just a minute, it would go a long way for all of us helping the two of you solve this." James didn't answer at first but still kept the line open. "James, you'd agree any mom would want to make sure her daughter was okay."

"I'll let Mary talk to her mom but only for a minute."

While King was negotiating a deal with James, Captain Hughes was prepping Mary's mom on what they wanted her to tell her daughter. The plan was to coax Mary to try to go along with the idea of getting back together with James and seek marital help. King motioned Mrs. Blankenship closer to him. "James, can you put Mary on the line for me."

"I want to hear from Mary's mom first."

"James, how about you letting Mary and her mom talk; then you can talk to Mrs. Blankenship. There wasn't an answer for a few seconds.

"You better not try anything, I'm not stupid."

"James, we know you're not stupid, and we also want nothing more than to help you and Mary out of this." King had succeeded in keeping James talking and occupied. The officer that was across the street on the roof top had reported to Captain Hughes that the front window view was clear and he had an unobstructed shot into the house if they needed. James had crossed the room a couple of times and the sniper was sure he had a clean target. King's plan was working so far and using the sniper was the last resort. "James, can you put Mary on the phone?" He could hear James talking to Mary and giving her some instructions. King thought the young lady was crying but not sure.

"Okay, Mary is coming but she can only talk to her mom for a minute."

"Thanks James, this will go a long way for you. My boss is pleased with your help so far. We're getting close to helping you get everything you want."

James handed the phone to her. Mary looked back at him and although she was crying, she called out, "Mom, mom, are you okay?"

King heard the sobbing voice and along with Mrs. Blankenship listened in on the conversation. "Mary, my name is King and I'm here with your mom, we need you to listen and help us."

"Mary, my baby, is you okay?"

After Mrs. Blankenship's question, both women started sobbing. "Mary, this is King again, your mom is fine now and our goal is to get you and James out of there soon. Can you help me?"

The young lady settled down and answered softly, "Yes."

"Mary," Mrs. Blankenship's voice seemed stronger. "James says he wants to get back together with you. It's important to give him that opportunity right now."

King was surprised how quickly Mrs. Blankenship got it together. Her statement was right on target.

"I understand mom, yes, James is a good guy and I know he's sorry all of this has happened." After that statement James came back on the phone.

"Mrs. Blankenship, I'm sorry this went so far. I just want to be with the woman I love."

"James, why don't you listen to what Mr. King is telling you and we can all help you and Mary." With that she handed the phone back to King and turned toward Captain Hughes. The lady did everything King could have hoped for and once she finished she broke down sobbing in tears.

_____Twenty-Nine

The harsh wind blew off Lake St. Clair and snow drifts hampered their progress as Dansforth and his wife tried to find their way out of the wooded area to get help. Although they weren't sure exactly where they started from, Kathy seemed to think walking away from the direction of the wind would be their best route. "I'm thinking that the wind is coming off the lake so if we go the other way we might find other cabins or maybe a store."

Tommy was glad that they found some jackets and scarves in the cabin to cover their faces. He continued to brush away their footprints with his free arm. "I'm sure that Bud and that big guy are close to getting back. We need to get as far away as possible." They were concerned about the path they chose hoping it was a direct line and that they weren't going in a circle. It was difficult especially when you have no idea where you were or what was out there. Trudging through the snow wasn't as bad as Tommy thought it might be. He had broken a branch off a small pine tree and at times walked backwards and brushed their footprints away as they kept moving along. Kathy was a real trooper. She was calm and focused as they weaved through the tree lined area about ten to fifteen feet just off the side of the gravel roadway. Keeping the road off to their right with shrubs and trees blocking them from clear view of the roadway was their best protection. "Honey if we can keep up this pace we have a great chance of being pretty far away from that cabin." Kathy nodded as she continued moving along the rough terrain.

***

Meanwhile back at the cabin Andrew struggled with the ropes that bound him to the radiator. *How did this happen, how could he let them overpower him.* He knew his uncle would go nuts when he got back. Pain resonated from his head and shoulders and Andrew was a bit foggy. Andrew's other concern went to the big man with his uncle. He knew that Sam was a killer. His uncle once told him that the big man enjoyed hurting people. He saw what he did with the two abductors and was sure that the man would kill him too. What could he do, his hands were numb and the pain in his head was tremendous. *How long had he been tied up?* Andrew needed to gather his thoughts. If his uncle wanted details he had to be able to supply them. *What kind of lead did Dansforth and his wife have? How long had they been gone?* Andrew was starting to panic and with good reason. His screwed up his only assignment. He just had to keep two people in the cabin who were securely tied up. He failed and failure wasn't an option in this profession. Andrew's head was throbbing and his mind ran back across the events before he was knocked out. *How could he explain this to his uncle? Could Bud hold the big man off?*

Andrew's fears came rushing back to reality when he heard the racket of gravel hitting the undercarriage of a vehicle outside. *They're back*! His breathing became rapid and he turned from side to side. Bud and the big man would soon come in and find out what happened. There was nothing he could do. Andrew hung his head and closed his eyes.

Voices outside were getting closer. "That wasn't as easy as I thought it would be. I had to send the car over a ridge hoping that it would crack the ice flows that covered the shoreline." The big man was bragging.

"All that and it's still visible from the shore. I could see the tail end of the car pretty easy. As soon as people start eating at the restaurant in the casino someone is going to spot it."

"If you're so sure you or that half breed nephew of yours could have done better than you should have done it."

It was clear the two men were arguing about dumping the vehicle that belonged to the two idiots that abducted Tommy Dansforth from the school parking lot. Andrew knew they were just outside the door and his life might be experiencing its final seconds. The sound of the front door slamming into the wall as winds rushed into the cabin broke his thoughts.

"Shit, what the hell!" Bud was yelling at the top of his lungs. Andrew slumped against the radiator with his head tucked in as tightly as possible looking like a turtle that was about to be attacked. "Where the hell are they?" Bud spun around and saw his nephew crumpled along the wall in the front of the small cabin, "Andy, what the hell happened?" The young man turned away from the sound of his uncle's question. "Son of a bitch, Andy, what the hell did you do?"

The young man didn't respond as tears trickled down his face.

***

Tommy and Kathy had been moving along the path off the edge of the roadside at a decent pace and figured they had been gone from the cabin for close to thirty-five minutes. If they could keep this up Tommy was sure they would at least be far enough away to make it impossible for Bud and his team to easily find them. Tommy continued brushing away their footsteps in the snow and the wind was becoming an asset in helping cover their tracks. The winds whipped their harsh frozen chill at the exposed body parts as the two kept trudging through the rough terrain. Tommy was concerned about his wife. She had been tied up for a long time and he knew she hadn't eaten for over twenty-four hours. Although they grabbed a few things from the cabin there wasn't time for them to rest and eat. "Honey, you need to eat some of those crackers you found."

"Let's get a little farther away and I promise I'll eat it's okay." Kathy Dansforth was stronger than Tommy ever expected she could be in this life and death situation. She was still walking about three feet in front of him as he brushed at their tracks in the snow. "Tommy, look out!" He didn't see the ridge ahead because he had his head down clearing their tracks and went tumbling over head first. "Tommy, are you okay?" Kathy bent down over her husband who was sprawled out over the bank of snow.

"I'm okay, didn't see that." He struggled to his knees as Kathy reached out to help him up. "I'm okay, really, I'm okay," he kept saying. Once he was back on his feet he rubbed at his knees. "Wow, that was dumb. Guess I need to pay a little more attention to what I'm doing."

"Do you want to rest here a little?"They had been through so much in the last day and half that Kathy wanted to make sure he was really fine, or at least as good as possible in this situation. She watched him rub at the sling holding his damaged arm.

"No, we need to keep going. I think we've done a good job brushing our footprints away and I don't need to keep doing that." The two held hands for a second and Tommy looked into his wife's eyes. "I love you, and promise we will get through this." They were silent as they hugged. "Point the way boss," Tommy said, to break the silence.

"Okay, but let's walk together so we can help each other." That was a good idea.

"Deal." They again started the journey along the rough path through the wooded area continuing to stay far from the gravel road but following its path hoping it would lead them to safety. The sun at times shone through the tall pine trees and helped shed light on their road ahead. The farther they traveled the better the chance that Bud and his men wouldn't be able to find them. "Maybe we should move deeper into the woods. If Bud and the big man start heading this way they would most likely follow the gravel road."

"What do you want to do?"

"I know it makes sense to follow the road but I'm afraid we might be too close to it."

Kathy suggested, "Why don't we cross to the other side? It might be good to crisscross through here. You could brush our tracks away on the roadway and the trees look a little thicker on the other side offering us more cover."

Tommy was really proud of Kathy. "Wonderful idea. I'll use the branch and you lead the way. He took the branch he was using and rubbed out the footprints as he and Kathy crossed the gravel road in front of them. Once they were on the other side of the path they moved a little deeper into the wooded area when the crushing sounds of an on-coming vehicle startled them. The sound broke the silence of their walk and Tommy looked back at his wife. Fear filled her face and he gripped her tightly as they crouched down into a thicket of underbrush that hopefully would cover them from the road. Once they were sure that they were covered, Tommy motioned with his finger to be silent to his wife. The on-coming vehicle slowed down and came to a stop. Tommy recognized the big man's legs climbing from the passenger side.

"They can't be this far, Bud. We've gone close to ten miles. We need to double back."

"I'll decide what we'll do." Bud was determined to keep checking this area.

"You mean like having your dumb shit nephew keep an eye on them." The big man wasn't going o let this go.

"Maybe it's our fault they got loose. Andy was hurt pretty bad."

"Sure, another excuse. Why did you leave him back at the cabin, we could use him out here."

"I told him to check in the other direction. He can walk along to make sure they didn't go the other way. I gave him a phone to call if he finds something. In the meantime I think we need to continue stopping along the route and looking for footprints. They had to travel this way."

"I'm thinking if we don't find them soon I'm headed the hell outta here." Big Sam was now gritting his teeth while looking back at Bud.

"You're not going anywhere. We started this together, and we'll end it together."

Tommy realized that not only were they being tracked but their trackers continued to be arguing about what they should do next. This might be the best news for him and Kathy. Tommy could see them get back into the car and the vehicle started moving again when suddenly it came to a sliding stop.

"Stop, I think there's something moving over there." The passenger door quickly swung opened and the big man jumped back out moving in the direction where Tommy and his wife crouched in the wooded patch. He stomping on low lying branches and kept moving in their direction when a loud noise from behind Tommy and his wife broke the silence. Bam! Bam! The big man ducked down and covered his ears. "What the hell!" he yelled.

Tommy turned his head toward the direction where the sounds came from. He was sure it was that of gun erupting. He couldn't see anything but a second round of shots rang out, Bam! Bam! *Is it hunting season*, Tommy thought, *who could be shooting and who were they shooting at?*

The big man retreated toward where Bud was standing as he opened his door. "Someone's shooting at us?" Big Sam was waving back to Bud. He ducked again as shots rang out a third time. The two men were now crouched along the sides of the vehicle and saw a small group of people moving up the gravel road toward them. The lead person was wearing traditional camouflage hunting gear carrying a shot gun in his arms and called out to them.

"Sorry, didn't see you both. Why are you out here and what are you doing on this road?"

Bud slowly lifted his head and waved his right hand in a

motion of surrender. Once he was sure that the on-coming group of hunters were waiting for an answer he stood and called back to them. "Guess we're lost. We are staying down the road at a friend's cabin and trying to head to the general store."

"Man you're really lost. No general store around here. This is private property." The lead hunter stood with his gun wrapped in his arms waiting for an answer.

Bud cleared his throat and looked over at his partner. "My boss owns a cabin just down the road," Bud pointed back at the gravel path they were on, "He told us to get some supplies from the general store. I must have got turned around somewhere. We'll just turn around."

"You have to be careful out here, there's been a black bear spotted. It's still hunting season in Ontario and when we heard one was spotted just yesterday, we all headed along this ridge near our hunting lodge." The man continued to approach Bud and Sam. He had a puzzled look on his face as he got within a few feet of the duo. "You're not dressed for being out here in the woods."

Bud knew that they looked out of place especially with it being hunting season and so damn cold. "I understand, but like I said, my boss sent us to grab some supplies. Maybe you can help us."

Tommy and his wife could barely make out what was happening. They heard some of the men talking but couldn't make out the conversation. Did Bud have more people searching for them? *Were these guys called in to help? Had they been spotted?* Tommy crawled along with Kathy pushing deeper into the pine limbs and thicket. They didn't want to be exposed. He and Kathy looked over at each other hoping that this wasn't the end of their attempted escape.

_____Thirty

Carole Newton stood next to the detective as he filled her in on the on-going hostage standoff. King hoped the conversation Mrs. Blankenship had with James and then Mary worked to their benefit. When James said that he was sorry that everything went this far, it gave King an opening he hoped for. He planned to parlay that into a way to get the couple to exit the home safely. Carole knew it was due to her new relationship with the detective she was being afforded first hand access to the events that were unfolding. Frederickson positioned her camera team safely behind a secure barricade that they had set up across the street.

"If we get any action, you need to move back behind that area too," he said pointing to the make shift wooded wall that the officers had constructed.

She knew this was critical for her coverage, "Thanks, detective."

King motioned to Captain Hughes and the two conferred for a minute. Frederickson moved closer to catch what they were planning. King said, "We're at a critical point. I need to get James to come out in the next few minutes or this could go south on us." Hughes and Frederickson understood. In every hostage negotiation there was a point where either you won the suspect over or you had to take extraordinary measures. The sniper was alerted that either James would be coaxed out or other actions would be put into place. King had given James with the best reason for him and Mary to come out, "If you come out now, you and Mary might be able to work everything out." Mary was now left with the prospect of convincing James that there was still hope for their marriage. King wanted to give the couple a few minutes before he called James back. He turned to the small group behind him. "This is it, either James takes advantage of our offer or we take other measures." He picked up the phone and dialed. It rang three, four, five times and no answer. He let it continue to ring as tensions grew. On the tenth ring there was finally an answer.

"King, please, I need more time. You need to give me more time."

"James, I've done everything I could to get you the best deal possible but time is running out. I'm going to cross the street and come up the front porch. How about you and I talk face to face?"

James was quiet, "No, you need to stay back."

"Can't do, James, I've already told my boss that you and I will talk this out in person. I've got a job to do and only want to make sure you get everything you want. You've got to help me here, James." King continued to move across the street as Captain Hughes listened on the second line. King was now on the front steps of the porch that had seven cement steps with large white wooden pillars on both sides. "James, I'm going to sit down on the stoop out here. I'm unarmed and only want to talk with you to finalize our agreement."

"I'm sure if I come out one of those cops is going to shoot me."

"No, I promise that won't happen. James, I've followed through for you and you've done everything possible so we can make this all work. Come on out and let's talk."

Carole turned toward Frederickson, "Is that safe?"

"He knows what he's doing. He's been talking to the suspect for over an hour and is one of the best negotiators in the department."

Carole turned to her camera team, "Make sure you get a close up of the front door." She turned back to the action taking place. Carole held her mike and pointed to the front of the home giving the Channel 7 viewers live details of what was happening in the standoff. She knew that the other stations would have coverage of the events taking place, but only Channel 7 was right in the middle of the action in the command center on Iroquois.

Everyone stood with baited breath watching as King continued to sit on the cement stoop next to the front door. King was still holding the phone in his left hand that was tethered to a strap that looped around his neck. The portable unit looked a lot like the typical cell phone with ear jacks that most people used. The major difference was that it had a head strap and ear loop that kept it all in place. King had been sitting on the porch for close to ten minutes still talking on the line to James.

Captain Hughes looked over at Frederickson, "This ain't going to work. I'm going to tell our man on the roof top to get ready to take action."

"Sir, I wouldn't do that. Let King try his approach. You can always use your man up there if necessary."

Hughes didn't want to lose the chance to end this but knew that in cases like this the lead negotiator was in charge. He also didn't like the detective giving him advice. He put a call out to the man on the roof. "Keep alert up there, don't do anything unless I signal or call you to move."

All eyes were glued to the front door of the home where King sat alone on the large porch. The front door was large, over seven foot tall and dark mahogany with a beautiful leaded glass oval center. Like most of the homes in this historic district, many of the original aspects were restored to the grandeur of yesterday. King turned and waved to the group at the command center as the front door opened about a foot. King stood up with his back to the street and looked at the door. He was obstructing the view for those on the street and appeared to be talking to someone.

The voice stated, "Mr. King, I'm Mary. James is standing right behind me and we want to talk to you alone but not outside, would you consider coming inside?"

King looked back at the group and then turned toward the door. "Mary, are you okay?"

"Yes sir, I'm fine. James thinks once he's outside you'll have an officer take him out."

"I promise, Mary, the only thing I want to do is get both of you out of here safely. The last thing anyone wants is either of you to be hurt. James, can you hear me?"

"I can hear you."

"You're so close to ending this just the way you want. Meet me half way and come out on the porch."

James called out from behind Mary. "If you really want me to trust you, I need you to come inside."

King again turned to the group on the street. "Okay, James, but I need to stay in contact with my boss."

"Okay, but leave your gun out there."

"I don't carry a gun, James. I'm not a cop, just a guy that works with the department in cases like this." King motioned with his right hand to the group of officers on the street and moved into the front doorway. The large door opened and King stepped inside.

"What the hell is he doing," Hughes was yelling and turned toward his men. "I'm taking control of this now!" King disappeared inside and Hughes clenched his fist and screamed at everyone within hearing distance. "Shit, is he stupid, now we have two hostages."

Thirty-One

The confrontation in the woods with the group of hunters and Bud created new concerns for Dansforth and his wife. They couldn't hear the exchange between the men and weren't sure if the new group was part of Bud's men helping search for them. Tommy and Kathy kept down under cover hoping that no one spotted them. Tommy had pulled some branches over their legs when the men had approached each other and was certain that they were well hidden.

One of the hunters told Bud, "You need to turn that car around and head back to where you came from. This is a private hunting preserve."

Bud quickly answered, "I told you, we're just on a mission to get some supplies and must have made a wrong turn," He was now agitated and didn't like the tone of the hunter standing in front of him. He turned and the big man standing next to the car slipped his hand into the side of his jacket. *Christ, don't pull a pistol out now.* Bud spun back toward the big man. "Hey let's head back and see if they can give us better directions. Sorry guys." He motioned to the big man to get back into the car. They climbed in and backed up to a clearing where Bud maneuvered back and forth to head back down the gravel road.

"Why in the hell didn't we just blast the shit out of them country bumpkins?"

"Shit, there was six of them, all with guns. Anyway we have more important things to think of right now. Unless we find those two who got away, our asses won't be worth a dime." Bud didn't want to panic yet but knew this latest run in with the hunters would only slow their search down. "Do you think they'd try to head to the ferry crossing?"

"I don't know if they even had any idea where we had them hidden, let alone that they were in Canada. Unless you're dumb shit nephew told them."

"That's enough about Andy. You've had it out for him since the beginning. I told you I'll take care of him." Bud now pulled back onto the path leading toward the cabin and pulled in the gravel drive. He slammed the vehicle into park. "Stay here, I'll be back in a minute. Maybe Andy's back and found out something to help." Bud pushed his car door opened and quickly moved to the front of the cabin. He turned the handle and opened the door looking for Andy. "Andrew, where are you?" There wasn't an answer and the cabin was pretty small that the only other place he could have been was the outhouse out back. Bud moved to the backyard and saw that the outhouse door was left wide open. *Now where in the hell could he have gone off to*, "Andrew!" Bud was now yelling at the top of his lungs with no success of finding his nephew. *Crap, where did he go?*

Bud walked around the right side of the cabin toward the front. He moved back toward the car when he saw the big man coming toward him holding Andrew with his huge arm wrapped around Andy's neck and dragging him to the cabin. "The little shit was hiding in the bushes. I should have killed him before when we found him tied up." Andrew was kicking his legs and sobbing to no avail as he continued to squirm in the big man's arms.

"Put him down, I said I'll take care of him." Bud clenched his fist.

"Don't think so. You both screwed this whole thing up. The dumb kid brought a cell phone with him."

Bud was shocked, he yelled, "Andrew, I told you no phones. Why in the hell did you bring one?" While Bud questioned Andrew, he didn't realize that Sam now held the kid a couple feet off the ground. "I told you put him down."

"Okay," Sam answered with a sneer on his face and the big man gripped and twisted Andrew's neck snapping it with one vicious thrust. He dropped the young man's limp body at Bud's feet. Bud was startled and looked down at the broken body of his nephew when the bullet pierced through his brain shattering his skull. Bud's body fell backwards in a puddle of blood next to that of Andrew. "I'm not hanging around with you two assholes." The big man said aloud searched through Bud's pockets for any money and his cell phone. He decided to hide the bodies and planned on making his getaway. Once he searched Bud he did the same with the kid and smiled holding the cell phone in his pocket. *Bud said no phones. Dumb kid, don't work very well without this.* Sam held a cell phone battery in his right hand and laughed aloud.

The big man planned to move the bodies and clean out the cabin of anything that would tie him to this whole thing.

* * *

Meanwhile the group of hunters continued along the path chasing their goal of finding the black bear that was seen earlier in the morning. Tommy and Kathy peeked out from their hiding spot watching the men moving out. Tommy said, "I'm not sure what the men were doing or if they were involved with Bud. "Do you think they're looking for us too?" Kathy stuttered as she whispered her question.

Tommy answered, "I'm not sure, but if they are, the odds really turn in their favor. Together with Bud and that big man there's seven or eight of them now. Let's wait here a few more minutes."

"Did you hear anything they said?"

"I'm not sure but eventually we'll find someone to help us, I'm sure of that." Tommy had to keep hope alive, but deep down he also feared what they faced. Once the hunters disappeared from view Tommy slowly got to his feet and helped Kathy up. He brushed her off and gave her a big hug. "Honey, I'm sure we'll get through this." Both of them nodded and he smiled. "Come on Mrs. Dansforth, let me take you home." She looked into Tommy's face putting her hands on the side of his cheeks that were red and flushed from the wind. It was a touching moment for two people struggling to find freedom. "I love you, Tommy."

"Ditto." Holding hands they stepped over the limbs and pushed the brush away that Tommy used to help cover them and headed away from the group of hunters that had gone in the other direction. They decided on moving a little deeper into the wooded area to avoid any possible contact with anyone looking for them. "Are you okay?" Tommy asked once they had walked for a few minutes.

"Yes, considering we're running from a group of madmen, out in the woods with no idea where we are or where we're going and it's cold as hell, I'm just great." Her frustration was evident, and rightly so. Kathy turned and continued to trudge through the woods and Tommy knew that things weren't looking good. Not much he could say, his wife was right, things would get much worse for them if these men with guns were joining the search. *If only they could catch a break,* he thought.

Kathy Dansforth was walking about ten yards to the right of Tommy and saw a clearing off to the far side. "Tommy, there's a large field over this way. I can see what may be a farm house or something that resembles one." Was this their break?

Tommy hurried to where she was pointing. "You stay here and I'll see if I can get closer without being seen." He moved to the right side of the field and turned back to make sure Kathy was clearly hidden behind the group of large pine trees. Moving at a calculated pace, he panned across the open field making sure that no one was watching. Once he was within clear view of the front of the long white wooden structure he had to make a decision.

Walk to the front door and reveal his position, or keep a watch for any movement around the place. The winds coming across the open field were wicked and snow kicked up in his face. He turned and waved back to where he had positioned his wife. Tommy Dansforth took a chance. Moving up the dirt path toward the front of the home he walked up the three wooden steps on the wraparound porch. Taking a deep breath Tommy knocked on the big red wooden front door. Once he did that he stepped back to the side of the door not knowing if he should stay or run. There wasn't an answer so he moved toward the other side of the large porch and peeked into the double window. The lace curtains told him that the place obviously had a woman's touch. That was a positive sign. He tapped on the glass hoping that the sound would carry better than the knock on the wooden door. Still there wasn't an answer from inside. Tommy moved off the porch and waved to his wife to come on up. He trusted her opinion and needed to know if they should use this as a temporary hiding spot, even if only to get out of the weather.

Kathy Dansforth started moving from behind the trees and slowly walked toward the home while keeping an eye on Tommy who moved from one side of the porch to the other trying to get a better view of the interior. Once she was close to make her final approach she heard a car or truck coming close. She called out, "Tommy, someone is coming!" Kathy panicked and hollered again. "Tommy, Tommy someone's coming." It was too late. Pulling into the opening was a large extended cab SUV pulling a flat bed stacked with bales of hay. Kathy ducked back into the tree line hoping Tommy heard her and either would be able to find a hiding spot or was prepared to meet whoever was arriving.

***

Killing Bud and his nephew was a spur of the moment

reaction that the big man hadn't planned on, however, he was done with Bud covering for his dimwitted nephew and he wasn't going to chance the prospect of being caught. His anger rose when he found Andrew hiding in the woods and the reaction was swift. After he shot Bud, he gritted his teeth looking down at Bud's bloody body. Either he had to leave them lying there out in the open or drag them to the cabin. *Got to get them hidden*, he figured. Dragging Andrew by the feet he kept mocking the broken body of the young man. *You never should have been brought him in on this thing. Bud screwed up, and it's all his fault.* He pushed the boy's body against the back of the cabin and returned to get Bud. The big man wanted to be careful not to get any blood on his clothes. He didn't want to attract any additional attention as he tried to escape, so he pulled Bud's body by the feet too. Pushing Bud next to his nephew he then kicked snow over the two of them. Covering the bodies with a thin layer of snow and leaves; the big man rubbed his hands together and sneered at his handy work. He made sure nothing was left on either body for identification and headed into the cabin to ensure that nothing would lead authorities back to him. The only tie in he had to Bud was that they both had done prison time together, years back at Jackson. They weren't even cell mates so he was pretty sure no one would connect them. He was convinced that he covered all his bases.

The big man made his way out of the wooded cabin after cleaning up. He pulled the vehicle out of the gravel drive and into the clearing spinning the tires and sending gravel flying everywhere. He decided to head directly back to the ferry crossing. It was a short ride and he figured that it would probably be busy. His vehicle pulled up to the loading area and was third in line to drive onto the boat waiting to load cars and trucks headed to Marine City. The crossing at the Marine City station was normally manned by two U.S. Border Patrol guards however with the new alert they received from their chief, additional personnel had been scheduled at every border crossing. The guards were supplied with descriptions of the possible vehicle in question along with the photos of the bearded man that their surveillance captured the other evening. The big man had no idea that the authorities were already searching for a fugitive that he resembled. Because he looked like one of the abductors seen in the border photo; he most likely would be detained. He had a pistol in the glove box along with one tucked into his right side jacket pocket. The ride to the ferry crossing didn't take long and Sam pulled into the short line of cars waiting to cross. The flat bed ferry continued loading as it bobbed up and down on the dock. The ferry captain waved the big man to pull up on the right side of the boat where he would be at the back of the group of cars and trucks. The short distance was cleared in the morning by the coast guard ice breaker that traveled from Port Huron down to the two ferry crossings at Algonac and Marine City. It also cleared the ice at the ferry crossing for Harsens Island; where there was no other option to cross except by ferry.

The crossing was a lot quicker in the summer, but winter was always questionable. The ice breaker had cleared the crossing earlier that the ferry traveled through but it still had to slow down when an ice flow blocked their way. The big man watched out the passenger side window as birds hitched a ride on chunks of ice headed south along the lake. He let out a chuckle at the thought of the Chevy he dumped in the lake north at Sarnia that might be floating right on by. Hopefully the two jackasses he put in the trunk wouldn't float by too; at least not now. He was confident that everything had been taken care of. Bud and his nephew would eventually be found and would be blamed for everything. The big man had no tie to them and was just hired by Bud to help with this assignment. Big Sam wished he knew who Bud's boss was. Maybe he'll try to find him and still collect that money they were owed. Having Bud's cell phone would let him put a squeeze on the sucker for more money. The ferry suddenly hit the dock ahead with pretty good force jarring the passengers. The big man jerked behind the wheel and was surprised that the boat hit with so much force.

The voice over a loud speaker barked out, "Sorry everyone, I didn't see that last chunk of ice, everyone needs to hold on. We might have trouble hooking up." The ferry swung side to side with ice flows slamming the small flat bottom boat as men on shore groped with the ropes pulling the boat toward the huge docking poles. It had taken the men on the ferry and shore more than fifteen minutes to finally secure the boat to the moorings at the dock. Everyone aboard cheered once they were hooked up and the ferry captain started the process of unloading vehicles. The first two vehicles on the front slowly pulled onto the ramp with the pick-up on the right going first and a minivan following. The big man watched as the border guards checked passports and identifications of the drivers and passengers. *The process seemed to be taking much longer than usual*, he thought. Once the first two vehicles cleared inspection the second row of vehicles headed to the check point. The big man re-started his vehicle and turned the car heater on full blast. The harsh winds ripped across the hood as he watched the next group again go through what was a very thorough inspection. *Really taking too long, why, what's up?* He turned looking back to make sure someone wasn't standing behind his vehicle. *What's going on here?* He didn't like what he saw. There seemed to be extra border guards working the crossing and once you were in line there wasn't any turning back. He had to go through the check point. Sam wanted to make an excuse to get through as soon as possible, but what could he say?

Thirty-Two

The station manager at Channel 7 was thrilled with the coverage that Carole was supplying during the live news feed at the hostage situation. Although the action was covered by all the local stations, only he had a reporter in the command area. Carole was in the process of updating viewers after the negotiator had gone into the home to meet face to face with the hostage and her abductor. Captain Hughes could be heard questioning the move and it was clearly being transmitted to the viewers. Hughes' remarks wouldn't be appreciated by his commander. Detective Frederickson tried to get Hughes' attention that there was a live mike right next to him but it was too late. Once he was inside the home King reached out to shake hands with James. James looked at the offer with an uncertain question on his face. "Is this some kind of trick?" he said.

"James, we've been talking for well over an hour and a half and I just want to thank you for letting Mary's mother and aunt go. Also for having the strength to meet with me personally." King kept his hand extended and Mary watched with anticipation. She also wondered what King might be up to. Finally James extended his left hand toward King while holding his gun still pointed at the negotiator. "Kind of awkward shaking like this, but James, we've come a long way and now we need to all walk outside together."

"I still don't trust the cops. You're up to something, but I just don't know what it is."

"First, I'm glad to see that Mary seems to be doing okay.

Second, no one has been hurt here and I want to keep it that way. Lastly, James, I've never lied to anyone and don't plan to start now. We can walk out and I'll be standing in front of you and let Mary walk behind us." King felt he was making solid progress because James let him in and now was still discussing how they can settle the standoff. "James, I have a car out there that can take us to a safe place where we can make sure you and Mary have the opportunity to talk. How does that sound?"

"Sounds too good to be true."

King turned and reached for the door knob.

"What are you doing?"

"We need to show the people out there that we're all okay. If they don't see me soon they might think that something is wrong." King continued to open the leaded glass door and stepped into the doorway with James and Mary standing behind him. He called out to the officers who had moved along the shrubs near the side of the porch. "We're going to be coming out in a few minutes. Everything is okay." King turned back to James. "Do you want to have me or Mary walk out first?" King knew by limiting James options of who should walk out first was the best way to move the negotiation along.

"I want to make sure Mary is okay, so maybe let her walk out first."

Success, King thought. "Okay, with a swift move King put his hand in the middle of Mary's back and moved her in front of them into the opening. "Okay Mary, you slowly walk out and James and I will follow you." The young teacher trembled as she walked out onto the porch and she could see her mom standing in the street with a group of police officers. King cautioned her, "just move slow I don't want you to fall or anyone to get hurt." Mary was standing on the top step and starting to walk down the cement steps as King moved into the clearing with James pushed up against him. King called out, "Everyone is okay here and we are going to head to my car. I don't want anyone to move from your position." Mary had reached the bottom step and was moving onto the walkway as James and King started down the same path. King motioned to the men who were behind the cement walls of the porch with his right hand. The signal had been planned if he could get James out of the home. Mary reached the street where her mother ran from Captain Hughes' side to hug her daughter. The two women held each other tightly and Carole and the Channel 7 News team caught every moment for their viewers. King had succeeded in getting James to free all three hostages without shots fired. King reached the final step with James still tightly behind him. "Watch your step," King said as he and James reached the bottom. When James took his eyes off of King, and looked down at the steps, the officers jumped out and wrestled him to the ground. "Don't hurt him," King said as he kicked the gun away that James dropped to the pavement.

To everyone's surprise, Mary left her mom's side and headed back to where her ex husband was sprawled face down on the pavement being handcuffed by the officers. She knelt down with King holding her back a little. "James, I'm sorry that this all happened, but I can't trust you and we just don't belong together." She stood up and hugged King sobbing.

"You lied, you son of a bitch, you lied to me." James was yelling as the officers started to pull him to his feet.

"James, I said I'll make sure no one gets hurt. Everyone is safe here. I'll go with you and make sure that you get the best opportunity to get help." He turned toward Mary who still hung onto his waist. "It's okay; I'm going to make sure I help James as much as possible."

The detective allowed Carole to move a little closer to the action in the street as she focused her attention on the scene taking place. No words were necessary. Viewers were in on every moment and the cameras kept sending the action back to the station with the only live feed of the events. The detective was watching when he heard his cell phone ring. He stepped back from the group and answered, "Hello." It was Jack Fox. "Detective, we just got approval from the RCMP in Canada to let us take a joint task force and cross at all four Michigan border crossings and start our search."

That was great news. He knew that it was a major accomplishment to get the two countries to agree so quickly to a combined search for the possible abducted witnesses. "That's great, what can I do?"

"Really not much right now, I'm supposed to be updated by the FBI once they start. I'm sure they'll concentrate on the crossings at Algonac and Marine City. That makes the most sense however, Port Huron, could also be a spot to check. The photo we saw earlier from the Border Patrol showed the two men in question making their way from the Marine City crossing."

"Wish I could be involved a little more but I understand. Jack, we got our hostage situation taken care of and the negotiator was able to get the man to release all of the people that he was holding."

"Great. Did you get a chance to talk to the sixth grade teacher about the events at the school?"

"Not yet, she's being taken to our precinct and I hope to ask her about it then."

"Guess she could still be a witness on what she may have seen at the school."

"Yeah, they're taking her and her mother to the station. I plan to go over everything with them. If something new develops I'll call you." Frederickson hung up and headed back to the Twelfth Precinct to meet with Mary Blankenship. He hoped that she saw something in the school lot that might help their investigation. Maybe she saw Dansforth with someone and could identify them. It had already been a long day and it was past two o'clock. Frederickson walked to his car thankful that the hostage situation had been solved. He saw King going over some details with two men and wanted to say something to him. "Excuse me, King, just wanted to say great job."

"Thanks, detective. Your precinct and you deserve a lot of credit for getting everything set up for me. Solid team work, detective."

"Thanks." Frederickson reached out and shook King's hand. The two men had a lot of respect for each other and it was great to see them enjoy a successful day. As the detective headed to his car he hoped that they would soon get some positive news from the Canadian search. He saw Carole waving to him.

She called out, "Detective, I promise I will owe you for getting me access to everything. My station manager also wanted to thank you for allowing us the scoop in the hostage situation."

"It's just what we agreed to."

"Well, maybe I can pay you back. My source at police headquarters just called me and with some interesting information and when he supplies me with this kind of detail, it's usually pretty accurate."

The detective was curious especially since Jack Fox said there was a suspected leak at headquarters. Frederickson calmly asked, "So what did your source tell you?"

"There's good reason to believe that the lieutenant governor or someone on his staff may be involved in something big. My source said the District Attorney's office is running an investigation into the guy's family and staff members. I guess the capitol is buzzing about what it all means."

The detective wondered who the source was. He wanted to probe her for more details. "This sounds a little wild, are you sure your source knows what they're talking about?"

Carole said, "He's never been wrong."

Frederickson thought about what Jack Fox said, someone was feeding the lieutenant governor information and now maybe they're working the news teams too. "Thanks Carole. If you find out more, I'd appreciate the heads up. So who's your source?"

"I can't reveal that, but promise to keep you in the loop."

Frederickson thanked the reporter and climbed into his car.

Frederickson needed to tell Jack that the investigations in the state capitol are out, and a reporter at Channel 7 knew about it. Fox better move soon or his case will crumble. He dialed the D.A. to give him a heads up. The phone rang three times before someone picked up. "Office of Jack Fox, District Attorney for Wayne County."

"I need to talk to Fox, this is Detective Frederickson, Detroit Police."

"Sorry, detective, but he just left a few minutes ago."

"Do you know where he went?"

"No, he didn't say. Do you want to leave a message?"

"Thanks, I'll try him later." Frederickson hung up and decided to head back to the precinct. *Got to get back to see what's happening with Mary Blankenship and her mom.* The captain was driving Mary Blankenship and her mom to the precinct and Frederickson wanted to find out if she saw anything the last night Dansforth was at the school meeting with parents. Maybe she can provide some clues for the case.

Thirty-Three

The big man thought the inspection of vehicles coming off the ferry at Marine City was taking way too long. *Usually they check papers and maybe a trunk search but what's going on.* He thought about the two bodies behind the small cabin and knew they wouldn't be found for a long time. It was now his turn to pull into the covered area manned by the border guards. The Marine City border crossing, like the one at Algonac was manned by a couple of guards that had the vehicles pull up to their inspection site. There wasn't anything to stop vehicles from driving right past the men that were doing the checking. No gate, no pylons, nothing, just uniformed guards on each side waiting for people to stop and hand over their documents. Sam proceeded at a slow pace and moved under the canopy, stopping next to where the guard motioned him to stop. He rolled down his window about half way.

"Name and Citizenship?" asked the border guard.

Calmly he answered, "Sam Jones, United States citizen."

"I'll need your identification and vehicle registration. Sir, could you please roll your window down all the way and turn the vehicle off please."

"Officer, I've got an important meeting and need to get going, can you help me here?"

"Okay, but first I need to see your identification and vehicle registration."

The big man knew that this was the normal practice but under the circumstances he squirmed in his seat. He turned and looked to the right and saw another border guard moving toward his vehicle.

He started to lower his window as requested and asked, "What's going on?" The first guard stepped closer and again asked, "Sir, please turn off the car and hand me your keys." The border guard stood firmly along the driver's side of the car holding his hand out waiting for the driver to hand over his keys and identification. Because the driver was hesitant; the second border guard who was now on the passenger side of the car moved forward to the front of the vehicle. It appeared to the big man, that the guard had his hand on his sidearm.

Sam again asked, "Like I said, I'm in a hurry, got a meeting to get to. How long this gonna take?" When the big man looked further to his right he saw two more border guards who were looking at a folder then back at him. *What were they looking at?*

"Sir," the lead border guard said more emphatically still standing along the left side of the vehicle. "You simply need to follow directions. I'll get you going as fast as possible. Now turn the engine off and hand me your keys." The guard reached toward the opened window.

"Okay, okay but you promise to get me going soon." The big man looked down at the ignition with the key chain dangling and moved his right hand toward the keys. The guard watched when suddenly the big man jammed the gas pedal to the floor, squealing through the border crossing, spinning tires and swerving to the right onto River Road. Two people crossing in front of Anita's restaurant jumped out of the way as the car accelerated to over seventy miles an hour within a few short blocks.

Pulling his firearm out the border guard ran into the street but there were people along both sides of the street and he couldn't take a chance on firing. "Call it in," he hollered back to his partner. The second guard was left standing alone on the passenger's side of the crossing.

His partner yelled back, "I got the plate number, OLF UO3, Michigan plate." The first guard headed back to where their SUV was positioned and jumped in. He pulled out onto River Road hoping to follow the path that the get-a-way vehicle took. The vehicle he was chasing was quickly out of sight and could have turned anywhere along River Road. The guard knew many of the streets were dead ends because the Belle River blocked passage north or west. River Road had many small businesses, mostly restaurants and gift shops along the street with a little bookstore on the corner of River Road and Broadway. Calls were sent out from the border crossing to the State Police Post at Marine City as well as the local police.

When the second guard ran into the office another border guard came running up, "What in the hell happened?"

"An older model dark blue Chevrolet pulled through the crossing without giving us his identification. We've got the plate number and Tim set chase. I need to call it in to the chief."

"Do you think it has anything to do with the BOLO we got earlier? We better compare the description to the bulletin." He looked at the photo of the car and driver in the email they received. It wasn't the same vehicle; however the driver could have been the same guy. He turned showing it to his partner in the booth, "What do you guys think?"

"Could be him."

"This might be the guy everyone is looking for."

People that were in line behind the vehicle that ran the crossing were now standing outside their vehicles. "What's going on?" was the common refrain.

The border guards secured the crossing. "We've got a situation here folks. Sorry but no one can pass for a few minutes." There were only two cars left in line and although one lady was heard grumbling, the man in the other vehicle said, "Better be safe than sorry." She grudgingly nodded.

The border guards at these small crossings knew that there was always a possibility of cars trying to pull through the check point but most times the people were caught pretty quickly because there were few escape routes in either Marine City or Algonac.

Water Street led to River Road and Highway 29 that ran north and south along Lake St. Clair. Unless you had a hideout off one of the small intersecting streets, the best escape routes were north toward Port Huron or down to Macomb County. Calls went out with an APB on the Chevrolet to every police department in the escape area. The chase for the speeding Chevrolet was taken up by three local cop cars along with another Border Patrol agent from Algonac. They were coordinating their efforts to cut off every possible escape route. When the call came into the Border Patrol Chief he contacted Jack Fox's office to let him know that they may have one of his suspects in a chase along Marine City.

***

Jack Fox was in route to meeting with the FBI when he got the call from the Border Patrol Chief and decided to cancel the meeting. The city's interim mayor, along with FBI, wanted to go over the details of the search that was approved by the RCMP in Canada. Fox knew the appointed interim mayor wanted to be involved but he was sure it was for political reasons. *He probably hoped to use the events to help his re-election campaign. Everyone has their own agenda*, Fox just wanted to get his witness back. When Fox contacted his office earlier, they told him that Detective Frederickson had called, at least three times. "What did he want?"

"He didn't say, sir."

"Okay, I'll try to call him."

Frederickson in the meantime returned to the Twelfth Precinct and along with his captain was interviewing Mary Blankenship and her mother. The two women told him that James had grabbed Mary when she was leaving her auntie's house for the evening class at Wayne State. "We decided to stay with my aunt because James had been watching our house. I was just getting in my car on Iroquois when he grabbed me and forced me back into the house."

The detective planned to ask Mary why she hadn't said anything about being at the school late or seeing Tommy Dansforth there. Just as Mary was explaining another officer interrupted, "Detective, you got an important call."

"Who is it?"

"Jack Fox is on line one and said it's very important."

"Excuse me," he got up and moved into the main office area, picking up line one, he said, "Frederickson here."

"Detective, we have a major development in Marine City. They had a guy crossing the border that resembles one of the men that we had in the photo crossing late the other night, he pulled right through the border crossing."

"He did what?"

"The Border Patrol said he appeared a bit suspicious, and when they requested his identification and keys, he took off through their station. There's an APB out for him and I'm hoping we get some results soon."

The detective appreciated the heads up. "What do you need me to do?"

"Nothing now, just promised to keep you in the loop."

"Jack, we're interviewing Mary Blankenship, the other missing teacher from the school along with her mother. The information she has supplied us with checks out. It looks like it's just a simple case of marital issues."

"Detective, maybe we'll get lucky with this event in Marine City."

"Jack, one more thing. My contact with Channel 7 knows about the lieutenant governor being involved in your investigation. She said her contact at police headquarters told her about it."

"Thanks, I knew there was a leak somewhere."

Thirty-Four

Tommy Dansforth had nowhere to hide. He didn't see the truck pulling up the long driveway until it was too late. *Where was his wife, did she make it back into the trees?* He realized the people arriving would easily see him standing on the front porch. Could they be the help that he needed? He watched as a tall man climbed out from behind the driver's seat. The guy lifted a shotgun from the gun rack on the back of the cab and pointed it at the stranger on his porch. "Stand still, I want to know what you're doing on my porch." The man moved cautiously toward Tommy, pointing the shotgun with a menacing look on his face. Tommy started to come off the porch. "I said don't move." There wasn't any place to run to. Tommy Dansforth put his hands up over his head and stood silently while the guy moved to within ten feet of him.

"Don't shoot, I need help." There wasn't anything he could do but hope that the man would believe his situation and come to their rescue. Tommy didn't want to reveal that Kathy was hiding in the wooded lot, at least not yet.

"Come on down from the porch, but do it slowly, keep your hands up in the air." Tommy moved forward keeping an eye toward the wooded area hoping Kathy stayed in there. The porch had three wooden steps and he made his way down to the base of the porch when the man stopped him. "That's far enough. What are you doing on my property?" The gun looked even bigger as Tommy now stood about five feet from the front of the barrel. The man was dressed similar to the men that Tommy and his wife had seen Bud and the big man talking to in the woods earlier. *Could he be with that group looking for the escaped couple?* The guy said, "Let's start with your name."

Taking a deep breath he said, "Dansforth, Tommy Dansforth." He lifted his chin and looked straight at the man as he continued. "I'm a teacher from Detroit." He knew that either he'd tell the truth and get the man to help them or tell the truth and be re-captured or worse. "Two men grabbed me from the school and brought me here."

"What do you mean here? This is my place. I've only been gone a day to get feed for my horses."

That news gave Tommy some hope. "I don't mean right here, what I mean is, they grabbed me from the school parking lot and brought me to wherever this is. I was tied up for a day or two, I'm not sure how long. I escaped a little while ago and they're out there searching for me. I've been trying to find a place to hide."

The man holding the gun lowered it a little and looked closer at his suspect. He could see that the man standing at the bottom of his porch wasn't young and appeared to have a cut over his right eye, one arm was in a sling and his clothes were muddy and torn. "Okay, lower your arm a little but keep it out to your side. Now tell me more about these men that grabbed you."

Tommy felt a rush of relief and brought his arm down to his side. "I'm not totally sure where I'm even at; just that once I got free, I made my way through the woods trying to get as far away as possible. I saw the men that held me along with another group with guns not too far from here."

"What kind of group with rifles?"

"They all were moving through the woods with their guns cradled in their arms, definitely searching through the woods. I feared that I now had more than the two original guys looking for me."

"Did the men you saw have hunting rifles like mine?"

Dansforth looked closer at the gun that the man was holding. "Yes, there were five or six of them. Could you please put down that gun?" Tommy was nervous enough and the rifle pointed at him wasn't helping.

The man lowered the rifle to his side but held it firmly. "The group you saw may have been guys in my hunting group. I know they went out earlier tracking a black bear that killed one of my horses and we heard it was spotted along the ridge."

This revelation caused Tommy to become both concerned and confused. Could the group he saw talking to Bud be the same hunters, or is there another group out looking for him and Kathy. "I'm not sure who or what the men with rifles were doing just that they were talking to the men that captured me."

The owner of the ranch was shaking his head as Tommy spun the story about men in the woods and Tommy still wasn't sure if he was friend or foe, just that the guy had his gun still pointed in Tommy's direction. He couldn't let Kathy come out of the woods, at least not yet.

***

The chase along River Road led to Highway 29 and the Chevrolet had been spotted heading west on Highway 29. The state police along with local law enforcement had joined in with the Border Patrol. The suspect was reported speeding up River Road, through the junction of Highway 29 and downtown Marine City. People were calling in with information that they had been either hit or run off the road by a dark blue older model Chevrolet. That helped the police determine the location and narrow where to set up road blocks. The interstate was six miles to the west and every highway leading in or out of the area had been cordoned off. Two troopers from the State Police post at Marine City had set up a perimeter along Marine City Highway just west of town. They had a blockade and guns drawn in case the escapee headed their way. Another set of troopers had done the same thing on King Highway that led to St. Clair. The big man didn't have any exits that weren't covered.

The Chevrolet's left front fender was dragging from the collision that happened when the big man hit a van coming toward him. It was sending sparks across the pavement that looked like a Fourth of July celebration getting started. There weren't any cars on the road now in front of him and Sam figured he needed to pull that fender off. Once he was out of the car he looked in both directions and the only thing visible were fields of pine trees and snow covered corn fields. "Shit, Shit. I gotta get out of here." He jumped back into the car and spun the wheels turning around headed back toward a gas station he had passed. *Maybe I can change vehicles*, he hoped. The station was just back a bit and he maneuvered the Chevrolet off the road into a culvert behind a group of large trees. The car wasn't any good to him now. Walking about one hundred yards along the side of the road he saw that there were three cars in the gas station lot. He pulled his cap down and pulled the jacket collar up over his chin. He entered the station taking notice of the people inside. "Cold as hell out there," Big Sam said entering the station with his head down.

The clerk, a young lady looked up and answered, "You broke down?"

"Yeah, my car had a flat and I had to walk a couple of miles."

"We ain't got no tow truck here. You need to use the phone?"

"That would be great." The big man moved to the far side where she had pointed to an old fashion wall phone that looked like something from the turn of the century. He chuckled to himself as he fumbled in his pocket for some change. While he appeared to be looking for change, he was checking out the place, hoping to grab another vehicle from someone inside. Sam slid his right hand into his jacket touching the handle of the pistol while pretending to make a call. One of the customers that was just leaving the station called out to him.

"Hey buddy, do you need me to drive you back to your car? If you got a spare, I can help you fix that tire." This might be the break he needed. Why try to overtake three people in the station when he could have one guy all alone. "That would be great, thanks." Big Sam turned keeping his head down and moved to the front door. The man who offered the ride was a slightly built guy maybe in his early thirties, he turned and asked, "Which way did you say your car was?"

The big guy pointed in the opposite direction because he didn't want his vehicle to been seen in the tree line. Both men climbed into the guy's Ford F-150 pick-up and the driver backed out of the station and headed in the direction the big man had pointed. "It's too cold to be out walking today."

"You got that right."

"Where are you from?"

The big man hesitated not knowing the area very well. "Just up the road." He was waiting for the opportunity to overtake the driver and steal the pickup.

The driver slowed down and looked back at his passenger, "Up the road where?"

Sam pulled his gun and pointed it at the driver. "You're too nosey pal, pull over." Sam pointed to a clearing ahead.

"Look, I didn't mean anything. How about you just get out and we'll forget the whole thing."

"I said, pull over now or I'll blow your head off." The gun was pointed directly at the driver's right ear. "Right here, pull over now!"

The driver eased off the pavement trying not to drive too far off the road. "Look buddy, you can have the truck. I got a wife and little kid at home. Please don't shoot me." Once they came to a full stop the passenger waving the gun motioned the driver to get out. The driver slowly stepped out of the truck glancing back at the man sliding over behind the steering wheel.

Sam hollered, "Lay down on the ground." The driver moved to his knees and again pleaded for mercy. "I said lay down!"

The driver could hear the man's feet hit the ground behind him. He begged one more time, "Please, Please..."

The big man clubbed the driver on the back of his head knocking him out. "Dumb shit!" He climbed back into the pickup and turned the vehicle around heading back out of town on Highway 29. Driving at the normal speed so as not to draw attention, the big man drove past the gas station on the right and continued down the road.

When he passed the station the attendant saw the pickup going by and was surprised. "Hey, that's Henry's truck, but Henry ain't in it."

The other customer in the station moved toward the large window and tried to see what she was talking about. "You sure Henry's not in there."

"No, looks like that guy that Henry gave a ride to." She grabbed the phone on the counter and dialed 911. It took only a few seconds for an answer.

"This is 911. What's your emergency."

"I'm calling from the Shell station on Marine City Highway and King Road. I think someone has stolen my friend's pickup and just drove on by."

"Okay, you say you think someone has stolen your friend's pickup. What makes you think that?"

"My friend gave this stranger a ride a few minutes ago. He lives in the other direction that I just saw his truck headed to. He wasn't in the truck."

"Can you give me a description of the truck and person you think stole it. Do you know the plate number?"

"It's a Ford F-150 bright red extended cab pickup, only a year old. I'll get you the plate number." She put the phone down and ran her fingers through some receipts on the counter. "Here it is, AAC 121, Michigan plate."

"That should be easy to spot. Can you describe the person who is driving the truck now?"

"He came into the station a little while ago, big guy, maybe six-foot-four, and over two-hundred pounds."

"What was he wearing?"

"Oh, I'm not sure, an overcoat, kind of long. Wait a minute. Bill, do you remember what that guy Henry gave a ride to was wearing?"

"It was one of those hunter's long overcoats, maybe medium brown."

She repeated the description to the 911 operator. "Please you've got to help; I know something bad has happened."

"Okay, I've alerted the authorities in Marine City and they will forward it to the surrounding areas. Let me get your full name and phone number."

The gas station operator was now starting to tremble but gave the operator her information. "Will you call us?"

"Yes, as soon as the police head your way I'll confirm that they are helping."

"Thanks." Once she hung up she turned to Bill. "Bill, we've got to do something. I can't wait here."

He said, "Okay, what do you want me to do?"

"Take your truck and head up the road toward Henry's place. I hope that guy just pushed him out of the truck and stole it."

Bill hurried out of the station and jumped into his truck, spinning tires and speeding out of the front of the gas station. He had to find Henry, hopefully safe and sound.

_____Thirty-Five

Rich Ellis, the Lieutenant Governor's Chief of Staff, made his way to the state senate majority leader's office. The two men were good friends and Rich felt something wasn't right with his boss. After he sat down with his friend he carefully asked, "Do you know anything that could be a problem for my boss?"

"Sean, no, he's rock solid, heard he's planning a run for governor's office next term. If so, there's no one in the party that would oppose him."

Rich knew the lieutenant governor's future plans and he and his boss had strategized to put themselves in position to win the governor's seat in the next election. Rumors had swirled that the sitting governor had plans to run for a U.S. Senate seat. "You're probably right, guess I'm just a little concerned because he seems pretty edgy lately."

His friend then asked, "The only question I had was we heard someone in the big city was running an investigation that could lead to Sean's staff. Also he's hired a few more people recently; maybe just beefing up his staff for the next election."

Rich didn't know anything about either issue that his friend raised. _Wonder where that came from_, he thought. The two men sipped their cup of coffee when Rich decided that his friend might just have rumors. He'd check them out.

Just as Rich started to get up, his friend asked again, "You sure that you haven't heard the rumors about someone in Lansing maybe involved in a crime down in the big city."

Rich sat back down, "No, what kind of trouble?"

"Not sure, but I heard that the DA down there, Jack Fox, has been seen in the capitol with the State's Attorney General, huddled in private meetings last week."

Rich immediately thought about Sean's younger son. How many times had he or his father needed to get the kid out of trouble? The kid had been sent to Colorado to a rehabilitation place for help. As far as Rich knew the kid was still there. *Please don't let him mess up our election plans.* "No I hadn't heard that." Rich got up to leave the office now wanting to make sure the lieutenant governor's son was still in Colorado.

As he got up his friend inquired, "How's the family?"

Rich cleared his throat, "Mine, fine, the kids are doing okay in school and everything is good at home."

"Let's get together with the wives once this latest bill gets through. We could use some time to blow off steam." The two men stood and Rich thanked his friend for listening to him. "Guess I'm just on edge with the prospect of running for the state's biggest office." Rich walked out of the building now with more questions than answers.

***

Information was flying across the wire to every police officer in Marine City; possible abduction and stolen vehicle, red Ford F-150 extended cab, new model, one driver maybe armed. Two officers manning a road block along Marine City Highway at the Belle River crossing were just getting the information when one of the officers pointed ahead. He called out to his partner, "Red F-150 headed this way and picking up speed." The two officers didn't have enough time to call it in; they took evasive actions behind the road block and drew their weapons. The F-150 had to be traveling over eighty miles an hour and heading right at them. "They were crouched down behind a barrier and could see the driver bearing down on them. One of the officers was crouched down on one knee pointing his weapon at the front tires of the speeding truck barreling down at them. The truck showed no sign of stopping or slowing down. Both officers started shooting at the front of the truck trying to take out the tires as the vehicle crashed through the barrier sending wood flying and the officers falling backwards. The Ford was now speeding past them as one of the officers rolled to his side and sent a last volley of bullets at the back of the truck's cab. "I'm sure I hit it. Did you see the driver?" Looking over at his partner he realized that the officer was lying motionless under broken and shattered wood. "No, no, Lyndon, you okay?" he crawled over to his partner hoping that he was still alive. His partner hadn't moved for minutes and the officer continued to hover over him. With his left arm under his partner's head he called for help.

The speeding F-150 continued flying down Marine City Highway with shards of wood sticking out of the front grill and steam coming out of the radiator. Bullet holes riddled the rear window that was blown out in the shoot out. The big man needed to get off the road but he wasn't familiar with the area. He had to get a new ride. There were a few homes set back off the road when he saw a driveway ahead with cars and pickup trucks lined in the circular drive. The F-150 slowed as the steam poured out of the front grill and the big guy guided it to the gravel path ahead. He hopped out of the vehicle and looked around, no one was insight. Moving toward the line of vehicles, Sam started checking for keys left in an ignition. The two pickup trucks at the rear of the line didn't have keys in them. As the big man moved down the line of cars he found a older model Chevrolet Malibu with keys hanging in clear sight. Jumping in, he started the car and maneuvered it quietly out of the driveway. Pulling back onto Marine City Highway, Sam continued driving west. He felt more confident that he would get away in this new ride.

Officers had come to the aid of the men that called for assistance along the road block with an EMS team working on the fallen officer. The injured man was being transported to St. John's Hospital on Highway 29, and initial reports were good. The information was being sent to alert everyone that the F-150 had the rear window shot out and possible damage to the cooling system, it would be easy to spot with a trail of steam coming from the grill.

The auction along Marine City Highway had just concluded when people noticed a vehicle that must have broke down along the roadside in front of the farm house. One couple was shocked to see their Malibu was missing. "Hey, our car is gone," the lady yelled. Others came over and suggested calling the police. The call was answered by a 911 operator who took details from the couple. Once the operator learned that a red F-150 was left on the side of the farm house with steam rising from the grill, she patched that information through to the teams involved in the chase for the person who ran the border crossing.

Trying to find a way out of Marine City, the big man turned off Marine City Highway and abruptly turned right onto Indian trail. That was a mistake; Indian Trail was a winding road that made a wide turn at the Belle River. Picking up speed again and looking for a way out of the area he didn't see the officers ahead, manning their position at the crossing over the Belle River. There wasn't a road block; just two officers stationed at each side of a short railed bridge. It was too late, he couldn't turn around and wasn't sure if the stolen Malibu had been reported. The big man planned to drive through this too if necessary. He continued at normal speed until he was one-hundred yards away and slammed down on the gas pedal charging toward the officers. They waved and fired shots in the air over the top of the on-coming Malibu but the car kept speeding toward them. A second volley of shots rang out shattering the windshield and riddling the big man sending him slumped over the wheel and the car flying over the short rail and head first into the bend of the river. The Malibu was standing straight up in the bend of the Belle River that was only three feet deep at this point as the two officers kept their weapons pointed at the car as they slowly approached from each side. There wasn't any movement from inside the car and they could see the driver slumped over the dash. One of the men climbed down the river bank making sure their suspect was dead or at least out cold. "We got him," he called out to his partner.

Once they confirmed the report that this was the stolen Malibu and knew the F-150 was found at the farm house, they were sure they had their suspect. Calls went out to all the officers pursuing the chase that the suspect fitting the description had been apprehended. The State Police were headed to the scene along with the sheriff from Marine City. The Border Patrol guard that was involved in the chase was on hand to identify the body pulled out of the car on Indian Trail. He confirmed that was the man that ran through their crossing. The officers on the scene waited as the body was pulled back to the surface and searched. They recovered a 9mm pistol that was tucked in the belt of the body and two cell phones were found in his overcoat. There was another pistol on the floor. "Bag these," the officer said. "Never know what they might find on them." The FBI was headed to the scene and Jack Fox was hoping that the capture would lead to finding his witnesses.

Back along Marine City Highway, Bill had been driving while searching for Henry whose truck was taken by the stranger. He slowed down when he saw a man kneeling on the side of the road. Pulling over Bill jumped from his vehicle and was happy to see Henry on his knees holding the back of his head. "Man, I'm so glad you're alive. We panicked when we saw your truck going by the station." He helped the slumping man to his feet and into his truck. "I'm taking you to the hospital." Henry was disorientated but thankful that he was alive.

***

Kathy Dansforth couldn't wait any longer as she watched her husband talking to the man on the porch who still held a rifle on Tommy. She moved out from behind the tree line and called out, "Hello, hello," while she calmly moved into the open. She was waving to her husband and the man who turned to see another stranger, a woman, now walking out of the pines toward him. The man stepped back a few feet and pointed at Tommy, "Stay put."

Tommy immediately stated, "That's my wife; we were both taken by the men I told you about. Please you've got to believe me."

"Listen pal, this is way too far out not to be true. Just stay there while I talk to her."

Kathy was now within twenty feet of the man and he motioned her to stop. "What's your name lady?"

She answered and pointed back toward Tommy on the porch. "Kathy Dansforth, that's my husband Tommy. We were both taken by some men who have been holding us captive in a cabin down the road. We got loose and have been running through the woods looking for help."

He could see that she resembled the guy on the porch; dirty and scratched up. "Okay, you need to move up on the porch next to your husband. We need to go inside and sort this all out."

Tommy and Kathy Dansforth looked lovingly at each other and she had tears in her eyes. Maybe for the first time in days they felt a rush of relief. Could their ordeal be close to being over?

Thirty-Six

The call came into the Ontario Provincial Police office in Sarnia. The caller indicated that he had two people, a man and woman that claimed that they had been abducted and held in a cabin along the hunting trail near his farm in Sombra. The description matched that of Tommy Dansforth and his wife that the Canadian authorities had from the FBI. The constable confirmed to the caller that the people were reported missing, "Hold them for us, we're sending officers." The caller gave them directions to his farm and said he believed the people.

Once the man called the details in to the authorities he helped Tommy and his wife clean up and put a new sling on Tommy's arm. The couple was cold, hungry and scratched up but considering the brutal weather and escaping through the woods they appeared in pretty good shape. Neither Tommy nor his wife had any identification on them, but their story and condition told the man that they endured many hardships. "There are at least two men still out there looking for us," Kathy said as they warmed their feet and hands in front of the fireplace. "We left a kid at the cabin, he's tied up."

"I told the constable everything that you said. They are on their way here and sending a team to look for the men that held you." He wanted to ask so many questions but didn't know where to start. "So where are you both from?"

Tommy looked back at his wife before answering, "Detroit, or at least that's where I teach school. My wife and I live in Macomb County, just off of M-59. I was attacked in the school parking lot."

Kathy looked over at her husband, "I just came back from shopping and making dinner for Tommy when a man came to the door claiming that he lost his dog. I messed up and let him in. That's when he made me get in my car and drive to a spot where another guy, a big man, with a beard, tossed me into the trunk. I don't remember much after that." The couple couldn't believe that they were finally safe.

The Canadian officials relayed the details to the FBI team in Marine City who were quick to relay it to the Border Patrol. Once the FBI Bureau chief had the details, along with the information that the suspect that ran the crossing was captured, he contacted the District Attorney in Detroit. "Mr. Fox, I've got good news for you. Your couple has been found and are safe in Canada."

Jack Fox was thrilled. "Who has them right now?"

"A farmer in the village of Sombra, across from Marine City, called it in. He said he had a couple claiming they had been abducted and escaped from the men that held them. They were on his front porch. He has them inside and both appeared to be doing okay, hurt, but safe. I'm sending a team to pick them up as we speak."

"Thanks Brian, do you think it's possible that the FBI could cross over into Canada and pick them up?" Fox wanted to make sure his witnesses were in his protective custody as soon as possible.

"We'd be better off letting the Canadian authorities handle things on their side of the border, you know, keeping the peace and cooperation thing. I'll make sure they are safely across the border and transported to the closest hospital. I'll have a team of FBI agents waiting to protect them."

Fox said, "Right now I don't want anyone to know that Dansforth and his wife have been found."

"Sure, I understand, but I have to close out the alert."

"That's no problem; I just need to make sure I have them in my custody first.'

Fox was glad he contacted Brian Sikorski, the Detroit FBI Bureau Chief, who confirmed that the FBI would handle protecting his two key witnesses. Fox had one more call to make. "Detective, good news; the Canadian authorities have our teacher and wife. They're safe and are being transported to the border crossing in Marine City."

"Great news, Jack, I know you've got to be thrilled. I'll call the school."

"Detective, not yet."

Frederickson was a little confused. "Why not, the school needs to know that he's okay."

"Detective, I know you're right, however until I make sure I've wrapped this up in a pretty little package and get the lieutenant governor's kid behind bars, I need to keep my only witnesses secret, at least for a few more days."

Frederickson didn't agree, but understood that with the implications of the lieutenant governor's kid's involvement, the DA was being extremely cautious.

Fox added, "Detective, I couldn't have done this without your help." Fox hung up and decided to head north to the hospital to meet with the FBI and his witnesses.

Detective Frederickson knew the case of the missing teacher was coming to a close, but wished he could let someone at the school know. With what Fox just said, he can't tell anyone. At least he had Mary Blankenship's husband in custody and he would be charged with abducting her and her family. Frederickson wondered to himself, *would anyone really know what part he played in this investigation.*

***

The ferry bobbed and rolled as it slowly hooked up to the crossing in Marine City. There was only one vehicle on it and two men in dark suits stood on the dock waiting for the ferry to be secured. Once it was docked the FBI agents boarded and the lead agent was happy to see the couple. "Mr. & Mrs. Dansforth?" Tommy and Kathy nodded as the two agents displayed their badges. The FBI took the couple into their protection, thanking the two Canadian officials who escorted the Dansforth's across on the ferry.

The Canadian officer told the first FBI agent that was signing the transfer papers, "We've got our men searching the area that your two people were able to help show us an approximate spot where they were held. When we find the cabin they told us about, who should I contact?"

"Our Bureau Chief, Brian Sikorski, is handling this." He gave the officer, Brian's information and again thanked them for their help. This had been a great example of international cooperation. The Canadian authorities had men combing the wooded area that the Dansforth's had pointed out on a map. There deep in the woods, not very far from the ferry landing, stood a small cabin about two-hundred feet off the main road hidden by huge pine trees. The gravel road wound through the trees. As they approached there wasn't a vehicle in sight, but the gravel showed signs that someone had recently driven on it. There were spots where the gravel had been tossed into a pile like a car spinning its tires. The men carefully approached the cabin with weapons drawn. Once the place was surrounded, one of the men carefully approached, holding his weapon pointed at the front door. The door appeared to be slightly opened and he slid the barrel of the gun into the opening and pushed the door wide open. "Anyone inside, this is the police."

There wasn't a response from inside the cabin. The others in the group had moved in closer and another man circled around the back. "I've got something back here!" he called out. The officer at the front of the cabin had moved inside while another officer moved in position to assist in case someone was still hiding. Two others circled to the back of the place to see what their partner found. The three men in the rear of the cabin looked down on two bodies partially covered with snow and leaves. "Better call it in, eh!" The Ontario Provincial Police had uncovered the bodies of Bud and his nephew.

The leader of the search party headed to the back of the cabin once they made sure no one was inside. He looked at the men standing over the frozen bodies, "I wonder what this was about?" They all looked at each other. "Well constable, looks like we've got a mess here, eh!" The men turned the two bodies over, stepping back as one of them was lying, eyes wide open."

"I'll give either of you a Toonie to shut those eyes." None of the men stooped down to do it. They stood over the bodies as the lead OPP officer called it in. The office in Sarnia dispatched a paddy wagon to pick up the bodies as the constable relayed the cabin location and address. The records would be checked to see who owned the cabin and they would try to identify the men via DNA, most likely with help from the Americans on the other side of the lake.

Once the information was received, the OPP office relayed the phone number for the FBI bureau chief. "Take photos of the bodies and forward them to their office. Maybe they will supply a fast ID for us." The constable took his Android phone out and patched the facial pictures with a text to the FBI. Nothing left to do but wait for the OPP group from Sarnia to pick them up. One man was stationed at the end of the gravel drive and two others waited in the cabin.

_____Thirty-Seven

Brian Sikorski had two of his best FBI agents running the information down that they received from the Ontario Provincial Police. They investigated the cabin's ownership through both the FBI data base and Interpol. Another group of agents downtown was hoping that they could identify the bodies of the two found at the cabin through facial recognition software. The FBI had contacted the District Attorney, informing him that they may have had a break in the case of who abducted the Dansforth's. Jack Fox was thrilled that his witnesses were escorted to safety and checked out at the hospital. He now knew that the bureau would be running checks on the man who ran the border crossing, as well as the two bodies the OPP found at the cabin. Fox was on his way to St. Clair to meet with the Dansforth's and called Frederickson to update him on recent developments.

Detective Frederickson just finished interviewing Mary Blankenship and her mother along with his captain and had to complete his report when the call came into the Twelfth Precinct. "Detective, I've got an update for you. The Ontario Police found the cabin and two bodies semi-buried in the back." Frederickson knew Fox was keeping his word, _I'll keep you in the loop detective,_ Fox had told him. "What do you need me to do, Jack?"

"Right now, I'm on my way to meet the Dansforth's in St. Clair. Once I make sure everything is okay, how about we meet?"

"Great, just let me know where and when. The drink is on me." The detective hung up and moved across the precinct to where the coffee pot was located. He was pouring a cup when someone approached coming out of the captain's office. Looking up he saw Sky King moving into the break room.

"Detective, I just wanted to say thanks for all your hard work."

"Hey, you did all the hard stuff. I was just there to watch and learn." The two men shook hands and King smiled.

"Sure, and if you didn't keep your captain at bay this whole thing would have gone down the toilet. I'll make sure you're mentioned in my report.

The detective knew it had been a good day; might be the first time in years that he didn't sit behind a desk watching everyone else on a case. The precinct was buzzing with the events and how Frederickson was key to solve it. As he walked back to his desk there were officers who reached out, back slapping and offering congrats. "Hey guys, it's all team work and the Twelfth did it." There was new respect for Frederickson around the office and he was happy to just be involved.

Meanwhile downtown in the FBI office, men were scurrying around having identified both the body of the captured suspect from the border crossing incident in Marine City and one of the bodies found at the cabin in the woods. Brian's team was trying to see if they could place the two identified men together. The third body, of a much younger man, maybe even a teen didn't fit, *maybe he was also abducted*, they thought. The body recovered from Marine City was Sam Ventimigilio, a known enforcer from Detroit. The big man had been linked to a crime family years ago and did hard time at Jackson State Prison. The list of crimes was extensive; ten years for armed robbery, twice pulled in as a murder suspect but nothing could be proven. Yes, this was a bad guy, but what was his part in the abduction, if anything. Could his capture just have been a coincidence? The second body, one that was found at the cabin, was that of Buddy Greco, known mainly as Bud. Greco was a small time hood from Lansing. He did time in several places including Jackson State Prison. Requests had gone out to the prison for inmate records. Maybe they could connect the two men to time served there. They tried to identify the third body but he didn't have a record and not in the data base. The next thing was to check the state data base for driver's license or passport information. The next phase was how did the three men connect to each other and who may have hired them.

Jack Fox had arrived at St. John's Hospital and was interviewing Tommy Dansforth and his wife. They were giving him the details of both their abduction, as well as what had happened at the small cabin during their abduction. Tommy told Fox about the evening he was grabbed from the school parking lot. Fox was surprised that he was able to almost fight off the guys that grabbed him, but Dansforth said one of them hit him from behind. The information that the men who originally took the couple had been shot at the cabin, and bodies dumped into the river, would create a new search off the Canadian shoreline. With the river still frozen and the car along with the bodies dumped into the frozen mess it might be hard for the Coast Guard to find them. Fox wondered why Kathy Dansforth hadn't called to report that her husband hadn't come home the night before.

"Tommy was going to stay at the Greektown Hotel. He had some comps and felt that it would be safer if he wasn't home. He became concerned because the other day he thought that he was being followed."

Jack said, "That's why my office wanted to put you both in witness protection."

"Yes, we knew that, but Tommy said let's see if maybe we were just being paranoid. We should have called you, I guess." Kathy looked over at her husband.

"Jack, Kathy told me to call you, it's my fault. I just didn't think someone would come after us."

"That's okay now, you're both safe and I'm going to protect both of you until the trial."

"But I've got a job to do and teaching is too important for me not to show up."

"I can appreciate that, however this may be the biggest trial in state history and that's pretty important too." It was agreed that the DA would place them in protective custody and that the school would know why or at least that the couple was critical to a pending case.

A nurse came into the room and handed Kathy Dansforth a small paper cup. "You need to take these. With those scratches and cuts we need to make sure you don't have an infection." She handed a similar cup to Tommy.

Jack Fox asked, "How are they both doing?"

"Surprisingly well, considering they've been trouncing through the woods in ten degree weather with those cuts and bruises. Mr. Dansforth will need to have that arm set; the x-rays show that it's broken in two places. Mr. Dansforth we'll have an orderly come in here and take you up to surgery for that."

"Surgery!" Kathy stood up. "Why surgery?"

"He'll have to be put to sleep so they can set his arm. Looks like they will have to insert a pin in it. It shouldn't be too long."

Fox put his hand on Kathy's shoulder, "Nurse, I'm sending someone up there with him."

"You'll have to talk to the surgeon about that."

"Kathy, I'll make sure everything is okay and someone will be with each of you the whole time." With that he had one of the agents assigned to the couple come into the room as he went to talk to someone from the hospital.

***

The FBI office in downtown Detroit was busy with researching the possible connection of the bodies that were discovered at the cabin and the one recovered in Marine City. They had to be tied together somehow but where. A package arrived in the bureau's office from the Marine City police with three cell phones in it. They were obviously burner phones, not unusual for people operating illegally to use. A group of agents were put on the assignment of tracing any calls that were made, either incoming or outgoing plus checking the serial numbers to see where and who may have purchased them. This would be a tough task because the cell phone industry didn't regulate these types of phones. They were often used by parents who wanted to control their kids calling expenses or criminals who didn't want any records of their calls or purchases. The agents handling the tracing of the calls made on the burner phones were surprised when they were able to recover the calling records from one of the phones almost instantly. One of the agents hurried into the Bureau Chief's Office. "Sir, I've got three calls from one of the burner phones. You're not going to believe who they called?"

Brian looked at the information and numbers that the agent handed him and jumped up from behind his desk. "Double check these one more time." When the agent headed back out, Brian grabbed his phone. "Jack, I've got something really big for you. You better come back in here."

_____Thirty-Eight

Jack Fox listened to the call from the FBI and knew it didn't make sense. How could this be? Where would this new information lead them? Jack Fox left the FBI agents in St. Clair guarding his two witnesses and drove back down Highway 94 toward downtown Detroit. It would take about an hour before he got there and his mind wandered, all over the place. His suspects had to be connected to the lieutenant governor's son, but now this news made the scope of the investigation double in size. Who really committed the Greektown murders or more importantly who ordered the murder. This new information would shake the whole case up? The aspects of corruption at this high of a level from what the FBI found would make national headlines. Fox wanted to hear the calls himself. How could a Detroit crime family become so powerful?

The bureau's office employed every agent possible to unravel the connections of Buddy Greco and Big Sam Ventimigilio. Records were coming in from Jackson State Prison and although both men had been inmates, neither of them served prison terms together. Data was gathered to see if either of them were arrested together or had any connection to each other's past. Everything was coming up empty. They still couldn't identify the body of the young man found next to that of Buddy, but Jack Fox supplied their office with the possible identification from the Dansforth's. He said that Kathy told him that the young man claimed that he was a nephew of Bud and that his mother was Buddy's sister. A team was working on gathering details so that they could make the identification positive. Fox also told the FBI agents that Kathy said the kid was just doing what his uncle told him to. She was sad that the kid was found dead. "Really seemed like a nice kid in the wrong place," she told Fox.

The bodies and car that were dumped in the river hadn't been discovered yet, but the Coast Guard had a cutter from Port Huron and another from Selfridge Air National Guard station combing the river for them. The Air National Guard had a helicopter flying low over the ice flows and traveled south along the river while the Coast Guard had two cutters heading downriver looking for any sign of either the car or the bodies. With temperatures in the teens and another snow storm on the way this would be a long tedious task.

Jack Fox just passed the exit for Interstate 75 and took the overpass that led to downtown to Highway 375. He decided to call the detective to let him know that the Dansforth's were okay and wanted to thank him for his participation. The call came into the Twelfth Precinct and the captain was surprised that Fox asked for Frederickson directly. "Detective, Jack Fox is on line one for you," the officer told the detective.

As Frederickson listened he saw his captain move into the main office and now standing about ten feet away. The detective lowered his voice as he finished talking to the DA and hung up the phone.

"What did he want?" Captain Hughes asked.

"He just wanted to let me know that our teacher and his wife were safe and checked out fine."

"Where did he take them to?"

Frederickson looked up, puzzled at the question. "I'm not sure what you mean."

"Where is he holding them," the captain asked. Hughes stood at the side of the detective's desk waiting for an answer.

The detective raised an eyebrow and slightly tilted his head to the side. "I never asked."

"How come we haven't informed the school that their teacher was found and safe? I think we need to do that."

Now Frederickson wondered why the sudden interest from his chief on contacting the school. So far the chief hadn't wanted to be involved, even feeling that the negotiator was handling the hostage thing all wrong. Why did his captain all of a sudden want to be involved in these details? He slid back in his chair and answered, "Fox told me that he would handle all of that. Guess they need to make sure that both Dansforth and his wife were okay first. Plus I guess because the Canadians were involved, there might be more hoops to jump through."

Captain Hughes stood at the desk for a minute and slowly answered, "Yeah, that makes sense, probably has them at a hospital somewhere." With that the captain quickly headed back into his office. Frederickson watched with renewed interest as the captain closed his door and immediately made a phone call.

***

Things in the bureau's office continued at a fast pace. Agents were adding names, places and mug shots to their crime board. The large white magnetic board had been moved into an office along the side of the room that agents referred to as the war room, with many agents coming and going. Brian Sikorski, the Bureau Chief, manned the information along with his special agents as they were connecting the names involved. They had pictures of the bodies found in the cabin at Marine City posted along with those of the Greektown murder victim and the lieutenant governor's son. They discovered the cabin was registered to a multi-national corporation and ownership showed it to belong to a European Company. That left them at a dead end.

Lines were drawn from one group or person to another with notes on their connection. Brian waited for Fox to arrive before adding the new details to the board. Jack Fox parked in the lower lot of the FBI downtown building and headed upstairs. He made his way into the bureau's office and was escorted to where Brian was meeting with two field agents.

"Jack, glad you're here. If you wait a minute we can head to my office."

Fox stood nervously, shifting his weight from one foot to the next in anticipation of the information he was about to hear. He studied the white board with names, photos and details. Brian turned and motioned him to follow into the small room next to Brian's corner office. "Jack, we got this package from the Marine City police and it contained these cell phones. My team began to search through them to see if we could pull call records, either incoming or outgoing. Of course they're all burner phones, hard to trace the purchase of them, as you know."

Jack stood there listening to Brian but didn't actually hear what he was saying, his total attention was on the one cell phone that Brian was holding in his right hand.

"Jack, this is the phone I told you about. It's different from the others and all the calls are still on the call log. Of course it's a burner but not a store bought one, it's government issue. Jack, one of the numbers in the log traces back to the Washington office of Eric Holder, the US Attorney General."

Fox was stunned, "The United States Attorney General?"

"Yes, and not only that number, but it appears there at least three times."

_____Thirty-Nine

Brian Sikorski, the FBI Bureau Chief, and Jack Fox were talking quietly in the outer office when one of the bureau's agents informed his chief that the call he requested had gone through. Brian waved Jack to follow him. The two men moved back into Brian's office along with the special agent that followed them.

"Thanks for calling me back," Brian stated. "I'm sitting with the Wayne County District Attorney, Jack Fox; we've been working together on an abduction case that has taken us over the border into Canada. We're pretty sure that we caught our guys, however, one of them had a cell phone with a few messages to your office, actually to you personally." Bill Lindquist was the Assistant Attorney General of the U.S. and reported directly to Eric Holder.

Bill didn't say anything at first then finally asked, "Have you got the guy in custody?"

"Sorry to say but all the possible suspects in our case are dead; unless you can tell me who your contact is. He may still be out on the run."

"Tell me, is one of your dead guys a kid, maybe twenty years old?"

"Yeah, no identification on him and so far the only link is he may be related to one of the other guys, Buddy Greco."

"Brian, I don't want you to misunderstand; we've been working a corruption case in Detroit for a while, then we got this call. Our informer said that he had reliable information that linked many high ranking police officers along with someone in the governor's office in a major cover up. Brian we're not sure how far up this goes."

"The Wayne County DA here is ready to prosecute a case involving a family member of the lieutenant governor. The people that these guys abducted are his primary witnesses."

Bill was quiet for a second, "We know about that."

Jack Fox jumped up from his seat, raising his voice he stated, "That's great, how in the hell does the U.S. Attorney General know about a murder in Greektown?"

Brian looked over at Fox, "Hang on Jack." Before Fox continued, Brian motioned him to sit back down. Moving from behind his desk, Brian shut the office door and returned back to the desk. "Okay, Bill we're listening."

Bill Lindquist informed them, "We had a link between high ranking members of the Detroit Police Department and certain local government officials. Two weeks ago we got a call from this kid who tells us that he and his uncle were being paid to abduct witnesses in a murder that involved the lieutenant governor."

Fox nodded with the details that he was already aware of except that one of the abductors had been calling Washington. "Why would the kid call you?" Brian looked over at Jack Fox. "Bill, initially I have the same question; why would a kid call the U.S. Attorney General's office?"

"That's a good question, I immediately had our people start working on it and the tie it to our current investigation of the police department fit. This kid had names and details that surprised even us."

Brian didn't like where this was going, "Did you know about the planned abduction and how did it still go down?"

"Our people met with the kid and he indicated that this was planned to happen in a few days, something must have happened that pushed the time table up. He texted us and said the order came through and his uncle didn't let him know until the couple had been taken. The text message said that it all had gone down, and was too late for us to do anything. The last text came in the other day then we lost contact. Our people tried to contact the kid but either his cell phone was off or he was in a dead cell area; even tried GPS but someone must have taken his battery out, because we couldn't find it on any grid."

Brian questioned, "How's this all fit in with your investigation of corrupt police?"

"The kid's information would have connected many corrupt individuals along with people in the governor's office. We offered protection and immunity for the kid with a light sentence for his uncle. We've been working with the feds legal people on this case. They were concerned because the information linked a group of bad cops in Detroit, that went all the way up the ladder to Lansing. When our people saw the television reporter breaking the case of the abduction of the teacher we scrambled for details and pulled out every stop to find them. I have investigators in Lansing right now."

"It sure would have been nice if you shared your information with us," Jack blurted out.

"Yeah, maybe you're right; however we didn't know how far this corruption went. Sorry but your office could have been involved." Jack bit his lip not wanting to stop the flow of information but mad that even he could have been suspected. "Okay, guess I understand. Where does this go now? I got my witnesses in protective custody."

"First thing, we want to spend time with the witnesses."

Brian jumped in, "Bill, I got my agents with them at the hospital in St. Clair, making sure they're safe and okay after the ordeal."

"I'm sure your guys are doing a great job. We'll need to go over all the details because once we bring charges with all the high profile people involved, this will really hit the fan, bigger than when we charged the mayor for corruption."

Jack Fox didn't like being in the dark and this federal investigation did just that as well as endangered his witnesses. He took a deep breath and asked, "What happens to my case?"

"Jack, none of these men, including those people in the governor's office are aware of our investigation. Once we bring charges, your case will be a key part of the corruption, linking key members of the Giambi family and their involvement with the police, along with their part in the abduction. We'll have you work with our people in bringing charges in both the trials.

"Both trials?"

"Yes, we'll want to try your suspects separate from those people responsible for the cover up. Jack, some important political figures in Detroit are involved."

"Okay, as long as my office is involved. With this many trials my team, will be busy for a long time." Jack suddenly had questions about Detective Frederickson. *God I've shared so much with him, hope he's not involved.* He asked Lindquist, "Can you tell us how many of your targets are in the police department?"

"My plan is to fly to Detroit later today and I'll meet with you, Brian and his team, and we will proceed accordingly. I don't want to do this on the phone."

The conversation continued with the plans to meet once Lindquist arrived in Detroit. Brian jotted down the flight information as Jack sat across from him going over his case and anyone that he had shared information with. Frederickson was the only possible link to corrupt police. Could all the trust Jack put in the detective backfire?

_____Forty

Detective Frederickson had placed three calls to Jack Fox, but hadn't heard back from him or anyone in his office. He wanted to know when he could let the principal at Kennedy Charter know that Tommy Dansforth and his wife had been found and safe and sound. He started questioning why Fox hadn't called him back. The secretary only said that he had been downtown in meetings all afternoon. *Guess the case is taking shape*, he figured.

Carole Newton called the Twelfth Precinct. "Detective, we'd like to do a follow-up interview on the progress with the Dansforth abduction and any details you may have discovered after the hostage case in Indian Village."

"I'd like to do that, but we might still have more work to do before I go on the air with details."

"Okay, but how's our case on Tommy Dansforth, the missing teacher from the school parking lot, going?"

Frederickson knew a lot but couldn't share it with the television reporter or even his precinct chief. He wished Fox would get back with him so he could close the case at Kennedy Charter. "Carole, I'm sure we'll have an update for you soon."

"Sounds like you're getting close to solving the case and have something you can tell me detective."

"Carole, the only thing I can say is we got some good leads and if they pan out; I promise I'll call you."

Once he hung up with Carole, he tried Jack Fox one more time. This time the secretary told him, "Sir, Mr. Fox just got back into the office and I'll see if he's available." Frederickson felt that he was put on hold for a really long time. Finally she came back, "Sorry detective, he has someone in the office and said he'd try to call you back as soon as possible."

Frederickson slammed down the phone. "Bullshit," he yelled, Officers in the precinct turned and wondered what had happened. This was a side of the detective they hadn't seen before; of course they hadn't seen him handling a case of any significance either. No one wanted to approach Frederickson. He shoved his chair into the desk and stomped toward the break room. Some of the men looked at each other not knowing exactly who should go talk to him, especially remembering the break room events from the previous day. Captain Hughes came out of his office and motioned to the officers. They knew he wanted one of them to see what happened. Frederickson stepped out of the break room and saw Hughes standing there. He finally asked, "Don, what the hell happened?"

Frederickson turned toward his captain, "When I know you'll know."

"What the hell does that mean?" The detective turned away from his captain. "Detective, do I need remind you that I'm ultimately responsible for every case in our precinct. Now where are we on this?"

Frederickson knew that he promised Fox that he wouldn't share anything about the tie-in to the investigation of the Greektown murder. He slowly turned back to his captain. Officers were worried, would this be round two. Frederickson took a deep breath, "I've been trying to find out from the DA when we can go to the press on the abduction case, but he seems to be in meetings. You know, just impatient, I guess."

Hughes wasn't sure that his detective was being straight with him. "That's all, you're sure?"

"Yeah." The coffee maker made a loud hissing noise signaling that it was ready. Frederickson turned toward the sound, "I'm getting a cup of coffee."

The captain watched him walk away before asking one more question, "Do you know where Fox is meeting?"

"No, just that when I called his office they said he was scheduled to be in meetings for the next day or two."

Hughes said, "Wish I knew where he was, I'd like to get more details on why the couple was taken." With that the captain turned back and made his way across the room. He walked through the main office and a couple of the men looked up and quickly dropped their head. The captain just waved his hands in the air as he passed them. Moving back into his office the captain closed the door and picked up the phone. He was standing with his back to the door and appeared to be engaged in a livid conversation with hands flying and his head bobbing up and down.

After pouring his cup of coffee, Frederickson stood looking out of the window from the break room. One of the officers in the squad room was watching the captain on the phone came in and saw Frederickson. "Hey Don, what the hell did Hughes say?"

"Why!"

"Well after he left you he got on the phone and looks like he's in one hell of an argument with someone. Thought you'd want to know."

"Thanks, I didn't have anything to tell him. I'm just waiting for an update from the DA so I can close my case. You know how that goes. We do all the hard work and once it's done they get all the glory."

The officer agreed, "You're probably right."

"Guess I need to wait a little longer, coffee?"

"Sure."

Frederickson poured the man a cup and one for himself. "Thanks for caring," he said and walked back toward his desk while peeking back at Hughes who was still on the phone. *Wonder what that's all about.* The captain continued his call not realizing that he was being watched.

***

Jack Fox finished meeting with his staff and called the local FBI office. He wanted to confirm the meeting time with the U.S. District Attorney. He wanted to see who in the Detroit Police Force was involved. His secretary came back into the room.

"Sir, Detective Frederickson called again, that makes four calls today."

"Thanks, I'll give him a call before I leave for my meeting." Jack Fox hated not being able to tell the detective what had happened. He just had to make sure that Frederickson wasn't involved. Fox dialed the precinct and was surprised that the detective wasn't in. They didn't know where he was; just that he had left about an hour ago. "Let him know that I called and will call back in a couple of hours." Fox planned to head to Wayne County Airport. He was actually kind of glad that he didn't have to lie to Frederickson. It would take close to forty-five minutes to get to the Marriott Hotel where he was meeting with Brian, the Assistant U.S. Attorney general and the Federal prosecutor that would handle the corruption case. Brian Sikorski called back to St. Clair to inform his agents that the U.S. Attorney's office was sending people to question the Dansforth's while in protective custody. "How are our two people doing?"

"The wife is better than her husband. He's just out of surgery after having his arm set. Mrs. Dansforth had a few contusions and cuts that were treated in the emergency room. They took care of what they could in the ER for Mr. Dansforth but the arm was real bad because it was broken for over twenty-four hours without any treatment."

"What did the doctor say about moving them?"

"I haven't talked to the doctor yet. I'm sure it will be okay. We can have a nurse treat them after being released. Boss, we've gotten quite a bit of attention here, so we've been lying low. I know you don't want any press around."

"Good job, you're right no press, no information to anyone about who they are or why we're involved. No problems, right?"

"Right, got it, everything's been going okay."

"Make sure you check the credentials of the people they send from Washington. It appears that there are a lot of people involved in a cover up and the Dansforth's are likely targets."

"Will do."

Brian knew his two agents were among his best and didn't worry about their ability to protect the Dansforth's. He was going to head to the airport to meet with the Assistant United States District Attorney and Jack Fox. Hopefully this would all be solved soon.

_____Forty-One

Detroit Police Headquarters downtown was buzzing with activity. Word began to spread, that a major crime syndicate was about to be rounded up and links to some prominent people in the state would be exposed. Carole Newton, from Channel 7, made her way through the Detroit Public Safety Headquarters building on Third Street. The building was once the old MGM Casino and had recently been opened with the mayor's offices, as well as police and fire departments headquarters. When the proposal for the move to the old casino building was first discussed many people were concerned. What would be the message to citizens with the city's offices being relocated in a closed casino? Once the MGM Corporation offered the building free to the city all the questions went away.

It was close to five in the afternoon and Carole was hoping to get a key interview to use for the six o'clock news. Initial calls from the news team were brushed off and once she arrived and had cameras rolling many high ranking officer's seemed to disappear. The Channel 7 News team had been on top of two huge stories over the past twenty-four hours, first with the abduction of a teacher from the school parking lot, then the hostage situation in Indian Village. Her station manager had calls from the national networks requesting footage and details on the situation still working at Kennedy Charter Academy. The missing teacher story was still in the front of most news stories.

Carole found her way up to the police chief's office and suggested that her camera team wait outside. She knew that she had a better chance for an interview without cameras rolling.

Maybe once she got to the new chief he would be willing to go on air with her; to her surprise he was standing at the entrance to his office talking to two men in uniform. Turning toward the well known local reporter, he greeted her. "Good afternoon, Carole, what can I do for you?"

"Good afternoon chief, my news crew is outside and I was wondering if we can interview you about recent events including any progress on the abduction at Kennedy Charter."

"Sure, could you give me a few minutes? I'm just finishing up with two of our captains here."

"Thank you sir, I'll wait outside, if that's okay." The chief nodded and thanked her for considering his schedule and willingness to wait. Her approach to interviewing key public figures was always professional and one of the reasons she was often well received and people were willing to talk to her. Carole stepped outside and told the crew that the chief will be out in a minute. They got their cameras ready and knew that until she gave them the signal; don't turn on the lights and cameras yet. It was maybe five minutes when the door opened and the chief along with two other officers that always were at his side came out into the hallway. "Thank you chief, is it okay for us to start?"

"Sure." The chief turned toward his two body guards and motioned one of them to move along. "Carole, Captain Allen was just updating me on our progress at the school."

Carole motioned to her camera crew and lights were turned on and the cameras were rolling as Carole opened the interview. "I'm talking to Police Chief Barry here at headquarters who will update us on the progress his team is making on the case of Tommy Dansforth, our missing teacher. Chief, what can you tell our viewers?'

"Carole, our teams have been working 24/7 since the 911 call came in. The detectives from the Twelfth Precinct have coordinated efforts with both my office and the county district attorney on the case. We're pleased to announce that officers, from the Twelfth Precinct, and a key detective have identified suspects and we've been able to narrow our search."

"Can you give us any details or descriptions on the suspects?"

"I don't want to compromise the investigation, however I can tell you that we've made great progress and are working with multiple organizations to resolve the case."

"What do you mean by that?"

"Our missing teacher is from Macomb County, we have the sheriff's office and their staff involved as well as the state police who have joined the search. Carole, it's a team effort and we've pulled out every effort to solve this and bring the teacher back safe."

"Along with that case, your team was involved and resolved a situation in Indian Village. Would you update our viewers on that case?"

"I'm pleased to say that through the efforts of our detectives and police negotiator we were able to get all the people out safely including the individual that was holding them in the home."

"I have just one more question," she turned facing the Chief, saving this question for last. "There has been an allegation that some key members of your team may be involved with a crime syndicate here in Detroit. Do you have an internal investigation going on this?"

The chief knew this issue might come up but didn't want to address it on air. He wouldn't want to talk about any internal investigation and definitely didn't want to expose any problems in his department. "Carole, I can't talk about any current investigations."

"I understand chief, however we have reliable information that a member of a known crime family has turned state witness and will reveal corruption in your department."

This question surprised him. "Again, I can't discuss current investigations." He abruptly said, "I need to get to an important meeting and when I have some details we'll keep your viewers updated." With that he turned and walked down the hallway.

Carole turned to the cameras and recapped the interview for her viewers. "You heard it here first, Chief Barry acknowledged that an investigation is ongoing and any officers linked to this will be prosecuted." That proclamation sent a tidal wave of questions throughout every precinct.

Chief Barry turned back to see the camera team still filming Carole in front of his office. He was half way down the hallway by now and turned toward his lieutenant pulling him closer. "What the hell does she know? I want you to find out what's going on now!"

He was visibly pissed and hurried past people in the hallway who tried to stop to talk to him.

***

The meeting at the Detroit Airport Marriott had become somewhat contentious as the Assistant Attorney General covered the details of their investigation. Jack Fox couldn't be held back. "My team uncovered the details of the events in Greektown and the witnesses are mine and mine alone." He was now standing in front of both of the men almost yelling.

"Hold on, Jack. I told you that your case will still proceed with the Dansforth's and the upcoming murder trial. Our case is much more reaching and will involve officials both in Detroit as well as Lansing. You have to understand that this is the kind of investigation that can ruin careers and gets people killed."

Fox was standing and shifting from one foot to the other without responding. Brian jumped in. "From what I know Jack, the only thing tying our two cases together is that the people that arranged the abduction of the teacher are tied into the corruption case. With the cover up charges and the link to organized crime the Fed's and U.S. Attorney General plan to bring, you'll find your case extremely critical to secure many warrants." Fox was cooling down and took a deep breath.

"I just don't want my case to go away, nor have people given immunity to testify in the federal case."

"Jack, the case the feds are planning will be huge, it may be the widest ranging case of corruption we've had in years. Your witnesses will only be mentioned because their abduction was part of the cover up part but they most likely won't need to appear."

"When are you bringing charges?" Fox was feeling better about the way things were going.

The U.S. Assistant Attorney General looked over at Brian, "Very soon, Jack, the FBI and I will be working on that today."

Forty-Two

The Dansforth's were guarded by two federal agents, that were now talking to a couple of men in dark suits. The doctor had entered the room and was explaining the surgical procedure to Kathy Dansforth. He told her, "We had to insert a pin in Tommy's arm because it was broken in two places." She shook her head when he showed her the x-rays that detailed the shattered humerus and ulna bone. "Mrs. Dansforth, without the pins we inserted, his arm wouldn't heal properly. It's going to be fine now, but will take a while to heal."

One of the FBI agents listened as the doctor completed his analysis of Tommy Dansforth's procedure. "How soon can we move him?"

"I wouldn't want him to leave the hospital for at least six to eight hours. The sedative has to wear off and I'd like to check him over a few times."

"Thanks, we'll make sure he's here for that. I'd like him to be moved as soon as possible to a private room so we can help watch over him and Mrs. Dansforth."

"I'll arrange that." With that the doctor moved down the hallway and stopped at the nurses' station. He gave them the request from the agents and plans were put into process to move both of them to a secure wing of the unit.

The agents called the updated information into to their Bureau Chief, Mr. Sikorski. "Good job." He told them. "Have the people arrived from the U.S. Attorney's office?"

"Two of them, a guy and woman, both of them from Washington. I checked their credentials and everything is in order. They want to talk to the couple as soon as possible."

"Once you have the Dansforth's secure in a room and Mr.

Dansforth is feeling okay, let them do what they need. I want one of you outside the door at all times and the other one inside the room. If the Attorney General's people from Washington object, tell them to call me."

The agents were good with the plan and waited for the doctors to have Tommy moved to the room that was being set up for them. One of the nurses moved down the hallway and asked, "The doctor said you'll need a large private room, do you want more than one bed in there?"

"Yes, Mrs. Dansforth should be able to lie down too."

"Okay, we're setting up room A109. It's down the hallway and pretty big. I'll have them put a few extra chairs in there too."

"Thanks, greatly appreciated."

The two people from Washington were going over documents and asked, "Is there going to be a place that we can use, we need a table and a place to set up our recording devices."

"It's being arranged right now."

Kathy Dansforth saw the nurse coming back down the hallway. "Can I see my husband?"

"Yes, I just talked to the people in recovery and he's being moved down to the private room we've set up. I'll be happy to walk you down there right now if you wish."

Kathy was happy that everything went well with the surgery and told the agents that she was going down the hallway with the nurse. "You'll have to be escorted by us, let me tell my partner that the room is ready." He turned and informed the others that they should follow to room A109 down the hallway. The nurse led the large group around the bend to the room that they had prepared for them.

Tommy Dansforth was still a little groggy but had a broad smile on his face when he saw his wife coming toward him. "You look good honey," he said.

"Boy they must really have you doped up." The couple nodded and smiled as Kathy bent down to give him a kiss on the cheek. "The doctor said you'll be fine in a few weeks."

***

The meeting at the Marriott Hotel was just breaking up

and Brian Sikorski walked out with Jack Fox. "In a few hours we'll have rounded up quite a few people both here and in Lansing. You know the news teams will be all over this with a lot of questions."

Fox told him, "I plan to give one of the reporters from Channel 7 a heads up on our part of the investigation, but only that we have a suspect in the Greektown murder, and are taking him into custody. Brian, you need to know that none of this was possible without the help of Detective Frederickson from the Twelfth Precinct. He's made sure that my case stayed in the background while we searched for the Dansforth's."

"I'll make sure he gets the credit he deserves. I know the Detroit Police Force will take a hit with this but having a good cop in the forefront will be a positive example and will do a lot of good." Brian wrote down the detective's name and information.

Jack added, "I've got men staked out at the lieutenant governor's house, and so far we haven't seen his kid, but the place is pretty big, so I'm still hoping he's there. How are you going to handle the other suspects in the case?"

Brian detailed his plan, "I've already dispatched my agents, along with the local police to the Giambi residence in Grosse Pointe, they'll take Vito and Vincent into federal custody. The two brothers, as I'm sure you're aware, run the Eastern Market trucking consortium and have been suspect for years. We'll also be rounding up various officers of the law, a Detroit Common Council member and three people in the governor's office including his lieutenant governor. Another surprise will be who else will be arrested as part of the Giambi crime syndicate. This is really going to be big, Jack."

They both had a huge grin on their face as they made their way back to the parking lot. Jack knew that soon the Free Press will have enough material to fill its pages for months to come. Jack Fox climbed in his car and smiled back at Brian, as he turned the ignition key. This had been his greatest success. Brian waved back but never saw this coming. The fire ball rose fifteen feet in the air as it consumed the Ford Explorer. Brian was parked about ten cars away and ran toward the burning Ford as soon as he heard the blast. There was nothing he could do. People were running both away and toward the scene as the flames rose above the cars parked in the lot. Two men came running carrying a fire extinguisher but it was too late. Everyone could see that a man was behind the wheel and engulfed in the inferno. Sirens could be heard coming from close by and Brian watched in horror unable to do anything to help.

Forty-Three

The blaze was captured on cell phone video by people that had been in the parking lot. Plumes of black smoke filled the sky. Brian immediately contacted his agents in St. Clair to make sure that their witnesses were safe. Once he had that confirmation, he called his office, informing them what had just happened. He was surprised when the agents said they were watching it all on television. "Get people to the Giambi residence now," he yelled. Brian knew this was the type of thing they would do. After all, it was Jack Fox, and his team that had been investigating the tie in to the governor's office and crimes uncovered at the Eastern Market. Brian then remembered what Fox had said about the Detroit detective that had worked the case with him. His next call was to the Twelfth Precinct. When the sergeant answered Brian immediately asked for Detective Frederickson.

"Sorry, but he's out right now. Can I give him a message?."

"This is important, do you know where he is or how can I reach him?"

"If you give me your name, I'll call him for you."

"Not going to be fast enough, I'm Brian Sikorski, FBI Bureau Chief. Give me his number now!"

The sergeant repeated Frederickson's cell number twice. Brian dialed it and waited for an answer. His phone went to the detective's message, this is Detective Frederickson from the Twelfth… Brian hung up. He didn't want to leave a message. He turned toward an police officer who was trying to keep people back from the area as fire fighters continued to battle the blaze that had spread to the cars on both sides of the Explorer. He flashed his FBI badge at the man and asked, "I've got to get in touch with a detective from Detroit, do you have a radio that I can use?"

"Sure," the officer handed his police scanner over. He put in the frequency used by Detroit cops and watched as Brian sent his message.

"This is Brian Sikorski with the FBI, I need Detective Donald Frederickson of the Detroit Police to contact me immediately. Detective, do not go anywhere or start your car until you call me. Here's my cell phone number, I'm working with the DA's office and this is life and death critical."

The officer could detect the panic in the FBI agent's voice, and thought that maybe the detective in question may have been related to the victim in the car bombing.

Once that message went out over on the scanner, many people, both officers and the general public turned to social media looking for the detective that was mentioned in the call. Frederickson's name was trending on all social media sites and his bio was popping up all over the web. Men from the Twelfth Precinct heard the information and had puzzled a reaction as to why the FBI would want to get to Frederickson, as soon as possible. It took only a few minutes when Brian's cell phone rang.

"This is Detective Frederickson, you're trying to contact me."

"Detective, Brian Sikorski with the FBI, I've been working with your local DA, Jack Fox. Where are you right now?"

"What the hell's going on? My cell phone and scanner is lighting up like a Christmas tree."

"Detective, I don't quite know what your relationship with Jack was, beside working on his case, but I'm sorry to tell you that Jack is dead. He was here with me meeting with the United States Assistant Attorney General and when we were leaving. Detective, his car blew up." There wasn't an answer from Frederickson for what seemed like a long time. "Detective, did you hear me?"

"I heard you, I just need a minute." Frederickson couldn't believe what he just heard. *Jack was dead. How could this have happened? Why did the FBI tell him not to start his car.* Frederickson asked, "How did this happen?"

"We walked out of our meeting and when he went to his car, as soon as he turned the key it blew up. It was terrible, flames shot up fifteen feet or more. Detective I'm concerned about your safety. Jack said you were very important to his case, and may be the only one outside of his office that knew many of the details."

Frederickson was still in shock. *Who did this? Could he really be in danger?* "Okay, I'm okay." Just then he thought back to the conversation with Captain Hughes in the office earlier. "Brian, this might be nothing but my captain asked several times earlier if I knew where Jack was having his meeting and with who."

Brian listened and couldn't believe it was possible, but was the Twelfth Precinct captain on the payroll of the Giambi family. "Tell me again exactly what he said."

"I'm going over it in my mind and he asked if I knew where Jack Fox was having his meeting. I told him I didn't know. Brian, I didn't know where the meeting was."

"I believe you detective. What did your captain do after you told him you didn't know where the meeting was?"

Frederickson thought about it. "He went in his office and instantly made a phone call. It lasted a while because I thought it was funny that as soon as he left my desk he had to call someone. Brian, I don't trust the guy, this isn't the first odd thing he's done."

"Detective where are you right now?"

"I'm outside about to head back into Kennedy Charter Academy. I wanted to tell the principal that we have her teacher safe and sound. Jack asked me not to do that but I know the whole school is hurting and could use some good news."

"Okay, but if you tell them, then you may be putting the teacher in more danger. I understand your point, but we can't lose our witnesses too."

Frederickson was standing outside the school and didn't know what to do. Brian was right, he knew that. *Why would he say he was there?* He asked, "What do you want me to do?"

"Nothing, just stay put, I'm sending an agent there to pick you up. Don't use your car. I'll have it towed in and checked over."

"That's not necessary, I'm sure it's okay…" Before he could finish Brian interrupted.

"Detective this is not a request, but an order. I'm also sending one of my men to your precinct. We can't take any chances. Do you understand?" Frederickson was nodding, still thinking about Fox. He had just started to like the guy. "Detective, are you still there?"

"I'm here. Tell your guy I'll be in the school. Got to give them some reason why I'm here, they've got outside cameras and I'm sure they've seen me out here." Once he hung up he moved to the front door and pressed the visitor bell. The bell rang and a voice answered, "Detective, come on in." Frederickson knew that he had to get a grip on himself, he'd seen many people killed and had to tell loved ones about a loss but this seemed different. Jack Fox was one of the good guys. How could this happen?

Forty-Four

Frederickson was standing in the principal's office at Kennedy Charter talking to Ms. Baker. "I decided to take the chance that you'd still be here. I knew it was late and pretty much everyone would be gone by now. My office has made progress on our case, and hopefully we will find Mr. Dansforth and his wife very soon."

"Detective, we were all so thrilled that your office was able to find Ms. Blankenship and get her and her family safely out of that situation they were in." Ms. Baker was pleased with what the detective had been able to accomplish, and the first good news regarding Mr. Dansforth's case that she heard. "I wish I could have announced something to our teachers before they left, they all are a little down since Mr. Dansforth's disappearance."

"When I talked to Ms. Blankenship at the precinct she said she'd call you."

"Oh, she did, maybe even when she was still there. I told her to take as much time off as needed."

"That's good, in situations like this it may take a few days just to feel safe again." Frederickson wanted to give Ms. Baker more details on the Dansforth case but he knew the FBI was right, couldn't take a chance on endangering the Dansforth's even more, especially after the events with the death of Jack Fox. *If those responsible for Fox's murder were able to get to him, what else could they do?* "I'm sure we're going to have a major development real soon." Ms. Baker sure hoped he was right. She heard the front bell ring and was surprised that someone was there at this time on a Friday. "Sorry, I meant to tell you that I'm expecting someone to pick me up here."

She looked over at him a little confused, "Isn't that your car parked next to the building?"

"Yeah, but something is wrong, I tried to start it but I think it's a battery. I called it in and the office will tow it in."

She moved to the door controller and saw the man standing at the door. He was tall, wearing a dark suit and stern look on his face. Baker turned the screen toward the detective, "Is this who you're expecting?"

Frederickson was on the spot, he didn't know who was coming to get him. "Let me walk to the door if it's okay and let him in."

"I could just buzz him in for you."

"No, he's from another precinct and I just want to make sure everything is okay." Frederickson excused himself and went to the front door. He slid his right hand on his holster and released the strap holding his gun. Not sure if he should pull his weapon, he looked through the viewer to check the visitor out, dark three piece suit, cropped haircut, and the detective could see the gun holster bulge in the left shoulder area, *has to be an FBI agent*, he thought. Frederickson pulled the door opened about three inches, "Can I help you?"

The man at the door announced, "I'm here to meet Detective Frederickson with the Twelfth Precinct."

Frederickson felt odd asking but he said, "Do you have any identification?" The man at the door turned his head slightly to the left and reached into his jacket. Frederickson placed his right hand on his weapon and kept an eye on the stranger. He watched the guy withdraw a leather folder and flip open the top displaying an FBI badge. "Sorry, I had to ask."

"Understandable, especially with everything that has happened, detective."

"Yes, come on in. I don't want to tell the people here that you're with the FBI. Is it okay if I just say you're an officer from another precinct?"

"No problem," he introduced himself, "I'm Carl Virgilio, Mr. Sikorski sent me to pick you up." Once they were inside, Carl asked Frederickson, "Is that your squad car along the building?"

"Yeah," and he reached into his pocket for the keys. "Do you want these?" He handed Carl the set of keys after removing his house key and two other keys from the key ring. The two moved into the office where Ms. Baker was sitting at her desk, separating a stack of papers. "Ms. Baker, this is Officer Virgilio from the Tenth Precinct."

Ms. Baker stood up and shook the officers hand. "Glad to meet you." She looked at Carl, and noticed how he was dressed, much different from Frederickson, who always looked nice but dressed much more casually. "Mr. Virgilio, how long have you been a police officer?"

Carl looked over at Frederickson then answered, "Actually I just was assigned to the same precinct as Detective Frederickson. I've been in law enforcement for close to ten years."

The detective turned toward his guest, "Carl, guess we should be going." He again thanked Ms. Baker. "I'm sure by Monday we'll be able have more information."

"Thanks, for coming by detective. Our district supervisor approved school to open again on Monday morning. They'll still have the security people guarding our parking lot."

He told her, "I'll make sure our precinct has officers placed around the area as extra protection for your students and staff."

"Thank you, detective." Ms. Baker walked them to the front door, still giving Carl the once over. There was something different about him, but she couldn't quite put her finger on what it was. Once they walked out of the front door she retreated to her office. When she looked out of the window she was surprised that both the detective and the other officer seemed to be looking under Frederickson's vehicle. *Wonder what they're looking for? If the car wouldn't start why not lift the hood and check the battery, strange, very strange.*

***

The FBI and Attorney General's office were scrambling, calls went out to key authorities alerting them to what was about to take place. The new police commissioner was on board with the plan and the FBI had their men strategically placed. The bureau would be in charge of placing those people suspected to be involved in custody. It would be a wide sweeping dragnet that could bring in as many as twenty police officers, as well as three high ranking political figures. Carl had brought Detective Frederickson downtown to the FBI office as requested by his bureau chief.

Brian was behind his desk with three other men when they entered the office. "Excuse me for a minute," Brian said. He moved into the main area and introduced himself to the detective. "Sorry to meet under these circumstances, detective. I wanted you to be here when things started to heat up around the city."

"What can I do to help?"

"According to Jack Fox you've been a great help. That information about Captain Hughes also came in handy. We've been running background checks and warrants have been issued for bank records, travel details and searches of residences. You'd be surprised but your captain has close to half a million in the bank and owns two homes, one in the city and a very large one in Grosse Pointe."

In Detroit, officers must live in the city, it's a requirement." Frederickson stated.

"We know, but the house in the suburbs off of Lakeshore Drive must be worth at least a million dollars. Your captain isn't the only one detective. In fact we've got people rounding up suspects around town now."

"How about the Giambi Brothers?"

"We have agents that will be picking them up too. There are officers in Lansing at the lieutenant governor's home with a warrant for his son, as well as another group of agents at his office, hopefully, bringing him in."

Frederickson wished Jack Fox was here to see it all come together. "Did your people find the detonation device in Jack's car?"

"Looks like a simple improvised explosive device magnetically attached to the bottom of his SUV. This one delivered its impact when the vehicle's ignition was activated. Once Jack turned the key the explosive ignited the fuel cell, causing one hell of an explosion."

Frederickson shook his head. The thought of Jack sitting in the car, then being blown to kingdom come, made him shudder. "Jack was a good guy; he'd been working on this murder case for weeks and was just this close to bringing all the suspects in."

"We're going to make sure all that happens. Jack will get credit for all his hard work. I'm sure that won't make what happened any better for his family, but I know that's what he would have wanted."

"You said, that your men were rounding up suspects all over the city, how about Captain Hughes, is he involved?"

"Yeah, detective, big time, my agents should be at the Twelfth Precinct right about now."

"Jack and I made a deal with a local reporter, Brian, can I give her a heads up?"

"He mentioned that to me. I can't allow any reporters to get in the way. Never know what could happen. How about if you wait until we have some of these guys in custody then give her a call."

"Sure, just want to keep my word."

***

Three agents from the FBI entered the Twelfth Precinct asking for Captain Hughes. The officer at the front desk turned and checked, "I'm not sure he's still in, let me call his office for you."

"We'd rather just go in alone," the agents said.

The desk clerk then pointed them in the direction of Hughes' office and they quickly headed into the large squad room. Captain Hughes was behind his desk and appeared to be packing something into a small cardboard box. When he looked up and saw the men heading toward him, he drew his weapon. "Don't come any closer," he yelled.

Officers in the squad room didn't know quite what to make of the events unfolding in front of them as the three agents moved into protective covered areas. One of the agents called out, "Captain Hughes, don't make this any worse. Put your weapon away and come out with your hands up."

Hughes answered with a volley of bullets that sent everyone ducking. "Never, he yelled out!"

_____Forty-Five

Information coming into the FBI office was that three agents were in a shoot out at the Twelfth Precinct with Captain Hughes. The captain had barricaded himself in his office and when anyone moved any closer he fired at them. The original goal to take him into custody was compromised with Hughes shooting back at the agents. The agents sent to bring him in were calling for directions on how to handle the situation. Brian still hoped to bring the captain in, but didn't want anyone hurt. His orders were clear, "Do your best but if necessary use any force you see fit."

Downtown at Detroit Police Headquarters on Third Street, the new police chief was involved with rounding up suspects and along with FBI agents had rounded up six captains, one lieutenant and eight officers. They were all taken into custody without any repercussions. Federal charges will be filed ranging from interfering with an on-going investigation to bribery. The FBI, along with the U.S. Attorney General's Office will be busy for years with trials.

Brian had told Frederickson that he could give his television contact a heads up about the men being rounded up downtown. The detective wished he could be involved, but understood that it was a federal case now.

Carole Newton was thrilled when she received the call from the detective giving her inside information about the corruption in police headquarters, along with the tie-in to the Giambi crime family in Grosse Pointe. She was soon on air with the news team as camera crews were filming officers being escorted out of the headquarters building handcuffed. The details were being broadcasted live and Channel 7 had the inside scoop. Frederickson didn't tell Carole about the events at the Twelfth Precinct or what the FBI had found after inspecting Jack Fox's vehicle. Carole had covered the car bombing along with the other stations and it was carried by many of the national news outlets. CNN along with NBC had specials running. Unfortunately, for the city, it would result in another black mark on its reputation.

Back at the Twelfth Precinct, the action had grown to a fever pitch with Hughes firing at anyone who moved. The captain's office had two large glass panels and a glass door that allowed the agents to have clear view of anything the captain may attempt. There was no way out. Officers in the precinct were updated to the situation and instructed to let the FBI handle this. The squad room was emptied except for the three agents and Hughes who had continued to stay behind his desk. "Captain, there's no way out; you're only making this worse."

Hughes was determined not to be taken in. He had fired at least six rounds at everyone that gathered outside his office and would soon be out of ammunition. Desperation gave way to reality. "I'm coming out," he yelled. "You all need to back off and I'll come out."

The FBI agents thought the standoff was about to end. "Throw your weapon out first captain." One of the agents had slid along the short wall that wound around the squad room while another agent continued talking to Hughes. They hoped once he moved out into the open that they could get the gun from him. "Captain, I need to see your hands up in the air when you come out!"

Hughes now moved from behind the desk. He could see that his office was surrounded and men from his precinct were watching the events unfold. The odds were stacked against him. His plans were so carefully made, but now it had all gone wrong. *What would his wife and kids think?* "Here I come." Hughes stood up looking out into the squad room. He could see his officers and detectives along the back wall watching as the FBI agent who was barking out orders, stood up moving closer to the front of his office. Hughes still had his gun in his right hand and it was held to his side. Once he was standing he looked at the agent who slowly approached and began to lift his weapon.

"Captain don't do it, put your gun down." The agent didn't want this to end up being suicide by cop.

Hughes was now standing to the side of his desk, he had tears in his eyes, "You don't understand. I didn't do anything to hurt anyone."

"Okay captain, just put your weapon on the ground, it will be okay." Hughes was now close to the doorway of his office and everyone anticipated that he'd drop the gun when suddenly he started to raise the weapon. Neither agent could get to him before the gun was pressed against the side of his head and he fired, sending blood and brain particles across the side of the glass enclosure.

"No, no," were the screams that could be heard from around the room.

Agents rushed to the fallen body of Captain Hughes that was crumbled on the floor in a puddle of blood. It was no use, he was instantly dead. How would they explain this to their Bureau Chief? "I'll call it in," the lead agent said. No one argued with him. They surely didn't want to do it.

***

In Grosse Pointe the local police along with the FBI had amassed outside the home of the Giambi brothers, Vito and Victor, who lived along Lake Shore Drive in a gated district along the water's edge. The last thing anybody wanted was a shoot out, with so many innocent people that lived so close by. The lead agent Dennis Montgomery, approached the guard who was stationed in a small brick building that controlled the gate access. Showing his badge he said, "We've got a warrant to bring in both Vito and Victor Giambi. You'll need to open the gates and leave them open. I'm going to have a car stationed at the entrance so no one can enter or exit." The guard looked down at the black phone that was positioned on the wall as the agent was giving him instructions. "Don't even think about it. Open the gate, step outside and we'll handle it from here." He had no choice. Pressing the button to open the gate, the agent watched carefully then took hold of the guard by the arm handing him to another agent standing along the entrance. Motioning to the other agents and police officers, one officer took control of the guard as the other men moved into the cul-de-sac. A police car blocked the entrance and another one was moved to the opposite side so that no one could leave. There were six agents along with eight local police officers. They weren't taking any chances but felt the Giambi brothers would more than likely surrender peacefully. These type of people always let their lawyers handle the fight for them.

The cul-de-sac was comprised of seven homes, all in excess of a million dollars. The Giambi brothers were at the top of the street, both facing the water. Vito's was a massive two story modern home with a lot of glass facing the lake. "Thank goodness all those windows look out over the lake and not the front," one of the officers was heard saying. The lead FBI agent instructed two officers to cover the garage side and another to move around the rear of the home. Montgomery and another FBI agent headed to the front door. They employed the same strategic manpower next door at Victor's home. It was easy to see both places had boat docks along the shoreline, but with the massive ice build-up along the shoreline no one was escaping that way.

The agent that now stood on Vito's front porch glanced to his right to make sure everyone was in position next door. Once that was clear he pressed the bell. The chimes from inside were clearly heard outside by those standing on the porch. It was close to three minutes when the door opened and a young woman, dressed in maid's attire, inquired what the men wanted. Her eyes grew wide as she saw men virtually surrounding the place.

"I'm Dennis Montgomery with the FBI, we're here to see Mr. Giambi."

She looked at the very tall handsome agent, and asked, "Which one?"

Dennis was taken aback by her question. "Vito Giambi!"

"Sir, he's in a meeting with his brother right now. I'll let him know you're here. Would you like to step inside?"

Montgomery turned back to the others waiting along the front porch, then he answered the maid, "I'll wait here, please keep the front door open." The maid turned and Dennis could see that she disappeared around a wall that ran behind the circular stairway that led upstairs. There must have been over thirty stairs leading to a balcony that ran across the front of the second floor. The agents hoped that both brothers were at Vito's house. It would make things much easier. Montgomery motioned to another agent to check with the second group at Victor's home to see if they found out where Victor was. Before Dennis got a response two men in obviously expensive three piece suits came to the doorway.

"What do you want with Mr. Giambi?"

"And who in the hell are you?" Montgomery asked.

The man standing closest to the agent answered, "I'm Mr. Giambi's attorney."

Dennis stood firmly in the doorway, "I have a warrant for Mr. Vito Giambi and his brother Victor. I'll need both of them now."

"Can I see your warrant," the attorney asked.

"I'll be happy to show it to you once the Giambi's are out here." Montgomery knew that the attorney wanted to stall as long as possible. He added, "The warrant also gives us permission to search both Vito and Victor's homes." Turning toward the group, he waved to the other agents, "Okay boys," He handed the attorney the warrant and stated, "Now step aside!"

The two FBI agents moved onto the porch, and proceeded to enter the front door as the attorney tried to stop them, but Dennis put his arm out, holding the three piece back. The second attorney disappeared into the home and the agents quickly ordered everyone out. "This is a legal search of the premises and everyone needs to step out of the way while we follow the letter of the warrant."

When the agents moved around the winding staircase they saw four men sitting at a large circular glass table. The table had plates and half filled glasses with a large vase filled with fresh flowers in the center.

"I need everyone to stand up," the agent demanded.

The men slowly pushed back from the table, and the second man that had been at the door asked, "Under the provisions of the law we are able to stay with your people as you perform the aspects of the warrant. I will need to see your warrant and read what areas of the house you're able to search."

"And who are you!" The agent asked

"I'm Mr. Giambi's attorney."

The agent was now joined by Montgomery who moved local police to the front door. "Mr. Montgomery, this guy wants to read the warrant first." The agent handed the warrant to Dennis. He addressed the attorney, "The first thing we need is everyone to step onto the front porch, then I'll show you the warrant."

One of the men that was sitting at the table jumped in, "Hell, it's cold as hell out there."

Montgomery laughed, "Then grab a jacket. Which one of you is Vito Giambi?" The guy who made the remark about the weather abruptly stood and answered, "I'm Vito."

Dennis walked over to him, "Put your hands behind your back, you're under arrest." Pointing at the other man sitting at the table, "Guess that makes you Victor?"

The younger looking man that stood back from the rest of them sneered at Montgomery, "Yeah, I'm Victor, asshole."

"Fine," Montgomery said, "You're under arrest too." Another agent handcuffed Victor as Vito was being led out of the home to a black SUV that had pulled in front of the home.

The attorney who was inside at the table quickly stated, "They're not going anywhere until I get a look at your warrant."

Dennis Montgomery had about enough. "Look jackass, the warrant is for the search of both homes, cars, boats and all buildings owned by the Giambi brothers. You're welcome to read it, if you can read. As far as them being arrested, you can come visit your client downtown in the Wayne County jail." Take them both away. The agents took control of the two Giambi brothers escorting them to the waiting SUV.

"Look agent," the attorney inside said, "I'll file a suit against you and your office unless my clients are read their rights."

Dennis had both brothers moved back into the large room. "Mr. Vito Giambi, you are advised that anything you say can be held against you in court. You do not have to answer any questions without the presence of an attorney. You are under arrest for bribery, and conspiracy in the abduction of federal witnesses." Dennis turned toward the attorney and had a broad smile on his face as he read the charges against Victor, just as he had with Vito, "Satisfied?"

The attorney hung his head. "I'll meet them at the Wayne County Headquarters," and he headed to his Cadillac Escalade.

Forty-Six

The large contingency of State Police along with the security team from the senate entered the Capitol Building and made their way upstairs to the office of Sean Johnson, the Lieutenant Governor. Their presence along with the Capitol Police heading upstairs had created a major disturbance with everyone wondering what had happened. People asked but the group continued on its mission without stopping. Once they made their way to his office they found out that the lieutenant governor was in the Senate chamber.

This wasn't unusual because the lieutenant governor, as his position dictated, was to preside over the State Senate when they were in the process of taking a vote. The group of officers now entered the back of the Senate Chamber and waited as the proceedings continued. The speaker along with the majority and minority leaders were tallying votes and no one had paid attention to the group, except the Lieutenant Governor, Sean Johnson, who saw them and recognized the head of security along with other officers. Sean turned and looked across the senate floor, only to see there were officers at both the doors along the side of the chamber. There wasn't any place he could escape to. He backed up along the wall and pulled a cell phone from his right hand pocket. Looking down at his phone he started making a call when a State Police Officer slipped up along his side and quietly said, "Sir, please put the phone away."

Sean Johnson looked up surprised, "Do you know who you're talking to. I'm the Lieutenant Governor of the State of Michigan."

"Yes sir, I know who you are, and if you don't want to create an ugly scene right here, I seriously suggest that you put the phone away and come with me."

The lieutenant governor swung his arm out and pushed the officer back about a foot when he was quickly spun around, pinned to the wall and handcuffed. Everyone rose from where they had been tallying votes at the speaker's table when the head of Senate Security stepped in, "Gentlemen, please continue with your business, the lieutenant governor is coming with us."

The officers escorted Sean out of the chambers and down the hallway as senators scrambled to find out what had happened. The man leading the lieutenant governor out had a stern grip on Sean and sternly stated, "Sir, you are under arrest for bribery, interfering with an on-going investigation and abduction of a federal witness. Anything you say can and will be held against you. You are entitled to be represented by an attorney."

"Get your hands off of me!" Johnson tried to get free from the officers grip and struggled with the man.

The officer pulled the cuffed hands back and up bringing a yelp from Sean. "One more move like that sir, and you're going to get hurt."

The lieutenant governor yelled back. "I'll have your job before the day is over."

The officer smiled, "That may be true, but you couldn't afford the pay cut."

***

In the posh outskirts of Lansing, the large group of men made their way up the long winding driveway of the majestic large white home that sat on a small hill accompanied by three State Police cars and a group of Federal agents. The young man who sat in the upper room watched as the cars and entourage completed its trip to the front of the house. "Don't answer the door, Sally," he yelled from upstairs." Too late, the maid had opened the front door and was already in a conversation with the group. He looked down through the opening in the railing and saw her pointing upstairs toward his room. There was no place to hide and he figured his father had taken care of everything. *Why were these men here and in his home?* The young man turned toward the spiraling rear staircase that led from his bedroom down to the kitchen. Grabbing his cell phone and wallet off the dresser he hurried to the stairway making a fast trip down the first flight when two men greeted him.

"Going somewhere?"

He turned but there were now men coming down the stairway and he was caught in-between.

"Sandy Johnson, you're under arrest for murder and collusion. Anything you say can and will be…"

"Shut the hell up, my dad is going to have all of you fired."

They pushed him against the wall, handcuffed him and the officer continued to read him his rights as Sandy yelled like a stuffed pig all the way to the back seat of the Suburban they put him into.

***

Brian Sikorski and the U.S. Attorney General's Assistant had their suspects rounded up from different parts of the state. Although the relationship of the suspects was convoluted, the FBI was sure they could connect the dots. The governor's office made a statement that evening to the press that he was sorry that a man he trusted turned on the good people of Michigan. He pledged to make sure his administration went through executive scrutiny and every effort to assist the federal authorities would come from his staff. During his speech the governor said he had no intention of leaving his position and would be seeking his second term in the fall. Political analysts knew that his administration was tainted and it would take a monumental effort to win a second term.

About the same time that the interim mayor and Police Chief were answering questions from the press about the number of officers that had been arrested, along with the events in the Twelfth Precinct that took place, Carole Newton stood front and center and asked, "Mayor, can you answer why a warrant has been issued for your personal records?"

He wondered how she got that inside information. *Had to be a leak*, he thought.

"Carole, I can assure you that every effort will be made to uncover anyone involved in this case. My office is cooperating with the investigation. We'll bring everyone guilty to justice."

"Glad to hear that." The knock-out punch was a left hook that Carole knew would rock the room. She added, "Our station has received documents that show your brother is on the payroll of the Giambi family, running the Eastern Market concession." The interim mayor stuttered a little, and Carole followed up with a second statement before he could come up with an answer. "I have reliable documents that shows you own a second home along Lake Shore Drive, just about a half-mile from Vito Giambi, that is in your wife's name. Looks like she's on the Giambi payroll too."

Reporters were jumping up and hands were flying in the air. Just as the mayor had cleared his throat and tried to answer, two federal officers entered the room and took him into custody. The police chief was left standing at the podium, alone to answer questions. Reporters screamed out as his press secretary rushed his boss out of the room. What was the next shoe to fall everyone asked? The entire press conference was telecast on national television. Other reporters were looking at Carole and wondering where she had got all her details. She'd never tell.

.

_____Forty-Seven

Although the trials would take years, newspapers would have enough material to fill the front pages and editorial section for a long time. The FBI had rounded up suspects and had them in custody from Lansing to Detroit. Detective Frederickson was invited by the FBI director to sit in as they went over details on the investigation as they put their case together. Jack Fox had given Frederickson a great deal of information about the Greektown murder and the detective became pivotal to the case. The governor also invited Frederickson to come to the capitol for a special ceremony recognizing Jack Fox and his work in the case.

Frederickson appreciated the opportunity and told Brian Sikorski, the FBI Director, that it would be an honor to recognize Fox and everything he did. Frederickson did have one request from the FBI. He detailed what he wanted from Brian, and the Bureau. "I understand, detective," Brian laughed but it let him know a great deal about Frederickson's character. "I'll be happy to make that happen."

***

Monday morning at nine in the morning, Frederickson walked into the bureau's downtown office. Brian Sikorski greeted him and escorted the detective to the conference room. There sat Mr. and Mrs. Tommy Dansforth, both looking pretty fair, although Tommy's arm was in a cast extending from his shoulder to his finger tips. Frederickson addressed them, "I'm so proud to meet both of you."

Tommy stood and gave him a hug. "Detective we know that

you and Jack Fox pulled out every stop to find us and spent every hour searching for answers to our disappearance. We're so sorry about what happened to Jack, he worked so hard to make this all go as easy as possible for us. We'll never be able to thank his family enough for everything he did."

Frederickson smiled and agreed that Fox would have loved to be present today. He told them, Jack Fox knew life is a journey, and he wanted his to be on the path of doing good. He'd be very proud when you testify in the case he put together. They smiled and held hands. Frederickson also told them, "I've asked the FBI for a favor, that they've agreed to, but we didn't want to tell anyone until everything was in place." He went over the details, and Dansforth and his wife were thrilled. Tommy asked, "When do we do this?"

"Right now," Frederickson said. "We're heading there now and we haven't told anyone about what we're going to do. Mr. Sikorski is sending a team of agents with us so we can assure your safety." Everyone stood as they finalized the plan and covered how it will all go down.

***

Kennedy Charter Academy was back in session for the first time since the abduction last week. Their superintendent had security guards in place both along the parking lot as well as where the students both arrived and would exit the school. The mood of everyone was down with students and teachers wondering where Tommy Dansforth was, and how was the investigation going. They hadn't heard anything over the weekend and their hope was disappearing. Ms. Baker was sitting in her office talking to Mrs. Peterson when she saw a large entourage at the front door. She right away recognized detective Frederickson who positioned himself in front of a half dozen or so people that were standing behind him. She remembered that he said, *maybe by Monday I'll have some good news for you.* "Detective, we're glad to see you. Come on in."

Frederickson walked into the main office followed by another tall man in a dark suit behind him. She focused on both of them and didn't pay attention to the small group moving into the office behind them. It took just seconds for everyone in the office to realize it, but when they did screams of cheers and a flood of tears filled the office. "Mr. Dansforth's name," was heard as Ms. Baker and Mrs. Peterson rushed to hug their middle school teacher and his wife. The secretary and other ladies in the office joined in the celebration as Baker cautioned everyone after glancing at the cast on Tommy's arm. "Oh, I hope we didn't hurt you."

Tommy and his wife were thrilled that they were allowed to visit the school before being secluded in a safe house. They weren't sure how the detective convinced the FBI to allow them to do this, but would be forever grateful. They knew they would be sequestered until the trial for the murder in Greektown. "We owe all of this to Jack Fox," Frederickson said.

"No, no, we owe both you and Jack Fox for everything," Kathy Dansforth stated.

Ms. Baker said, "Everyone would want to see you but I don't know if that's possible."

One of the FBI Agents said, "We really have to be careful but what do you have in mind?"

Baker thought for a minute, So many teachers and students have expressed concern, and they'll be disappointed if they didn't get to see Mr. Dansforth."

Frederickson jumped in with an idea. "When all this started last week you called a special meeting in the gym. Could you do that?"

"How much time do we have," she asked.

One of the agents said, "Could you put it together in the next fifteen minutes?"

"Absolutely." Baker hurried into her office and got on the intercom. "I need all teachers to gather your classes and bring students quietly to the gym for a special meeting. Have students take their normal position as they do for all our assemblies." The teachers were as much in the dark as the students, but got their groups in line and headed down to the gym. Speculation was abound with many asking each other what was going on. Some feared that there was bad news regarding Tommy Dansforth. Others thought that they would get an update on the situation. The first group in the gym was Mr. Banner's class. Of course that was normal because his classroom was just outside the gym. Students filed into their designated spots and Ms. Baker was in the front of the gym reminding everyone to be quiet. Once everyone had gathered in their spots Baker addressed them. "First I want to thank all the students and teachers for your quick response to this special assembly. I have a guest that wanted to talk to you today. The teachers have met him last week but students have only seen him on television." With that she introduced Detective Frederickson.

The detective made his way up the center aisle that the students left in the room. When he made his way to the front of the gym there was a nice round of applause. "I don't deserve your applause but appreciate it. I want to thank your teachers, Ms. Baker and Mrs. Peterson, for all their help in our investigation. I also wanted to be here today to be able to introduce someone very special to all of you. It's my great pleasure to bring back Mr. Dansforth and his wife." The gym broke out in bedlam, students were jumping up and down and eighth graders hugged Mr. Dansforth and his wife as they made his way down the middle aisle. Harrison and LaShanda wrapped their arms around him and wouldn't let go.

The detective handed the microphone to Tommy as the students continued enjoyed the showing of joy and sheer pandemonium. Holding his good hand up in the air, everyone quieted down. "I can't tell you how much Kathy and I appreciate your thoughts, prayers, and everything you all tried to do to help us. My wife and I will be alright, and I'll soon be back in my classroom." That brought out some cat calls and cheers from everyone. Dansforth again quieted the assembly, "I have a special message for my eighth grade class. While I'm recovering I'll have plenty of time to prepare homework assignments for all of you." That got a lot of laughter and cheers from all the students. "I love you all," Tommy said as he hugged his wife.

Ms. Baker moved closer to Tommy and gave him another hug. The gym was close to the happiest place in the city as Frederickson looked over at the group. Ms. Baker peeked a glanced toward him and they both smiled at each other. She was sure that she saw tears in his eyes as he moved off to the side watching it all with a big smile on his face.

Acknowledgements

Thanks to Beverly Styles, for the outstanding editing. You've been a great friend and your work has made my novel better in many ways.

To Carl Virgilio, for the all his detailed work on the cover back page, and book marks. You made sure it jumps off the book rack. Thanks, especially for your friendship, and great work with our writers group.

Thanks to Ms. Shawn Walkiewicz, for supplying the photo that was used on the cover..

Thanks to my daughter-in-law, Merritt, for excellent resource material, it was a nice help and I plan to share it with my writers group.

To the members of the Shelby Writers Group, you have been an inspiration to me and to each other.

I hope my guest enjoyed the parts they played in this story. Thanks to Carole Arnone, Don Frederickson, Brian Sikorski, Randy Hughes, Harrison McCutchen, Chris Kawiecki, Dennis Montgomery and Carl Virgilio for their roles.

Tony Aued

Tony Aued

THE AUTHOR

About The Author

Mr. Aued is the creator of the *Blair Adams, FBI Thriller Series*. The four books take his fans on a thrilling saga of a young woman whose husband was killed in Iraq in the first book, *Blair Adams, The Package*. The three following novels are sequels to the opening story, and send the reader on a wild ride as Blair's character becomes involved with the FBI. The series has received acclaim from The Times Herald, Macomb Daily and Shelby Source as riveting. Reviewers stated that the books reads like a movie script with fast exciting action.

Mr. Aued's new novel, *Murder in Greektown*, is set in Metro Detroit, where he grew up and taught school. His plot brings the readers into the action, guessing who did it, as a whirlwind of potential suspects are introduced. The investigation leads to potential police interference as the case of the missing teacher expands and takes surprising turns. The reader is introduced to Detective Frederickson, who as a main character, has to deal with constant interference from his captain, and the District Attorney. The story has many twists and turns and has the reader involved in solving the mystery.

Mr. Aued and his wife have lived throughout the Midwest and Southeast with their dog, Baxter.

Tony Aued

Made in the USA
Middletown, DE
08 November 2019

78015794R10161